DARK SIDE

DARK SIDE

Margaret Duffy

This first world edition published 2013
in Great Britain and the USA by
SEVERN HOUSE PUBLISHERS LTD of
19 Cedar Road, Sutton, Surrey, England, SM2 5DA

Trade paperback edition first published 2018
In Great Britain and the USA by
SEVERN HOUSE PUBLISHERS LTD
Eardley House, 4 Uxbridge Street, London W8 7SY

British Library Cataloguing in Publication Data
A CIP catalogue record for this title is available from the British Library.

ISBN-13: 978-0-7278-8340-7 (cased)
ISBN-13: 978-1-84751-897-2 (trade paper)
ISBN-13: 978-1-78010-481-2 (e-book)

ONE

There were several loud bangs and the ornate partition that separated the café-style front of the establishment from the wine bar at the rear where I was sitting, and through which the sun had been shining so beguilingly, plunged down in a waterfall of thousands of glittering shards of glass. It seemed as if I stared at this, fascinated, for quite some time but actually it must have been only for a second or so. In the next moment I was thrown over sideways on to the floor, my head colliding heavily with the leg of another chair. Everything became very confused, women screaming, men shouting, the pounding feet of panicking people. Then, the weight that had knocked me over lifted off and I found myself looking into someone's eyes, green like mine, only a matter of inches away.

'You OK, Ingrid?' he asked.

'I think so,' I said.

Somewhere outside, a motorbike roared away.

'Police!' another man's voice called, penetrating the hubbub. 'Everyone please calm down. Is anyone badly hurt?'

My very near, and also prone, companion, Commander Michael Greenway, formerly of the Metropolitan Police and now Patrick's boss at the Serious Organised Crime Agency, got to his feet, extended a hand and yanked me briskly to mine. It immediately became apparent that several people had been cut by flying glass, which was everywhere as a side window appeared to have been smashed as well. I grabbed a waiter, who was rigid with shock – I already knew his command of English to be limited – and managed to convey to him that we needed a first aid kit. Slightly to my surprise the bar possessed one and Greenway and I got to work, leaving the third member of our party, my husband Patrick, to police the incident.

'They got away – far too many people for me to risk a shot,' Patrick said a little later, speaking to me over the heads of several people we had seated while they recovered from the shock and had small cuts dealt with. One woman who had been sitting quite close to the window was bleeding heavily from a gash to her face and Greenway was with her, trying to stem the flow with a dressing. Miraculously, no one had actually been hit by the bullets fired seemingly at random into the premises.

Rapidly approaching sirens blared and very shortly afterwards professional medics arrived and took over, followed, five minutes later, by the Metropolitan Police. The detective sergeant in charge went pale when confronted by a furious Greenway, brandishing his Serious Organised Crime Agency ID and demanding to know, with lavish use of expletives, what had kept them.

Patrick had been questioning bystanders and now returned to report that the driver, a man, or perhaps woman, had been wearing a crash helmet, its tinted visor making identification impossible, as had the gunman, riding pillion on the bike, a black Kawasaki with no number plates.

Greenway introduced the pair of us to the DS as 'Patrick Gillard and Ingrid Langley,' adding that we were 'colleagues' and leaving it at that.

We made brief statements and then left. It was then that I noticed the commander had a small piece of glass sticking out of his neck, blood trickling down and soaking into the collar of his shirt. Patrick and I steered him, protesting, back inside to have it removed and the wound treated.

All this while we were on leave, too.

I am an author by trade for most of the time. My ex-lieutenant-colonel husband's job description is that of 'adviser' to SOCA, soon to be merged into the National Crime Agency, and my own part-time role that of 'consultant'. To him, that is. He sometimes jokingly refers to me as his 'oracle'. Patrick's experience after serving in special forces, followed by a period working for D12, a department of MI5 – we both did – seemed to be the desirable assets when he was offered this job. Also in mind, no doubt, was his ability to have an immediate affinity with any weapon handed to him, a talent for adopting all kinds of personas, and being able to get right inside the criminal mind.

On reflection, he would have made a very good, and uncatchable, crime lord, there being a dark side to his character that even John, his father, has recognized in him. I sometimes wonder, had he not been offered this position, whether he would have stayed on the straight and narrow or turned himself into some kind of maverick law-enforcer.

This went through my mind now as we sat at a table outside a coffee bar some fifty yards from the scene of the incident, not involved in the investigation for once, waiting for Greenway. Flocks of London pigeons which had been put to flight by the shots were still wheeling around the tops, and reflected in the many glass windows of the buildings. Patrick was seated at my side, his gaze ostensibly on the police personnel who were cordoning off the area with incident tape and shepherding away gawpers. Scenes of crime people were arriving. But in reality I knew he was in a world of his own. A serious face – grim now after what had just occurred, but transformed when he smiles into the boy I fell in love with at school – is a little careworn now, the thick black wavy hair greying. No, not a maverick – not now.

As if sensing that I was looking at him he turned, seeming to try to read my thoughts.

'You wouldn't though, would you?' I said, speaking them aloud.

'Wouldn't what?'

'Ever work independently to the police to, say, bring mobsters to court that the conventional forces don't seem to be able to touch.'

A smile twitched at the corners of his mouth. 'Life gets quite stimulating enough working as I am, thank you. Besides, I've done all that.'

I was aware that while a serving soldier in Northern Ireland he had been sent after wanted terrorists, bombers and murderers. And, sometimes, been under orders to 'remove' them.

I said, 'But if you were asked to?'

'It could happen.'

I didn't feel that he had quite answered the question. Perhaps I shouldn't have asked. 'Do you have any theories about this shooting – other than the obvious ones?'

'Yes, I do, actually.'

He got to his feet and walked off, back in the direction of the café bar. I watched as he showed his ID and ducked under the incident tape, then stood in the road opposite the entrance and walked up and down a few times, having to go around a couple of ambulances, three police cars and a paramedic's motorbike, his gaze fixed on the inside of the building, perhaps working out the exact line of fire. Back on the pavement he crouched quickly, arms extended as if holding a weapon and aiming it. After standing still for a few seconds he went back inside the café bar, again showing his warrant card. They weren't taking any chances. When he reappeared a minute or so later he was with the commander.

'Considering that you're on leave and this was supposed to be just a bit of socializing on our part, it was quite exciting,' Greenway said. There was an adhesive dressing larger than one might have thought necessary on his neck, which he now touched.

'Coffee?' Patrick asked.

'Why not? We can sit here in the sun and criticize what they're doing.'

'I suggest the place in the arcade over the road. They do very good tea as well.'

Greenway looked a bit surprised but then shrugged and said, 'Whatever you fancy.'

It was actually an Indian tea house, cool and peaceful after the summer heat, noise and traffic fumes outside. Patrick led the way, glanced around and made for a somewhat dim corner. We placed our order.

'How often do you use that café bar?' Patrick asked his boss.

'Quite frequently. As you're well aware, it's near the office and they also serve coffee in the rear bar where it's a bit quieter. I sometimes meet Erin here if she's up in town shopping as she likes the ambience of the place. But I'm careful not to stick to any kind of routine, if that's what you're asking.'

Erin, a one-time DS with the Met, is his wife.

'You've already said you didn't see the gunman.'

'No, I must have been looking the other way.'

'Logic tells us that there are two or perhaps three possible reasons for the shooting. The first one is the most obvious, that it was a gangland attack against, say, a rival drug dealer who was in the building. I don't actually go for that as surely they'd have gone in looking for him, not just shot through the open doorway. The gunman had got off the bike, by the way. Or, second, that the proprietors hadn't paid protection money. The third is that you were the intended target.'

'So that's why you wanted to come in here away from the street. It's far more likely that *you* were the target.' This was a reasonable comment given that the pair of us are known to be on several terrorists' hit lists and it is why Patrick is permitted to carry, at all times, a Glock 17 in a shoulder holster. Needless to say, it never makes an appearance while we are at home but is rarely far away from him.

'I don't normally sit opposite doorways. Think.'

He nominally only has the rank of constable to enable him to arrest people, too.

The commander did not mind. 'There's always the risk,' he acknowledged, not thinking.

'I'm speaking from memory but I'm fairly sure that there were several areas on that Art Nouveau-style screen that were clear of pattern. I reckon you were sitting on a line just about opposite the doorway and would have been clearly visible to someone standing just outside through one of them. I think the first shot smashed the screen, the second and third went through the window behind, all on roughly the same trajectory. And, forgive me, you're a good target.'

He meant from the point of view that the commander is a tall man, taller than Patrick, who is six foot two and, as a former rugby player, broad-shouldered and well-built.

Greenway laughed. Then he said, 'You're on leave until next Monday, which is five days away. If we've time from other work then we can find out if the Met's turned anything up and go from there.' Unconsciously, perhaps, he again touched the dressing on his neck. 'What I don't want is for word to get around that there's a theory I might have been in the firing line.'

'Damn, I was just about to call the *Sun*,' Patrick said, but he wasn't smiling.

We had come to London for an exhibition of Chinese art at the Victoria and Albert Museum and also to enable me to walk round Soho, during the day and after dark, to soak up the atmosphere for my new novel, *Death Asks No Questions*. I'm not a particularly nervous person and have explored parts of London on my own in the past, but having a meaningful escort did have the advantage of being able to visit, as Patrick put it, 'the more interesting places', meaning pubs with low-life customers.

'Please don't start playing poker,' I had pleaded when this idea was first mooted. 'You nearly always win, and/or spot the in-house professional cheats and it hardly ever fails to lead to some kind of fracas. You even got involved in a brawl last time and were arrested!'

'But I was undercover on the job!' Patrick had protested. 'Getting arrested was a damned good idea at the time. *And* I won almost two hundred quid.'

I had given him a look that showed I had definitely rested my case.

That afternoon there was a thunderstorm bringing rain of monsoon proportions. We went to the exhibition and, the deluge continuing into the evening, I had to content myself with a quick tour of Soho huddled inside an anorak. We then had a drink in a dingy subterranean bar followed by a meal in a Greek restaurant before scurrying, dripping, back to our hotel. I was fairly happy, though, having spent the evening people-watching. There had been the added entertainment provided by a lady, a real one of very senior years, who had had far too many G and Ts, trying to chat up my husband. In the face of promises of all the money he wanted and a stately home in Buckinghamshire that needed a real man to run it, he had told her that I had bagged him first.

That had happened very early in life when we were at school in Plymouth together. Before he had been made Head Boy he had merely been, to me and my female friends, that is, one of that sub-species into which we lumped together all boys. Then, when everyone had grown up rather a lot I suddenly noticed the tall, dark individual who, together with a girl of Nordic beauty who shone at just about everything, had been accorded the school's highest honours. Patrick, I knew, was the son of a clergyman, sang in the church choir and went fishing in the River Tamar with a boy called George. He was rumoured to regard all girls as an irrelevance. My contemporaries' reaction to this was acute disappointment amid worries that he might be gay. What a terrible waste, we thought, if he was!

Our fathers knew one another as there was a Parochial Church Council connection. John, Patrick's father, was utterly delighted that mine, upon being made treasurer, had discovered an old bequest to the church in a forgotten savings account – quite a lot of money – and had suggested that his eldest son could help

me with my physics homework. It was the summer holidays and
the physics was a project at which I had been staring in a kind
of numbed horror on and off for days, proclaiming loudly to all
who would listen that I did not understand one word of it. No
internet in those days.

Patrick had duly arrived and sat opposite me at the kitchen
table, simmering. I had gazed back in what I hoped was a cool
and detached fashion, knowing that if I dropped my gaze and
giggled I was finished. For here, the knowledge booting me into
full womanhood in one split second, was the man I wanted for
ever and ever.

He had thawed and explained the physics. No good – I was
too busy looking into those grey eyes, the irises rimmed with
black and flecked with gold . . . Finally, he worked it all out for
me to copy later but made a couple of small mistakes – deliberate
ones, I discovered quite a while afterwards – so the teacher would
not suspect I had had help.

Our friendship grew and for the rest of the holidays we walked
the dogs and took picnics up on Dartmoor, Patrick producing a
bottle of wine from his rucksack and putting it in a stream to
cool. His main attraction, other than those wonderful eyes, was
his ability to make me laugh. Then one day we laughed until we
cried, hugging one another under the hot summer sun, and I had
felt the way his wiry body moved under the material of his shirt.
He had held me even closer and kissed me.

I can remember nothing of us removing clothes. Just friends
one minute and then as close as two people can become the next,
the pair of us shocked speechless by the pleasure our young
bodies had just given us. Finally, after quite a few such picnics
– that summer broke all sunshine records for Dartmoor but we
might not have noticed had it poured – Patrick had a crisis of
conscience and asked me to marry him. He had been, after all,
very strictly brought up. My reply that I was only fifteen caused
him to attain a shade of pale that up until then I had assumed to
be humanly impossible. But he had repeated the offer right then,
come hell, horsewhips and jail, and I accepted.

Oddly, we 'behaved ourselves' after that, which was just as
well as we both had the notion that children – we still thought
of ourselves as sort of kids for some strange reason, even though
Patrick was eighteen by then – couldn't make babies. Naive

wasn't the word for it – my mother refused to talk about such things. It was a miracle that I didn't get pregnant.

We married when we were both in our early twenties. But by then my new husband was in the army, a junior officer rising through the ranks like bread dough on a hot day. There was a whole world out there for him to explore, and he did not really want to be tied down. After a very stormy relationship there was one last terrible row which ended with me throwing his classical guitar down the stairs and then him out of my cottage – bought with my writing earnings and money left to me by my father – into the rain. We got divorced.

He served abroad, the second youngest major in the British Army, and was horribly injured in an accident – not his fault – with a hand grenade, finally having to have the lower part of his right leg amputated. Just before this, out of hospital and in agony as the pins in the repaired smashed limb were not holding, he had turned up on my doorstep to tell me that he had been offered a job with MI5. A stipulation was that he had to find a working partner, female, as socializing was involved and it was thought that lone men did not merge easily into a crowd. We had always got on famously in public, he had reminded me brightly – which was perfectly true – so did I want the job? It was well paid, and there would be lots of potential for ideas for future plots in my novels, he had wheedled.

I had found all this utterly unbearable and not just because he had fainted at my feet from pain and weakness not five minutes after crossing the threshold. It was somehow knowing that the real reason he was right here in front of me, almost literally on his knees, was to ask me, although he was maimed, to take him back.

I had taken him back and accepted the job offer. We rediscovered the old magic that had been between us and I soon found that I needed him just as much, if not more, than he needed me. These days he is almost as mobile as he was before his injuries thanks to a man-made construction below the knee with its tiny in-house computer, powered by lithium batteries, that reacts to his every movement. It cost roughly the same as a family car.

'So you'd left the bother magnet switched on,' Detective Chief Inspector James Carrick of Bath CID said darkly. He seems to be convinced that we go looking for trouble. We were in the Ring o' Bells, the pub in Hinton Littlemoor, a village in Somerset where we live, having returned home from London the previous day.

Patrick chuckled and shook his head. 'Not this time.'

'D'you really think they might have been after Greenway?'

'It's not impossible. He wasn't interested in giving it any thought at the time but as we know all too well head mobsters are using rogue private investigators to access police files and have even had incriminating and sensitive information deleted courtesy of bent cops. Mike's name has to be on several inquiries into enforcement operations where there's been insider criminal activity – inquiries that have actually been very successful. The empire has struck back and the gang leaders don't like it.'

Carrick pulled a face. The police attitude to private investigators tends to be that of toleration as long as they stick to checking up on straying spouses and searching for lost relatives or stolen dogs.

'Another pint?' Patrick asked him.

The Ring o' Bells was under new management, having been closed down for a while after the previous tenants had been convicted of using the business for money-laundering purposes. The DCI, an old friend, had called in to have a drink with us on his way home from work. A fondness for real ale notwithstanding, he never thinks it a bad idea to maintain an occasional personal presence in hostelries on his patch to demonstrate to the landlords that they are on his radar.

'No, thanks, I must away,' he replied, getting to his feet.

I did not ask the proud new father if he was dashing off to help his wife Joanna bath baby Iona Flora as I knew he would eagerly produce his phone and show us the latest photographs – 'She's going to have red hair, just like her mother!' – of his daughter. And he had initially said he couldn't stay long, hadn't he?

'Did I ever mention a man by the name of Benny Cooper to you?' Carrick said on an afterthought as he put on his jacket.

'I don't think so,' Patrick answered.

'Remind me to sometime.'

'Why, is he someone I ought to know about?'

'You talking about private investigators brought him to mind.

He used to work for *The Bath Times* as a crime reporter and also wrote a gossip column: In The Know, it was called. I got him for being an accessory to GBH and, with the Vice Squad, for peddling child pornography some years ago. He's out of prison now, set himself up as a private eye and been seen locally with a mobster known to the Met. *He's* been linked to a case in London where police files were tampered with. No pointers to Benny as yet, though – more's the pity,' Carrick finished by grimly saying.

'Do you have a name for this character known to the Met?'

'As usual, he has more than one identity but because of pressure of work I've had to postpone investigating further.'

'Can you give us a few minutes Monday morning first thing to give us what you do know?' Patrick asked.

'I thought you were back off to London.'

'This sounds like being work-related. We can travel up later.'

'Fine. Eight thirty?'

'I know about Cooper,' I said a little later. We had stayed to have a meal in the pub's restaurant. 'Joanna told me a while back. She was the victim in the GBH case.'

Patrick looked up from the menu. '*Really?*'

'Cooper'd had his knife into James for a while as he knew he was on his case and somehow, some time previously, had got hold of the story of how he and Joanna, who was James's sergeant at the time, had an affair while his wife was still alive – she died from a rare form of bone cancer, if you remember. The super, now retired, hated women in the job and she was forced to resign by being moved to a dead-end posting.'

'I can't imagine that happening now.'

'No, nor can I.'

'Sorry, go on.'

'Cooper was knocking around with a man whose name I think she said was Paul Mallory – they had some kind of porn outfit together – and started shadowing James when he went out in the evening, trying to spot him drinking heavily or picking up a prostitute – anything that he could use to try to blacken his character. Apparently he already sneered anonymously at Bath CID through his newspaper column. Eventually, because James was closing in on the pair of them, he persuaded Mallory to rough up Joanna to muddy the waters of a murder investigation involving another woman with red hair, to act as a distraction. Only he almost strangled her and when James found her he had to give her the kiss of life.'

'Bloody hell!' Patrick whispered. 'I'm not surprised he's got him in his sights now he's out of jail and seemingly back in business. He'll be wanting, very badly, to nail the creep to the wall by his ears.'

The fact that men who have laid a hand on me during our time working together have ended up either in prison or extremely dead, mostly the latter, is never far from my thoughts.

We bought the old rectory in Hinton Littlemoor when it became apparent that the church authorities were about to put it on the market and move Patrick's parents John and Elspeth – John is the incumbent of St Michael's Church – to a small bungalow on a cheap and ugly new development at the lower end of the village, the site of one-time railway sidings. After a lot of building work had taken place at the rectory – including an old stable, harness room and garage turned into living accommodation which serves as an annexe for Elspeth and John, and an extension to the first floor above it – we moved in.

We have three children of our own, Justin, Victoria and baby Mark, and two adopted, Matthew and Katherine, known as Katie, Patrick's late brother Laurence's children. Their mother is under seemingly permanent treatment for alcoholism and/or drug abuse and wants nothing further to do with them. Our three youngest are looked after mainly by the nanny, Carrie, and we could not manage without further help from the children's grandparents. My dear father died at a tragically early age of a ghastly creeping illness, my mother is another basket case and again, has no interest in her family, so the children have just the one set of grandparents.

'Can I count you in for the choir on Sunday?' John asked his son, putting his head out of the annexe's front door as we entered the back way, through the conservatory. 'We're very thin.'

'Counter tenor or bass?' Patrick said with a grin.

'Whatever you like as long as you *sing*.' John's fuse as far as Patrick's sense of humour goes is sometimes very short.

'I'm a thin alto,' I offered, but inwardly quaking as I had never done anything like this before.

'Delighted, my dear! Thank you. Elspeth'll find a robe that fits you.'

Seated in the choir stalls for the first time on that Sunday morning with a full view of the congregation, I noticed a man I had not seen before. When Joanna had told me about Benny Cooper she had quoted a woman who lived in the same square as Paul Mallory who had described him as being 'sort of smarmy with dark hair and shades'.

So who was this man sitting almost at the back of the church who looked sort of smarmy with dark hair and shades? After the service I asked John if he knew him.

'Oh, that's Jeff Bates. He and his girlfriend have recently moved into the one-time forge. He's a landscape painter but the poor chap's been having treatment for some kind of eye trouble. Everyone's hoping it won't affect his career.'

It appeared that the odious Cooper was preying on my mind.

TWO

There had been a suspected murder overnight and Manvers Street police station was in organized turmoil. Carrick, with his assistant Lynn Outhwaite hurrying just behind him, was descending the stairs from the top floor. As we approached a third person caught up with them, the new Detective Inspector, David Campbell, whom we had not previously met. After quite a long time without one a new DI had finally been appointed to Bath CID and it was his second week in the job. He had come from HQ in Portishead and everyone had assumed that another Scot would meld very nicely with the boss. Everyone, that is, except Derek Woods, the custody sergeant who, having read the history books, had warned darkly against making such presumptions. For the MacDonalds still hated the Campbells after the massacre of Glencoe, didn't they? Perhaps others did, too.

We had already gathered that Carrick, who had undertaken to mentor Campbell for a couple of weeks to show him, in his words, 'how Bath ticked', was not particularly impressed.

Apparently this was nothing to do with anyone being put to the sword but merely an apparent lingering prejudice on Campbell's part that everything in England was vastly inferior to the land of his birth. I thought there was every chance that James had merely disliked the man at first sight.

The DCI was annoyed now and I had an idea that our mission was already in ruins. We waited until they arrived on the ground floor where, upon seeing us, he came to a halt, causing Campbell to almost cannon into him and Lynn. Carrick gave him a look and the other man apologized.

'Sorry, I have a possible murder case on my hands right now,' he said. 'A woman's body was found near Oldfield Park railway station three quarters of an hour ago.'

'We've just been told,' Patrick replied.

Carrick's normal good manners surfaced and he introduced Campbell to us, just giving our names. The DI smiled thinly and gave us a little nod. He was older than Carrick, stocky, possibly in his early fifties, with hard, pale blue eyes and coarse grey hair cut brutally short.

We stood aside and they went off in the direction of the side entrance to the car park.

As they departed I heard Campbell ask, 'Who are they?'

'SOCA,' Carrick answered tersely.

'Right,' Patrick drawled as we strolled slowly in the same direction. 'Tell me, oh, oracle mine, what is the chemistry going on there?'

I said, 'Your guess is as good as mine but it could be something to do with the fact that although he's been desperate to be given someone permanent to spread the workload, James has been king of all he surveyed for quite a while now. Campbell's older, probably been in the force far longer but from what we hear has probably never really acclimatized to being down south. James is irritated, that's all. He'll get over it. He was probably looking forward to our chat this morning.'

'You have to get on with your staff, though, don't you?' Patrick remarked disapprovingly.

I paused in my stride for a moment. 'You can talk! I can distinctly remember you and one of yours fighting like tomcats on a village green after he'd taken a swing at you because he found you utterly insufferable.'

Patrick smiled reflectively. 'You fell off a horse on to him too. That didn't exactly *help*.'

'And shortly afterwards, still presumably all shades of black and blue, he left MI5 to live with an American divorcee who had four children.'

The pair of us hooted immoderately with laughter, causing the trio ahead of us to turn round and stare.

'No real leads,' Michael Greenway announced without further preamble. 'Not as far as any connection with yours truly, that is. The Met's convinced it was a gangland shooting, mistaken identity or whatever. The bike was found, burnt out, on waste ground and three boys, playing truant, presumably, were spotted and questioned. One of them said he saw a couple of youths running away from the area on the day the crime was committed – one thin, the other on the overweight side. They were carrying their crash helmets but he didn't recognize them. He may well have done, of course, but was too afraid to say so. There are local suspects and I understand they'll be questioned – if they can be run to earth. People like that, the odd job boys, tend to disappear as though they never existed. I suggest we let the Met get on with it and tackle more pressing matters.'

'How is the woman who was injured?' I asked.

'I'll find out for you,' the commander said with perhaps the merest hint of exaggerated patience. He hit keys on his computer, swore under his breath as a chunky forefinger landed on a wrong one and then remedied the mistake.

OK, so I was a bit annoyed with the way men sometimes airbrush things like that from their mindset.

'Three stitches in a cheek wound and kept in hospital overnight as she was suffering from shock and has a heart condition,' Greenway reported. He flashed me a big cheesy grin, as though he knew his irritation had surfaced. 'Now then . . .'

'One thing,' Patrick said.

'What?' Greenway grated.

'I have a name for you. Benny Cooper. He used to be a crime reporter for a Bath newspaper and had his knife into DCI James Carrick, rubbishing the CID anonymously in a column he wrote and snooping on his private life. This was mostly because Carrick knew he had a porn business and was pulling out all the stops to close it down.'

'Is it relevant to this?'

'It might be insofar as you've been involved with CID cases in Bath.'

'There's something I really think we ought to get on with. Right now. You have one minute.'

The commander had picked the wrong man to get flustered and almost certainly knew it. Patrick made himself more comfortable in his chair and said, 'Carrick mentioned him to us in connection with police officers, especially those in charge of cases, being targeted by serious criminals, whether directly by personal attacks on their characters or through the use of dodgy private investigators who bribe dodgy cops in order to get evidence removed from case files or details of witnesses for the intimidation thereof. Cooper went to prison some years ago for being an accessory to a serious assault on Carrick's wife Joanna – this was before they were married. She almost died. The aim was to muddy the waters of an ongoing murder investigation at the time, to make Bath CID – and James – look bad. The man who attacked her, Paul Mallory, an oppo of Cooper's, also went to prison, obviously with a longer sentence. Carrick told us that Cooper's out now, and so is Mallory – I checked and read up about the case. Moreover, Cooper has set himself up as a private eye and been seen hobnobbing locally with a mobster involved in a case in London where police files were tampered with.'

Greenway knows James Carrick quite well and respects his judgement. He frowned for a few moments and then said, 'I agree that it's interesting. Do we know who this mobster is and whether his name's cropped up in relation to any of the same cases that I have?'

'Not yet. As is the norm these days, he has false identities,' Patrick replied. 'We had to postpone a meeting with Carrick about it and I haven't been able to delve into it as I was told to remain on leave.'

A very small smile twitched at Greenway's lips, a sort of silent *touché*. They both really enjoy these exchanges. Then he said, 'Make a note of it. Until we're asked for help or a good connection's made I think we ought to let Avon and Somerset do any work needed. Now then . . .'

*   *   *

I had gone along to this back-to-work briefing partly out of courtesy, to show my face, and also to learn of any important updates. My role only involves working part time, otherwise I would not be able to write a word, and anyway, most of what Patrick does on a day-to-day basis is just that – routine, involving liaising with and issuing orders to people 'on the ground' who are mostly carrying out surveillance operations or working undercover. For this is he eminently suited, having worked in army special operations, and feedback from those under him shows an appreciation of his knowledge of exactly what is involved.

The real reason for my return to London for a couple of days was to meet an old friend – she lives very handily in Kensington – go shopping and generally have time off. That was today; tomorrow I was hoping to undertake a little more writing research in the Soho area, hopefully in the dry this time. So I excused myself from the briefing and left the building. As soon as I switched my mobile phone back on there was a text message asking me to contact Julia, my friend, immediately.

'I've been trying to get hold of you for *ages*,' she complained.

I apologized, telling her that I had been somewhere where I'd had to switch off, which is perfectly true under most circum-stances. She has no knowledge of my second career.

'Look, I'm terribly sorry, Ingrid, but I can't go shopping and have lunch with you today. Mummy's been taken ill and I'm throwing things in a suitcase right now. There's a taxi coming in around ten minutes and I have to get a train to Oxford as the car's in for service today, which is a damned nuisance.'

I soothed her as best I could and said I hoped that her mother made a speedy recovery. I felt really sorry for her as her demanding mama is often 'ill' at the most inconvenient moments with an uncanny way of seeming to know when her daughter has taken a day off work for an outing or something similar. I had a nasty feeling that the old lady was working towards moving in with Julia, who's divorced, which would mean she'd have no life of her own at all.

I found I was walking in the direction of the café bar where the shooting incident had taken place. It served coffee and food so why not have lunch there?

When I arrived I saw that the window had been boarded up,

and the glass partition screen had been replaced by something a lot less attractive so perhaps was only temporary. I was slightly surprised that the violence did not seem to have dampened the enthusiasm of the local clientele and it was very busy, the serving staff expertly weaving their way through the narrow spaces between the tables with loaded trays.

I sat in the café area and ordered what I wanted, coffee first, and then sent a text to Patrick with my whereabouts and change of plan, one of our working rules. Fine, I then thought, but I did not actually have a plan for today. There was no response from him but roughly ten minutes later, when my cappuccino had arrived, he turned up.

'Roast beef and horseradish panini with salad?' I hazarded as he seated himself.

'Sounds just right. I told Greenway I couldn't concentrate while I was famished.'

'This isn't the right place for you to feel happy sitting – near the door.'

He glanced around. 'Can't be helped, the place is packed. Perhaps if we change places so I've a view outside . . .?' This we did. Then he said, 'It occurred to me that although the Met will have interviewed everyone who was working here on the day of the attack, there's a chance one of the members of staff might have remembered something else since.'

'I thought Greenway had something he wants you to work on – another case?'

'He does, but this is my lunch hour, isn't it?'

A diminutive woman of Chinese appearance approached from somewhere at the back to stand by our table and I quickly realized that she was not one of the waitresses.

'You were here when we were attacked by armed criminals,' she said very quietly in perfect English, but with a slight American or Canadian accent.

'That's right,' Patrick acknowledged.

'I want to thank you, that's all. For helping the injured people and . . . organizing things. And the big man, your friend. I – I ran into the office when it happened. I stayed there until the police came.' She blinked nervously a few times. 'I thought that gunman would kill me.'

'Why was that?' Patrick went on to ask.

'Just . . . a feeling.'

'I have to tell you that the three of us work for SOCA, the Serious Organised Crime Agency. We just happened to be here for a—'

But she had fled.

'Leave her to have a think for a few minutes,' Patrick said when I had half-risen from my seat, expecting him immediately to follow her.

'She might just bolt for home,' I pointed out.

'No matter. We can find her as if she stayed in the office until the police arrived and was interviewed they'll have her name and address.'

After we had eaten our lunch and settled the bill we moved to leave and, as already quietly arranged, I mimed to Patrick that I would visit the ladies' loo which was signposted to somewhere at the back. He mimed back that he would wait for me outside and went out.

There was a maze of little corridors, doorways and staircases, both ascending and descending, at the rear of the premises and, having done a virtually tiptoed recce, it was easy to take a 'wrong' turning and enter a room with a very faded *Staff Only* notice on the door.

'Oh, sorry,' I hastened to say, having caused the Chinese woman to start violently.

She was sitting behind a cheaply made, rickety-looking desk on which were spread various papers, invoices, perhaps. Resting on top of them, like an incongruous paperweight, was a handgun. I braced myself as the woman snatched it up but she opened a drawer and thrust it within, out of sight.

'Would you care to talk to me?' I enquired.

'You'll arrest me.'

'No.'

'I don't trust you.'

'It looks as though you don't trust anyone.'

'I don't. You can't now.'

'Look, I didn't see the gun.'

We gazed at one another for a few more moments and then she said, 'I won't talk while that man you're with is here. He's not . . . kind.'

I longed to tell her that sometimes he can actually be downright soppy. 'No, all right,' I agreed. 'But I shall have to tell him where I am or he might come looking for me.'

'I would prefer you to phone him from here.'

'Of course.'

'Come in and shut the door.'

This I did, taking my time to draw up a chair, seat myself and find my mobile in order to take in my surroundings. The room was very scruffy; peeling paint, cobwebs in the corners of the ceiling, most of the floor space taken up with piles of boxes of what appeared to be coffee and stacks of disposables such as paper napkins and kitchen and toilet rolls.

The same could not be said for the occupant of the room. As I had already noted she was neatly dressed in a crimson blouse and black silk trousers and was, I supposed, around thirty-five years of age, and petite, probably only just reaching my shoulder – I am five feet eight. Her hair was dark as one might expect but fine, swept up into a bun on top of her head. Her eyes were brown and, right now, fixed on me in a hard and suspicious stare.

I rang Patrick, who said that he would hang around. Then I said, 'Are you the owner of this business?'

She nodded. 'There's just me now. My husband is dead.'

'I'm sorry.'

'Don't be. He was rotten right through.'

I decided not to probe about that just yet and asked her if it was all right for me to take a few notes.

She nodded again.

'Do you mind telling me your name?'

'The other police asked that. It is Sulyn Li Grant. Li was my mother's family name in China. My father was American, Spencer Horatio Grant the Third.' The last information was uttered with pride.

'You didn't take your husband's name?'

'No.'

I decided that the reasons behind that were none of my business. 'Do you think the shooting was carried out by Chinese criminals?'

She shook her head. 'No.'

'You seem very sure about that. Could it have been anything to do with a Triads group?'

'No. I have nothing to fear from them.' Then, obviously feeling that some explanation was required, she added, 'I am protected.'

Again, I felt I should not pursue the matter. 'Who, then?'

Sulyn shrugged.

'Something to do with your husband?'

'I don't *have* to answer your questions,' she answered defiantly.

'No, but it might save you from being bothered by the police again.'

She thought about it. 'OK.'

'You said just now that you were frightened the gunman might kill you. Had your husband been involved with criminals?'

'I knew he was, but he told me nothing – I didn't want to know anything.'

'Was *he* paying protection money to anyone?'

'He promised me that he wasn't.'

Perhaps because he knew she was already doing something along those lines, I thought. But that did not mean that he hadn't been under pressure from another criminal gang to do so.

'D'you mind telling me how he died?' I asked.

Silence.

'Did the other police ask you about that?' I persevered.

'No, why should they?' Sulyn answered with a toss of her head.

'I'm guessing that his death wasn't as a result of illness or accident.'

'I don't know.'

'You don't know!'

'There was no body. He just disappeared.'

'When was this?'

'A little under a year ago.'

'He might just have run out on you?'

'No.' Then, after a short pause she continued, 'He was too stupid with drink half the time to try to conceal from me that there was another woman or that he planned to go. Who would have wanted him? What would he have lived on? What was the sense of leaving a good business? He just went out early one evening and didn't come back. And then about three weeks later a man came to see me who said that he was dead and I was to ask no questions. When I agreed he gave me a thousand pounds. I needed the money badly as there were bills to pay.'

'Did you know this man?'

'I'd never seen him before.'

'So you have no idea why your husband was made to disappear or even killed?'

'No. But I'd known from the way he behaved that something was wrong. He was drinking even more, and jumpy. I'm sure it was something to do with the people he was involved with – the criminals. I didn't ask.'

'But the same people who gave you the money couldn't have wanted to kill you, surely?'

She shrugged. 'They might have changed their minds, if they thought I would talk to the police about it.'

'Was your husband violent towards you?'

'Yes, sometimes, when he was drinking heavily.'

'Had you told the police he was missing?'

'No! I didn't want him found – I just hoped he was six feet under somewhere.'

A completely irrelevant and crazy thought went through my mind: why the hell had I divorced Patrick when we were married first time around? Things had never got *that* bad.

I said, 'May I have his name?'

'Only if you promise that, if you find him, you don't tell him I told you.'

'I promise.' The thousand pounds 'compensation', I thought, said it all. This man was dead.

There was another short silence as she hesitated. 'Sometimes he called himself Bob or Bill Hudson, sometimes Bob Downton. I saw letters that came that were addressed to all those names. I think they were stolen names, stolen identities. I just called him Bob.'

'You don't have a photograph of him, I suppose?'

'No.'

I laid down my pen. 'Please, off the record, tell me why an intelligent woman like you married a man mixed up in crime.'

'You'll think me a fool. My parents were killed in a road accident – in the States, you understand – and I soon discovered that although I'd always been given the impression that they were wealthy there was no money, only debts. By the time I'd sold the house and settled everything there was only enough for me to come to Britain. I wanted to go to university here but didn't find out enough about it before I came. I knew there was an aunt in London, my mother's sister, but couldn't find her. My visa expired and I couldn't get a job so I ended up working . . .' Here she dropped her gaze and mumbled, '. . . on the streets in order not to starve. That was where Bob found me. I think he loved me, or if I'm honest, lusted after me to begin with and of course there was security for me – this business and a home. And now I might be found and deported as an illegal immigrant!'

'Did you go through an official marriage ceremony with this man?' I enquired.

'No, I was what you call a common-law wife over here.'

I explained that I did not know enough about the law to be able to help her with this but could put her in touch with people who did. But, as I had anticipated, she wanted nothing to do with officialdom in any shape or form.

'Can't you tell me anything at all about these criminals Bob was involved with?' I asked, preparing to leave.

'Sorry, no, nothing. It's really best for me not to know.'

THREE

'What sort of handgun did this woman have?' Patrick asked.

'I'm not sure as I only caught a glimpse of it. Possibly a Beretta of some kind.'

'Imported in pieces from China and assembled here, no doubt. We need to do some research on her husband.'

I reminded him that he had been given another job.

'But we don't want to just hand this on a plate to the Met, do we?' His gaze focussed on me. 'Do we?'

'At the risk of becoming tedious . . .'

Patrick sighed. 'OK, I'm supposed to be working on something else.'

'I have a suggestion.'

'Which is?'

'You get on with what Greenway told you to do, I write a report on my interview with the woman and, you having read the full account of what was said so you're fully briefed, I then put it in Greenway's in-tray without further comment.'

'Fine – if you think it'll achieve anything.'

The commander phoned me the next day. 'Thanks for that, Ingrid. We'll leave it on file now I've sent a copy to the Met – I don't know what she told them but it never hurts to cooperate. I think you already know that I simply don't buy the theory that I was the one in the firing line in this shooting and from what she said I would guess that her missing man had stirred up some mobsters who don't, for some reason, yet know he's presumed dead.'

'But your name must be on reports into investigations into private investigators obtaining information from corrupt police officers.'

'Along with dozens of others. If more evidence comes along to strengthen that idea I'll take another look at it. Meanwhile, if you want to go home please do so as Patrick's going to be tied up with this mostly desk job for a while.'

Roger and out, I thought, having achieved absolutely nothing.

There was no reason to leave the car in London, besides which I would need it, so I collected my things from the hotel and set off for Somerset, in no mood to stay in the city now, book research or not. I could not remember the last time I had felt sorry for Patrick other than when he had been hurt in some way. Greenway's instructions to him had been more, to quote my husband, 'pithy and to the point'. A little sympathy is due to Greenway here, too, as Patrick has always been a loose cannon, the commander having been told by Richard Daws, our one-time boss in MI5 and now in some unspecified, and possibly secret, senior position in SOCA, that it would take fifteen years off his life if he had us around.

Having dealt with domestic matters for a few days and taken the four older children on outings – it was half-term – I suddenly remembered the meeting with Carrick that had never happened. Acting on a whim is never a bad idea and after breakfast the next morning, Friday, I drove into Bath. It was pouring with rain and very windy, petals from the battered floral displays speckling the pavements like confetti. Probably because of the weather the city was unusually quiet, and this state of affairs was reflected at the Manvers Street police station. Even the old ladies who regularly bring small gifts and people who sleep rough who, high on something or the other, come in for someone to talk to, were missing. I can remember James Carrick once severely reprimanding a constable who referred to such people as 'cop botherers' in the hearing of one such person.

On climbing the stairs to the floor where the CID offices are situated the first person I met, in a corridor, was the new DI, David Campbell. He stared at me in perplexity, not remembering for a moment who I was, and then looked worried.

'The DCI has asked me to handle his workload today,' he replied to my query in his strong Glasgow accent.

'This isn't about work or any of his current cases,' I informed him. 'If you remember we were unable to see him about a week ago because of the murder investigation.'

'That's still ongoing, although we have a strong suspect. But nevertheless . . .'

'He doesn't want any visitors?'

'It's not that. He's asked me to oversee present work and handle anything serious that comes in, that's all.'

Lowering my voice I said, 'I'm not here on behalf of SOCA. James is a friend of ours. Is he here?'

'No.'

'D'you mind telling me where he is?'

'I don't know where he is.'

We gazed at one another for a few more moments and then Campbell added stiffly, 'He said he had a private matter to deal with, Miss Langley.'

I gave him a big smile. 'Thanks, and it's Ingrid.'

'If you don't mind I prefer to keep matters on a professional basis. I originally joined Strathclyde Police and that's how we run things in Scotland. It reflects better on the role of the police.'

I left, resolving to ask Patrick to try to iron out that particular problem, perhaps by inviting him to share a few drams.

James's mobile was switched off so I tried his home number. Joanna answered and I could hear little Iona wailing in the background.

'She simply won't settle,' lamented the new mother after we had exchanged greetings. 'We've had very little sleep for about a week now.'

'It's no good asking me for advice as I was useless with Justin and spoiled him terribly but do phone Elspeth and ask to speak to Carrie,' I urged. 'She knows absolutely everything about babies. I wanted a word with James. Is he there?'

Sounding very surprised, Joanna said, 'No. Isn't he at work?'

'I expect he'd just popped out for something,' I answered lightly. 'It was only a friendly call.'

'Patrick's in London, I take it.'

'Chained to a desk.'

'James hasn't yet resigned himself to the fact that that'll be his fate now Campbell's on the job.'

We rang off. No first names there either, then.

I am an impatient and stubborn sort of person and hate to be left in a state of limbo when I have decided to do something and am forestalled. It was obvious that Carrick had not merely gone along to Boots to buy some aftershave or had an appointment to discuss financial affairs at his bank or there would not be such an information blackout. To try to find him, though, seemed impertinent at best.

I rang Patrick and explained the situation, wondering if he had any ideas. He did not, and suggested that I leave it for twenty-four hours. So here I was, all fired up to talk about Benny Cooper and my day now had a very large hole in it. Fine, I would brace myself and seek out Mr Sort-of-Smarmy-with-Shades and see what he had to say for himself.

Sergeant Derek Woods has been stationed in Bath for a long time, having arrived before James Carrick, and what he doesn't know about the running of the place, the more important past cases from his colleagues in CID, and local villains must be infinitesimal. At one time a bastion on the desk in the public lobby, this now an enlarged and refurbished reception area, these days he is in charge of the custody suite. For the second time that morning I entered my security code on the number pad by the door that opens into the main part of the building, enquired after him and was told that he was in the canteen having his morning break.

'Can I get you a coffee?' Woods offered in his soft West Country burr when I asked to join him.

I smiled my thanks. 'Lovely, thank you.' The stuff wasn't but I really needed to talk to him.

'The governor's in London?' Woods enquired on returning. He had somehow persuaded the canteen staff to use a china cup and saucer instead of the usual polystyrene thing. He has always liked Patrick.

I nodded. 'In the office.'

Woods drew in breath through his teeth. 'Not happy, then.'

'No.' I stirred the sludgy-looking brew. 'Derek, I was wondering if you knew anything about Benny Cooper and Paul Mallory.'

The lines on Woods' craggy face deepened as he ransacked his memory. After several long moments had elapsed, he said, 'They were involved when a Mrs Pryce was killed at around the same time the Chantbury Pyx was stolen from a display case at the art gallery. The old lady was a real nasty, complaining kind of biddy and had crossed the square to have a go at Mallory, who played very loud music in his flat with his windows open. Terrible modern orchestral stuff, apparently – someone said it was like a plane crashing on a concert hall. It was the last straw, I guess, and she was beside herself with rage. She met the bloke who had stolen the Pyx just inside the entrance – Mallory lived on the first floor – grabbed the hammer that he'd used to attack the security guards and break into the glass cabinet while he was apparently wrapping it up more securely, and dashed off upstairs, presumably to batter on Mallory's door with it. She met another old lady on the way and must have thought she was going to try and stop her. The second lady, Miss Braithewaite, I seem to remember her name was, thought she was going to be killed and tried to get the hammer away from the woman. She got hold of it, there was a tussle, Mrs Pryce slipped and the hammer hit her on the head. Her skull was paper-thin and that was the end of her.'

'I hope Miss Braithewaite didn't end up in prison.'

'No, it was a complete accident, although apparently the Pryce woman had looked mad enough to have attacked *anyone*.' Woods grinned. 'Especially as Miss Braithewaite was the DI's old English teacher – Carrick hadn't been promoted then.'

'I was told it happened around the time the girl with red hair was murdered.'

'That's right. The bloke who had nicked the Pyx, who had form and was dressed as a woman, had thought he had been seen by a girl with red hair as he came back with his loot. He had:

Joanna Mackenzie, now Mrs Carrick, was working as a private detective and engaged by Mrs Pryce to find out who was nicking some of the plants in pots from the front of her house. But there was another girl with red hair working over at the nursing home in the same square – can't remember her name. The bastard – if you'll excuse my language – killed her shortly afterwards. Mistaken identity.'

I was wondering how the hell Carrick had managed to sort all this out. 'And Cooper and Mallory?'

'Cooper's a right little s— so and so. He persuaded Mallory to rough up Miss Mackenzie as he'd been lambasting Carrick and the CID here for failing to catch Mrs Pryce's killer – it was assumed to be murder at the time – in his newspaper column and thought it would mess up the investigation, thereby giving himself more good copy. But Mallory almost killed the girl. He was lucky not to be charged with attempted murder.'

'I understand Cooper had been watching Carrick, hoping to catch him with a prostitute or drinking heavily.'

'That's right. Although, you must appreciate we ordinary bods didn't get the full story on that. You probably know more about it than I do.'

This had only just occurred to me. 'I understand that Cooper and Mallory were already in the frame for some kind of pornography business?'

'Child pornography,' Woods said disgustedly. 'Personally I'd like to see people like that strung up – but please don't tell anyone I said so.'

'Where did all this happen? You mentioned a square.'

'Yes, right here in the city. Beckford Square.'

'Have you any idea if Mallory still lives there?'

'No, sorry. Whether he owned the flat or rented it . . .' Woods shrugged. 'He wouldn't have paid rent while he was inside, though, would he?'

'And Cooper? Where does, or did, he live?'

'No idea. But, I can have a look in records for you.'

'It's OK, thank you, I can do that myself. Apparently he's set himself up as some sort of private investigator.'

'I can just see him in a little back room somewhere digging dirt,' Woods muttered disgustedly.

'I suppose you wouldn't know who this mobster is who's

known to the Met that Cooper's reputed to be knocking around with in Bath?'

'You'd need to ask CID about that.'

'Derek, you're the eyes and ears of Bath. No wild guesses?'

He shook his head slowly. 'Sorry, no, Miss Langley. This is all pretty recent stuff and as far as I know word hasn't got to local snouts. And I don't advise you checking up on Cooper on your own, or on Mallory for that matter – he used to be right under Cooper's thumb and all the worse for it, never mind attacking Mrs Carrick, as she was to be.'

I thanked him, finished my coffee and took Woods' advice by deferring going to the last address listed in police records for Cooper, setting off instead to locate Beckford Square.

It was situated just north of the Royal Crescent and the Circus, the latter of which consists of three crescents that form a circle. Between one of these is Nash Street leading directly to Beckford Square which, belatedly, around eighteen months previously and after years of neglect, was designated a conservation area and scheduled for massive renovation. This has now largely been achieved and West Terrace, which I knew had been semi-derelict and boarded up for a very long time, was in the final stages of being converted into up-market retirement apartments. In the centre of the square was a little garden surrounded by ornate cast-iron railings with a matching gate. These were newly painted and the worn grass and overgrown dusty-looking ever-green shrubs which I seemed to recollect had been within had been replaced with neatly raked gravel, a new bench and a multi-stemmed birch tree.

I had consulted Records before I left the nick and looked up the Pryce case. She had lived at number 3, South Terrace, one of a row of much smaller houses that had only two storeys. That side of the square looked as though it had been added as an afterthought, when perhaps the original builders had almost run out of money. Here there were no Ionic columns or friezes, no Palladian ornamentation, just double-fronted houses with, even more oddly in such a setting, small front gardens. These, as one might expect in Bath and from what I could see between the parked tradesmen's vans, were picture-perfect with tiny lawns and jewel-bright flower beds.

I had not read all the case details but it was logical that Paul Mallory's flat had been, or still was, in North Terrace, as Woods had said the woman had crossed the square to complain about the noise of his 'music'. If there were any intrusive sounds emanating from the terrace now they would be drowned out by the sound of nail guns and power tools on the building site over to my right.

One might have imagined that the little garden in the centre would be accessible to residents only with keys to the gate issued. But this appeared not to be the case as a man whose appearance – tattered jeans, filthy sweatshirt, matted hair full of twigs and leaves – gave every indication that he was living rough, was seated on the bench, a bottle to hand from which he now took a mouthful. His gaze came to rest on me as I drew level and he gave me a revolting leer, followed by an obscene gesture.

OK, point taken, I thought, and abandoned my mission.

Patrick came home for the weekend that evening, hurrying upstairs for a shower and change of attire with the manner of a man hurling his working clothes aside and sluicing off all boredom together with city grime. He reappeared remarkably quickly, having said hello to everyone else at home, poured himself a tot of whisky and dropped with a sigh of contentment into an armchair. Vicky, who had followed him in, climbed into his lap to show him her new teddy bear, a present from Elspeth. The previous one had come to a bad end after being offered to a village fox terrier to admire only for it to be snatched, triumphantly carried away and shredded. This had had the effect of poor little Vicky now being terrified of dogs.

'What's his name?' Patrick asked her.

'Eeyore.'

'I thought Eeyore was a donkey.'

She shook her head, giggling, and I said, 'I think she prefers it to Pooh.'

'Pooh's rude!' shouted our daughter.

Carrie came into the room. 'Oh, that's where little madam is. Sorry, I just wondered where she'd disappeared off to.'

It was past the child's bedtime so Patrick carried her upstairs. Justin was staying overnight with a school friend, having been threatened with complete and for ever stoppage of pocket money

if he misbehaved – his past record is not good – and the two
older children were in the annexe with their grandparents to share
their evening meal. It is the Friday routine and I understood that
chicken pie, homemade, of course, was on the menu.

'Anything interesting in your few days at home?' Patrick asked
when he returned to the room.

'Well, as you know I went to talk to James this morning but
he wasn't there and David Campbell didn't know where he was.
So after I rang you I found out where Beckford Square is – a
flat in North Terrace there was the last known address of Paul
Mallory – and went round for a snoop. There was a down-and-
out sitting on a bench in the square. James, obviously doing the
same thing.'

'You didn't approach him.'

'Of course not. I came away. I didn't go to have a look at
Benny Cooper's last known address either as I didn't want to
interfere with anything James might be doing. But he did see me.'

'Have you contacted him since?'

'No. I thought you'd like to be in on that.'

'Too right.' Patrick took an appreciative sip of his single
malt. 'Is it just the kids having dinner or are we invited as
well?'

'I thought you might prefer fillet steak and all the trimmings
for two with a bottle of claret here tonight. All the family's here
tomorrow evening.'

After we had eaten, Patrick rang the DCI suggesting a meeting,
whereupon Carrick said he could be at the pub in fifteen minutes'
time. This made me wonder if his darling daughter still wouldn't
'settle'.

'I really want to apologize to you, Ingrid,' was his opening
remark when we saw him on the village green and were still
yards apart, he obviously having had to park somewhere else.
The building was packed to the doors, people spilling out into
the road and across on to the green. I suddenly remembered that
a skittles match against Wellow was scheduled for tonight.

'No need,' I hastened to assure him. His face had lack of sleep
written all over it.

'Mow you down with his car, did he?' Patrick queried.

I made light of the leer and gesture and then said to James,

'Patrick's done far worse things than that to preserve his cover. Is Paul Mallory still living there, then?'

'If being dead drunk or out of it on drugs for most of the time can be described as living, yes.'

Both men then eyed the Ring o' Bells with practical gaze.

'We'll never get a pint in a thousand years,' Carrick lamented.

Patrick frowned. 'If we go round the back and ambush someone . . .'

They went off, leaving me standing. It was a lovely evening so I found an empty bench a bit farther away and wondered, not for the first time, why Carrick had not told his new DI what he was doing that day. Surely their working relationship hadn't actually crashed already.

Not long afterwards, in a staggeringly short space of time in the circumstances, the two came back into view, Patrick carrying what appeared to be a heavy cardboard box that clinked. I had a quick guess from the apparent weight and came up with a bottle of wine, four to six bottles of bitter plus the relevant glasses.

'A visiting beer from Dartmoor!' he exclaimed. 'Jail Ale, no less, and a special offer on a dozen bottles to sons of the soil – some tonight, some tomorrow!'

'How terribly suitable,' I commented, my own version of this being most tonight, not much tomorrow. 'But you aren't sons of any kind of soil. What about me?'

They stopped in their tracks, clearly having forgotten all about me.

'It's so warm we were thinking of going home and sitting in the garden.' Patrick then said, adding with the smile of a man under wifely siege, 'There's a good bottle of Chablis in the fridge.'

Just the smallest bit offended, I replied, 'It's for an emergency – like unexpected visitors.'

They looked at one another and Carrick said, 'I reckon this is an emergency, don't you?'

No point in falling out with both of them.

'I knew you'd want to ask me about it but it's not official – yet,' Carrick said. 'This is just me doing a little homework on a couple of local ex-cons.' As he spoke his voice had thickened with anger.

'Far be it for me to advise moderation,' Patrick said softly.

James gave him a straight look. 'No.'

'Or urge you to consider that getting emotionally involved can affect judgement.'

'No – again, I reckon you'd think it none of your business,' the Scot said, taking a fierce swig of his beer.

'It's not.'

There was a little silence.

'But?' Carrick snapped.

'I suggest that your judgement has been affected insofar as it obviously hasn't occurred to you that it might be, taking into consideration his previous behaviour, exactly what Cooper wants.'

'*Wants?*' This incredulously.

'The DCI, still raging over the attack on his one-time girl-friend, now his wife, has admitted under questioning that he targeted those responsible in a private vendetta. One of them, Paul Mallory, now an alcoholic, has recently been found with severe injuries having been savagely beaten.' Patrick looked at James pointedly.

'Bloody hell! You don't imagine I'd—'

Patrick smoothly interrupted with, 'That's the beginning of an article in a gutter national newspaper under the headline "cop gets revenge on yob who injured his wife".' And when the other carried on staring at him, appalled, he added, 'As you're more than aware he's done something like it before and all the signs are that Mallory's right under his control. And now you say Cooper's big buddies with a serious criminal?' He shrugged. 'All it would take is a phone call for Mallory to be seriously done over.'

There was a much longer silence this time. Eventually Carrick, gazing into space, breathed out hard through his nose and muttered, 'Perhaps I shouldn't have come out tonight.'

'Perhaps you don't need friends.'

The DCI turned to face him. 'Look, Patrick . . .' Then he got to his feet and strode away for several yards, his back to us. Patrick merely smiled into his beer tankard, waiting.

With a gesture of despair Carrick came back and reseated himself. 'This man's like a running sore to me,' he said through his teeth. 'I've seen him twice lately when I've gone out at around midday. He doesn't bother to hide himself, just stands around seeming to know where I'm going to be. And it's worse than that: Joanna told me the other day that there was a red sports car parked in the lane outside our house with a man sitting in it. She's never actually come face-to-face with Cooper but from her description it was him all right.'

Patrick said, 'I've already mentioned to Greenway that Cooper and Mallory are back in circulation as we were discussing the subject of career criminals recruiting dodgy private investigators to get corrupt cops to leak information and delete files. You've already had the experience of having Cooper trying to interfere with an investigation and he also took it to a personal level. As you know, Greenway doesn't think that he could have been the target in that London shooting. He did, however, ask me to put the incident on file, leaving the responsibility of looking into this mobster chum of Cooper's who's been involved with interference to evidence elsewhere to your lot. James, you're on SOCA's radar with regard to this matter, which means that if you go in alone there's every chance that things'll go pear-shaped. If you bide your time and out-think Cooper, everything will be a hell of a sight better.'

I had already said to Patrick that in my opinion a large part of the problem was the DCI's chronic lack of sleep.

Carrick said, 'So, assuming I'm actually listening to you, where do I go from here with this little shit? Ignore the fact that he's been sitting outside my house while Joanna's there on her own?'

'From what I know about your good lady,' Patrick drawled, 'she has a pretty devastating right hook. Once bloodied the nose of one of her DS successors when he made some kind of dirty remark about your relationship, didn't she?'

'Who told you that?' Carrick demanded to know.

Patrick smiled. 'Only a little bird perched in a grape vine.'

My money was all on Derek Woods.

'Seriously,' Patrick continued, 'I do understand your worries. But, if it *was* him I can't imagine that Joanna's in any danger. Would you like me to watch Cooper and Mallory for you?'

'How the hell can you? Just now in the pub you said you'd been given a desk job that would last a while.'

'I'll disobey orders – besides, I can do most of the desk job from home.'

Slowly, Carrick shook his head. 'No, but thanks all the same.'

'Do you have any more info about the mobster Cooper's involved with?'

'I simply haven't had the time to go into it. But, there's a rumour, courtesy of a London snout, that he likes to be known as Raptor.'

FOUR

'The biggest advantage is that Cooper's not previously clapped eyes on us,' Patrick remarked, noting down a few figures on his clipboard.

'No, but James has if we bump into him,' I pointed out ruthlessly. Despite James's refusal of our offer of help we were doing a little investigating.

My partner handed me a large tape measure and began walking away from me towards a lamppost holding the end of the tape. Having arrived and noted the distance I gave him, he let go of the end and I wound it in again. Eyes on the ground as if following a trail, he then set off towards where a side street joined the main road.

'He can always tell us to sod off if we do,' he observed mildly when I caught up with him.

We were dressed in blue overalls, part of a collection of 'come in handy' garments we keep in an old kit bag in the car for when we want to assume any kind of role. It includes dark tracksuits for being invisible at night and jeans and baggy sweatshirts for loafing around as Joe and Mrs Bloggs. Most have been acquired from charity shops. Patrick did ask me to dispose of a black lace Teddy-style bra that transforms my modest bust into something quite amazing – I had worn it as part of a 'tart rig' – on the grounds that when I wore it his concentration on the job in hand went overboard. It is now safely in a drawer in the bedroom at home, as you never know when you will need to generate some raw lust in your man.

So, as utility company jobsworths, it being Saturday notwithstanding, no one gave us a second glance as we measured this and that, lifted small manhole covers and peered within, shaking our heads and writing a few sentences along the lines of, 'Rain water in cavity not draining away' and 'This water meter is filthy. How do they read it?' in case we were challenged. Until this moment, we had stayed in the close vicinity of the house last given as Benny Cooper's address, a thirties semi in East Twerton, just off the Lower Bristol Road in Bath.

'He's probably moved,' I said as we reached the street corner and turned left.

'Well, someone's at home. As we saw, there was a red sports car parked in the drive – such a vehicle was mentioned by Carrick last night, if you remember – and I saw the bedroom curtains being drawn back,' Patrick replied. 'The place is also in a fairly bad state of repair, which might suggest the owner spent a period of time away detained at Her Majesty's pleasure.'

'And we're walking down here why?'

'Just to move away from that area for a few minutes to look normal and also, for future reference, to find out if there's a back way.'

There was not and we wandered back the way we had come, Patrick writing down the numbers of the telegraph poles. The registration of the vehicle had also been noted for later checking.

'No, to hell with this, I'm going to ring the doorbell and tell him we can smell gas,' he announced.

We returned to our original scene of operations in time to see another car draw up outside the house. As is the case in most of the city there were double yellow lines on this section of road, which would explain the driver's subsequent haste, hurrying to the rear of the car, a black hatchback, throwing up the door and grabbing several heavy carrier bags of shopping. He then kicked open the garden gate and tottered up the short path, almost falling after catching his feet in something – the overhanging weeds? – and, having dumped down the bags, rang the bell, following this with a good battering on the door with a fist. Hastening back to the car he collected two full cardboard wine carriers and, having already placed a twin toilet roll pack beneath his chin, returned to the house, the door of which still remained shut.

'Come on! Come on!' he yelled after more ringing and banging.

We, meanwhile, were exhibiting enormous interest in a drainage grid in the gutter.

Some moments later the door was wrenched open, wrenched

seemingly on account of having been stuck in the frame, setting the old-fashioned letter box clattering.

'I'm not bloody deaf!' a man yelled. 'I was in the shower!'

'And I'm on double yellow lines! I can't wait any longer!' the other bawled back.

'Then why not just leave it and go?'

'Money! That's why. Money!'

'I'll give it to you when I see you tomorrow.'

'That's not good enough. You haven't paid me for the last lot yet either.'

'I haven't got that much money in the house.'

'You're a bloody liar! No cash from your little drugs business lying around? No takings from—?'

'Shut *up*!'

'I'm warning you that if you—'

'You'll what, you stupid little git? I'll see you tomorrow. Go on, get out!'

The door slammed. And then there was another bang, as if whoever it was had had to shoulder-charge it to make it close properly.

We continued busying ourselves with grid examining as the man got in the car and drove off, tyres squealing.

'Did you get his picture?' Patrick asked.

I told him I had – several, in fact – having achieved this by crouching down, concealing myself behind his legs and using my mobile phone camera. Then I said, 'The shopping must still be on the doorstep.'

Patrick crossed the pavement to stand behind – no, mostly inside – the overgrown front hedge. Then, a quarter of a minute later the door was hauled open again and there was a short pause – only one item of shopping hitting the ground, possibly the toilet rolls, to a chorus of muttered expletives – before it thundered shut again.

'Cooper,' Patrick reported. 'I got a good view of him. Let's go before someone reports us to the police for snooping around.'

Back in the Range Rover, parked several streets away, we discovered by accessing police files that my photographs were definitely of Paul Mallory. One was particularly clear as he had glanced fleetingly in our direction on the alert for traffic wardens.

'You know, that was quite fantastic,' Patrick exclaimed. 'When I first joined D12 I can remember people sitting in phony utility vans in the vicinity of addresses for *days* without so much as glimpsing their targets.'

'And with all the kit, too,' I recollected. 'Little red and white barriers to put around lifted manhole covers. Flashing warning lights. Even bunches of wires disappearing underground but nothing to do with the real thing to pretend to work on.'

'A lot of money is always thrown at national security.'

'The pair were well in character, weren't they?'

'Scum's the word,' Patrick commented.

'What does Cooper look like now? Presumably he wasn't wearing his shades.'

'No. Overweight – although to be fair he had an overlarge dressing gown on – five feet seven-ish, dark hair, small dark eyes and a pointy nose, giving him the manner of a nervous ferret.'

I thought this hardly surprising given that Mallory had just advertised to everyone within earshot that he was dealing in drugs and getting money from some other unspecified source – illegal almost certainly. Cooper was obviously using him as an errand boy. The man must be very sure of himself.

'What do you think he hopes to gain as far as James is concerned?' I queried.

'Perhaps he's just enjoying winding him up by sticking up two fingers, demonstrating that he's around. I just hope Carrick doesn't put a foot wrong.'

Patrick was too impatient to wait for Carrick to investigate the identity of Cooper's new mobster associate and, that same afternoon, accessed various secure Metropolitan Police websites, looking for anything about a man who liked to be known as Raptor. He also has the added advantage of being able to get into SOCA files, some of which are shared with MI5, his high security rating meaning that information not necessarily readily available to the forces unless requested by a very senior officer is at his fingertips. Other, more sensitive information has to be accessed in person, in London.

Nothing so tortuous was required, however, and he soon established that the serious criminal most likely to be the man in question had at least four aliases and, indeed, liked to be

known as Raptor. Reading a book in the same room, I heard a
snort of derision from my husband when this came up on the
screen. This individual had recently been seen in Bath. Although
thought to be deeply involved in a case where evidence against
another London gang leader, his brother-in-law, had 'disappeared'
from both computer and paper files, the Met had been unable to
make any charges stick. One of the reasons for this was that a
detective involved, implicated in corruption, had been found dead.
The subsequent inquest finding had been that he had committed
suicide having taken an overdose of sleeping tablets, a verdict
about which his family had been very unhappy. No details were
available. In another case names and addresses of witnesses had
somehow been leaked, several of whom had received threats
and changed their evidence or refused to testify. That case had
collapsed.

'This villain, who incidentally is a strong suspect in a jewellery shop raid in the West End a few days ago, has not only
created for himself several identities,' Patrick continued after
giving me the previous information, 'but would appear to have
several addresses. It's known he has a flat in Ealing and another
in Manchester. He was spotted by a keen-eyed off-duty detective
in Glasgow who tailed him to a tenement block in the Broomielaw
but it's not known whether he sometimes lives there or was
merely visiting someone. The thinking is that he's on the move
for much of the time, staying with family, friends, cronies, what
have you. There's no real evidence for that – but taking into
consideration the experience of those doing the investigating
there's every chance they're right.'

I said, 'I'm wondering how he keeps tabs on his henchmen if
he's flitting around all the time.'

'The main theory is that he commutes between various centres
of operation and doesn't just travel around in order to keep giving
the police the slip. One scam has been selling so-called assas-
sination kits to other gangs – weapons, mostly handguns,
imported from abroad and assembled over here. Apparently
they're supplied to customers packed in DIY power tool cases.
This appears to be a personal project – but it's been done before.'

'You said Sulyn Li Grant's Beretta could have entered the
country that way.'

'Along with many others,' Patrick replied wryly. 'After receiving information the Met raided a lock-up garage that turned out to be a workshop used for putting weapons together. But other than a few bits and pieces that pointed to the previous presence of firearms the place was empty.'

'That suggests he could have been tipped off, too.'

'It does. He also dabbles in exporting stolen top-of-the-range cars to Europe but that might be coming to an end as his agent oppo in Le Havre has recently been arrested by the French police. I hope they keep him securely locked up so he can implicate this self-styled Raptor before someone puts a bullet in him.'

'Is there a real risk of that?'

'It never hurts to prepare for the worst with these people when they become desperate. I'm also asking myself if that implicated Met cop really committed suicide.'

'But don't you think we should leave that to the Met and the Independent Police Complaints Commission?'

'Oh, yes. I'm just interested in the Bath connection – if there is one – with regard to our Jockenese friend. I think I shall take Monday off.'

With that in mind and not really wanting to go against Greenway's orders, Patrick slogged away at home with his assignment through most of Sunday, even declining with apologies his father's request to sing in the choir for the morning service. John, unused to being countermanded on such matters, was not pleased, even though I helped out.

Patrick went out on Monday morning and did not come back until early evening. I had stayed at home, writing and dealing with family matters. We have a home help two mornings a week, who also gives Elspeth a hand, but with a large house and extended family there is always plenty to do. These 'normal' activities also salved my conscience as I worry about the amount of time I spend away engaged on my other career.

'I paid a visit to Miss Braithewaite,' Patrick started by saying. 'The old lady who was involved in the Pryce case Sergeant Woods told you about. She lives in the flat above Paul Mallory.'

'The lady who was James's one-time English teacher.'

'That's right. She told me he played the part of Lord Peter Wimsey in a school play she wrote that was an adaptation of one of the Dorothy L. Sayers stories.'

'He must have been just perfect with his fair hair,' I said. 'But I have to say, before I spoke to Derek Woods I hadn't thought he spent any of his youth in this area.'

'She told me that his mother moved south when he was in his early teens and when he left school he trained to be a physical education-cum-sports teacher. But it wasn't exciting enough so he joined the Met. James actually came *back* to Bath. Anyway, after I'd finished cleaning Miss Braithewaite's living-room windows—'

'*What?*'

'She'd been up a really tall set of steps cleaning the insides of the windows. She must be all of eighty-five so I offered to finish them for her.'

'You're a saint. I take it you made it an official call.'

'Of course. It's not a security risk as there's no love lost between her and Mallory. She was praying he wouldn't come back after he was released from prison but he has. And he's playing his music again. She can hardly hear it normally because she had her flat soundproofed and he hasn't had his windows open.'

'Did she tell you anything useful?'

'Only that she can just about hear him having huge rows with another man who I can only guess is Cooper. She hasn't seen him and made a point of telling me that she doesn't stand by the window spying on everyone else in the square. That's what Mrs Pryce, who everyone hated, used to do.'

'Has she met Cooper?'

'No, but his picture was in the local paper after the trial so she has an idea what he looks like. The reason she hasn't seen him might be because there's a back way that leads into a small car park for residents only. A path from that takes you into a little lane that joins another on the west side of the Circus, probably intended for the use of servants in the old days. Which means that Cooper doesn't have to enter the square in order to visit Mallory.'

'Cooper said he'd see Mallory tomorrow. That was yesterday.'

'Miss Braithewaite didn't hear or see any movement yesterday. They probably met somewhere else.'

'We're really no further with this then, are we?'

'Patience. Then I went to the council offices and tried to track down this Raptor character. One of the surnames he's been using recently is Kingsland. Lots of Kings and names beginning with King on the council tax register but not that one. Obviously that might not mean he doesn't live in the area as he could be renting a room, or flat, where council tax is included in the rent. I've already checked the local electoral roll and he's not there either. Nationally, of course, there are thousands of Kingslands. I then abandoned that line of enquiry and went to the nick where I looked him up in Records – if you remember this mobster uses at least three aliases.'

'I hope James didn't spot you.'

'It wouldn't have mattered as I also needed to check up on something for my official project that I can't access on a home computer. I didn't see him, nor Campbell. Anyway, as I already knew – had made a note of, in fact – in the past Kingsland has also called himself Craig Brown, Shane Lockyer and Nick Hamsworth, the latter of which is thought *might* be the one on his birth certificate. Digging a little deeper I discovered that the first of those was definitely a stolen identity created using personal items taken during a burglary in Hounslow. That came out when he was convicted of handling stolen property: computers, TVs, jewellery and other stuff, the hauls of various burglaries. He served three years so has almost certainly dropped that alias.

'The second, Shane Lockyer, was the name he used years previously to that, when he first started on a life of crime in his late teens. Lockyer was his mother's maiden name. When he came out of prison, where he had served five years for his first serious offences, committing several robberies with violence together with other members of a gang calling themselves, believe it or not, The Raptors, he used the third name, Hamsworth.'

'Super chap, to use his mother's name to drag through the mud,' I murmured.

'She's probably proud of him, having done time herself for drugs dealing and forcing girls into prostitution.'

'OK, delete that last remark. So he might have gone back to using Hamsworth then if Kingsland got a bit hot.'

'Or another one he's dreamed up.'

'D'you have the addresses of the flats in Ealing and Manchester?' I enquired.

'I do. And of the tenement flat in Glasgow.' Thoughtfully,

Patrick added, 'Hamsworth's proud of this Raptors thing, isn't he? Otherwise he wouldn't have assumed that nickname. There's every chance he'll resurrect them at some stage – in his mind, his past glories.'

The rest of the week went by, during which Patrick applied himself to what he was really supposed to be doing at HQ. While he was thus engaged and knowing I had little chance of success, but also that these things have to be thoroughly investigated, I checked locally on the name Hamsworth. I discovered that there were not very many of them: an elderly married couple living in Radstock, a teacher at a prestigious private boys' school on the outskirts of Bath, two spinster sisters sharing a cottage in Priston, a retired police sergeant and his wife who had an apartment in Midsomer Norton, and a family butcher's business in that same town, the proprietors of which might be related to them. This was just a guess as the name originates in the northeast and is not common in the West Country.

No, as I had thought, this man must either be using another name or was not trying to establish for himself an outwardly respectable identity in the locality and was, as Patrick put it over the phone one evening, 'hiding away somewhere in a rat hole'. I felt investigating that possibility fell to him.

In between the more important writing sessions I turned my attention to the missing, presumed dead, husband of Sulyn Li Grant, the man who had called himself either Bob or Bill Hudson, and sometimes Bob Downton. Accessing police records for the London area I discovered with no surprise whatsoever that as Bob Downton he had a criminal record and had served three years in his early twenties for gang-related crimes and then another four for similar activities not long afterwards. If he was no longer alive the Met had no knowledge of it. The name Hudson only featured in connection with three shoplifting sisters, a couple of murderers who had been dead for ten and twelve years respectively, an animal rights teenager who had been party to the bombing of a laboratory and a seventy-five-year-old man who had driven the getaway car in a jewellery shop robbery.

The address for Downton at the time of his conviction had been in Bethnal Green, London, but I looked at more recent listings and discovered that his café bar business was given as the most recent known address. It was pointless to examine local registry records as if his common-law wife had not registered his death, who would? Not whoever had finished him off, that's for sure.

I changed tack and looked in the Metropolitan Police records with regard to bodies recovered from rivers and other associated watercourses that remained unidentified. I was a little shocked to discover how many there were. I emailed the force with the physical details and a mugshot of Downton, this unfortunately taken at the time of his first offences so probably completely useless by now. I did not get a reply for over twenty-four hours, by which time it was Friday afternoon.

'There's one extremely dead body with a bullet hole in its skull in a mortuary in East London that just might be that of Sulyn Li Grant's husband,' I disclosed to Patrick later after he had arrived, had his shower and was relaxing with Vicky on his lap, something she was making her routine.

'By that I presume you mean there's not a lot left.'

'Yes. It was disinterred from a flooded ditch on waste ground during the re-development of a warehouse at Woolwich. Having been put into a large plastic bag pierced with holes the body had then been weighted down with bricks, possibly because it wouldn't sink. It had probably been there for several months.'

'How long ago did he disappear?'

'About a year.'

'And when was the body found?'

'Three months ago.'

'Fits, then.'

'So we have the corpse of a white male who wore dentures thought to have been in his fifties when he died. Otherwise it remains impossible to identify unless someone can produce some DNA to compare the remains with.'

'I take it these folk don't have any kids.'

'That's fairly safe to assume but we can check. How's the job going?'

'I might finish it next week – unless someone else screws up.' Patrick smiled. 'Perhaps I ought to go and take a pot-shot at Greenway to make him change his mind.'

I wagged a forefinger at him.

'I wasn't all that serious, although the theory has a lot going for it. But mobsters so far have concentrated mostly on getting bent cops to delete files or give them info on witnesses and so forth. James's problem with Cooper and Mallory a while back took it several stages further but as far as I know no one's gone in for that kind of personal attack on the police since.'

'Unless Cooper's given the idea to his new buddy, Kingsland, Hamsworth or whatever he's calling himself now.'

'It would still be an amazing coincidence as far as Greenway's concerned.'

The house phone rang and Patrick, who was sitting nearest, answered it. I could hear that it was a female caller and that she was agitated but not speaking all that loudly.

'OK,' Patrick said. 'Act quite normally. We'll be there in a few minutes. Don't mention that you've called us and when you answer the door act as if we're friends expected for supper.'

He slapped the phone down, gathered up Vicky, who was almost asleep and said, 'The Carrick's place – now. That was Joanna. James is about to detonate as Mallory's parked nearby this time and although he got the crew of an area car to ask him to leave a while ago, which he did for a while, he's back.'

FIVE

James and Joanna live only a few miles from us in a farmhouse they restored from a semi-derelict condition. After leaving the main road at the top of Hinton Littlemoor the Somerset lanes we had to use to reach it are twisting and narrow, with passing places, and there is no room for error. Patrick drove the Range Rover as fast as he dared with me acting as look-out on the tight right-handed bends. We met a tractor but luckily were near the entrance to a house and Patrick swung the car into the open gateway to enable it to pass.

Nearing our destination, he slowed as we did not want Mallory to think us anything but ordinary visitors. With this in mind I had made a quick detour to the kitchen on the way out and grabbed a bottle of wine from the rack, placing it in a small carrier bag containing a pair of sandals I had bought that afternoon, tipping them out unceremoniously on to the worktop. Poor Vicky had fared little better, dumped, with apologies, in her grand-mother's arms just as she was about to serve their, and Matthew and Katie's, dinner.

We drove into the farmhouse drive, not looking again at the same black hatchback we had seen outside Cooper's house parked close by. Acting all jolly, we got out of the vehicle and Patrick secured it while I headed for the front door. Joanna opened it before I got there.

'Lovely that you could come!' she cried, arms wide.

We hugged. Then Patrick hugged her amid cries of 'Darling!' and lots of 'Mwaa! Mwaa!' sound effects, he playing the complete idiot.

Once inside, the door shut, Patrick stood with his back firmly against it, Carrick having just emerged from one of the two large living rooms. One did not have to be very clever to realize that he had been hitting the single malt.

'What's this then?' he queried.

'I invited them round,' Joanna said.

'I see,' he replied, adding, 'good,' unconvincingly.

'To dinner,' his wife added. 'Sort of a last-minute decision.'

To Patrick, James said, 'Now you're here, I'd like you to help me get rid of Mallory. He's outside this time.'

'That's why I asked them to dinner,' Joanna went on. 'To stop you getting rid of Mallory.'

The DCI was still looking at Patrick.

'No,' said Patrick.

'Then I'll go and speak to him myself.'

'You won't because he'll be all ready to wind you up. You must get the area car crew back to talk to him more forcefully.'

'But—'

'All they have to do is tell him that there have been a spate of rural burglaries lately, which I happen to know is true, and that behaving in suspicious fashion is not in his best interests. They'll need to remind him that he has a criminal record.'

Carrick made no response to this.

'James, I do *not* want Cooper or Mallory to know I'm with the law,' Patrick continued. 'Not yet. Not only that, I'm in a position to prevent you from causing a breach of the peace which would be highly damaging to your career if you were to lose your temper and assault him.'

'How the hell are you, other than by not permitting me to exit through my own front door by sheer physical force?' Carrick snorted. 'There are two back ways out of here, you know.'

'I do know and it's quite simple. I shall arrest you.'

There was quite a long silence.

'You can't handle much more of this, can you?' Patrick whispered. 'Not with all the other pressures at work as well.'

'No,' Carrick acknowledged, no louder.

'If I promise to do everything in my power to sort this out for you on condition that you completely ignore both Cooper and Mallory's provocations from now on, except to take steps through strictly legal channels – as you're going to do right now – does that help?'

'I don't know,' he said after another few seconds' pause.

'All you need is patience and to rely on me.'

'Patrick—'

'Have I ever let you down?'

'No.'

He could hardly forget that Patrick had also saved his life on one occasion when he had been bolted inside an industrial boiler in an old brickworks in Wemdale and left to die. Realizing that the DCI would not have gone down without inflicting damage on the mobsters responsible, Patrick had combed the grim northern town's most disreputable pubs for ne're-do-wells showing signs of having come off worst in a fight. He had found a group of three: a strapped-up broken nose, a closed eye and a fat lip, put money on the table and they had led him to the factory. They had then decided that they would steal the rest of his money, wristwatch and anything else of value and he had had to do a lot more damage to them before he and James could get away.

Patrick said, 'I want your solemn undertaking on this. You can't play into the hands of these scum.'

'You won't be able to fit it in between all your official work.'

'I shall make time. Ingrid and I have already been watching Cooper's house.'

Carrick registered surprise and then said, 'Greenway won't like it.'

'Tough,' Patrick responded with a shrug and then held out his hand.

'Sometimes you're a bastard,' Carrick said through his teeth.

Patrick knew exactly what he was referring to and gave him a big smile. 'You don't want to be marched through the door of your own nick, do you?'

After another agonizing pause Carrick swore – probably, I could not be sure as he always swears in Gaelic – grasped the hand and at least two of those present breathed out.

The phone call was made, the area car arrived very shortly afterwards, advice was given and Mallory drove away. He did not return, at least, not that night.

'Paul Mallory,' Patrick said early the next morning when he first woke up. I knew this because I had been awake for some time and was scraping together the will to go downstairs and put the kettle on. I had been lying there, exceedingly comfortable, gazing at the man in my life. He was very peaceful, the slightly austere features in repose, those mesmeric grey eyes veiled. We were both getting older, I told myself, probably too old for the kind of things we did in connection with our SOCA job. We have five children.

Ye gods.

'What time is it?' Patrick continued muttering.

'Only six-fifteen. Tea?'

For answer he rolled over towards me, not saying anything and not having to, his actions demonstrating an immediate personal preference with regard to the next activity. Sometimes prone to these pirate tactics he would nevertheless have desisted instantly, or at least undertaken a little gentle persuasion, had I not been willing. Yes, I was willing – very. Afterwards, when my husband had muffled my whoops of pleasure with the quilt – I have always been very noisy when thus engaged – we clung to one another breathlessly.

Perhaps we weren't too old after all.

'I'll get the tea,' Patrick then said, preparing to get out of bed. He crashed off to sleep again instead.

'Paul Mallory,' Patrick said for the second time that day, staring at the computer screen. 'Forty-two years old, five feet seven inches tall, receding light brown hair, pale complexion. An only child, born in Norfolk to wealthy parents. Home was a slightly run-down estate. But his father wrote him out of his will and everything went to a cousin when his mother died. What is a bit odd is that this man had no criminal record until after he met Benny Cooper. Of course, that doesn't mean he wasn't a bit dodgy before that – perhaps he just never got caught. Obviously, he never got on with his father.'

'Did he have an actual trade or career?' I wondered.

'Nothing about that in his records. From what Carrick said he doesn't appear to work now, so he must have some saved money.'

The rest of the previous evening had gone well, considering, and Joanna had managed to stretch her cooking to serve four and added a cheese course. The 'wee one', as Carrick now referred to his daughter, had remained soundly asleep throughout and I gathered that advice from Carrie about changing the baby's routine and milk formula had made an improvement.

We were working in the living room, handy to supervise the two older children's homework, the house rule being that they do it on Saturday mornings if at all possible so as to leave the rest of their weekend free. Matthew and Katie were seated at an antique gateleg table belonging to their grandparents that can be folded up when not in use. Both were wrestling with English essays that had to be handwritten.

Patrick glanced up from the screen and caught my eye. And smiled, and then chuckled. Then proceeded to carry on chuckling in a bloke version of the giggles.

'What's funny, Dad?' Katie immediately wanted to know, all ready to share a joke.

Patrick could hardly tell her that her adoptive mother's very own choral symphony earlier, swiftly stifled, always makes him laugh and he left the room, still chortling.

Four eyes gazed at me blankly.

'It happens to the best of people,' I told them solemnly. 'What's with the essays?'

'My day at the seaside,' Katie lamented. 'So *boring*. I haven't even started.'

'Does it have to be true?'

'No, you can make stuff up.'

'OK, you're building a sand castle—'

'I'm too old for sand castles!'

'All right, you're helping your little brother build one, when you dig up what looks like a large human hand.'

Her eyes shone. 'What, all rotten – green bones with bits of skin hanging off?'

'Yes, and the police are called and the beach is cordoned off and dug up while people look for the rest of the body. Only eventually the hand turns out to be the remains of a turtle's flipper that had been washed up.'

'That's fantastic!'

'I haven't started either,' Matthew said hopefully. 'It has to be about one of my hobbies.'

'Which are?' I queried, knowing the answer full well.

'I don't have any really – only my computer and it has to be something else.' He looked quite upset. 'I'm really worried about it as it should have been handed in last week.'

This lack of hobbies had been a point of contention for quite a while; he was steadfastly disinterested in joining in with the sporting interests of his friends or anything else we had suggested. Even an offer from James Carrick to coach him in rugby seemed to have cooled after initial enthusiasm.

I said, 'Perhaps you ought to go and find one – quickly.'

'Would Dad help?'

'Well, as you know he's already tried to – but do go and ask him again.'

The boy went away and I wondered what Patrick would make of *that*. As it happened the solution would probably not earn Matthew any cred with his chums but after a slightly shaky start he would grab at it with real keenness. I'm sure Patrick, a bit exasperated by now, reverted to lieutenant colonel, took him to the livery stable, ordered him on to his horse George and started to teach him to ride, which up until now Matthew had always insisted was only for adults and *girls*. The essay, penned at some speed later that day, was mostly about not quite falling off.

On Monday morning, Patrick having departed by train for London earlier, I rang Sulyn Li Grant to ask her if she had any of her husband's possessions that might hold traces of his DNA. At first she said that she had thrown out everything he had left behind, got rid of 'all his rubbish', but then remembered an old rucksack he had used that she thought might still be in a cupboard some-where. She said she would look for it and phone me back so I gave her the number of my official SOCA mobile. In this job you don't give personal phone numbers to anyone other than close friends and family.

I had to wait for over two hours for a reply but when it came she said that she had found it after much searching. I asked her to put it in a safe place in a plastic bag of some kind so it could be collected and then rang Patrick. He promised to contact the relevant Met department. This seemed to be the best course of action; after all, they were in possession of the body. DNA testing normally takes around a week but Patrick asked for it to be fast-tracked.

It was very important, for friendship's sake if nothing else, that Patrick was seen to be doing something on the Cooper/Mallory front. A round-the-clock watch on Cooper and tailing him everywhere was really the only way that his new-found mobster friend could be identified but, from our point of view, completely impractical right now as neither of us could spare the time. Carrick could hardly justify police time and expense for such an exercise either when no actual crime had, to our knowledge, been committed. I was fully in sympathy with his anger and frustration.

Almost three days dragged by, during which I found myself unable to concentrate on writing. My main character, a middle-aged DCI of outwardly placid manner, kept morphing in my imagination into a dark-haired sort of smarmy-looking man wearing shades. Finally, unable to put up with this any longer, I shut down my computer mid-afternoon and went outside through the front door, hoping to find inspiration if I went for a walk around the garden.

Parked across the end of the drive was a red sports car.

My first reaction was to stand and stare but I did not, following the advice given to Carrick by ignoring its presence after the first glance and wandering away. I told myself that it could easily be another vehicle, not Cooper's – someone might have stopped to answer their mobile or to look at a map. Not everyone uses a satnav. But why had I got the impression that someone was taking photographs of me?

It goes without saying that writing inspiration, or that of any other kind, failed to arrive and shortly afterwards I returned to the house, using the back way through the conservatory. Going upstairs, I was about to go into Patrick's and my bedroom as it is at the front and overlooks the drive, when it occurred to me that I would still be visible to whoever was in the car if I looked out of the window. If it was still there. I peeped around the edge of the curtain.

It was.

My mobile rang and for a moment I looked wildly around the room for it before realizing that I had put it in my pocket. It was Patrick.

'Wildly bored here,' he reported briskly. 'Just completed the job, Mike's out somewhere, just about everyone else in this department seems to be on hols and I've tackled every crozzy I can lay my hands on – without a lot of success.'

'How much leave do *you* have left?' I asked him. I don't get paid leave, the understanding being that my role is part time and I do not work while Patrick is on leave except in exceptional circumstances.

'Oh . . . dunno. Some of that last lot was sick leave after we were chucked out of the van on the last case. Why, d'you fancy jetting off somewhere?'

'I think we ought to get on with this Cooper and Mallory thing.'

'I'm not sure I want to use up leave for that.'

I told him about the car, adding, 'But it's bound to be somebody else.'

'Please don't go out to check or challenge whoever it is,' was the immediate reply. 'If it is Cooper, Mallory could have taken our car registration the other night, given it to him and he's asked a dodgy cop friend who's looked up the ownership details for him. I'll come straight home and have the rest of the week off anyway.'

I then remembered that the two eldest children would be home very shortly from school. I decided that to avoid them approaching the car I would meet them off the bus and bring them through the lychgate into the churchyard, and from there through a side way into the garden. This was a most natural thing to do on a sunny afternoon, even though they are old enough to walk across the village green and cross the road on their own, and usually do.

As I approached it began to look as though the car was parked so tightly across the width of the drive entrance that there would be barely room for anyone on foot to squeeze by at either end. This, I felt, was deliberate provocation, as though the driver intended to force some kind of argument, and I suddenly remembered that John was out, visiting a couple of parishioners. To retrace my footsteps would not appear natural and the action of a coward. I began to see the wisdom of Patrick's words and wished I had taken the side gate into the churchyard from the garden in the first place.

I reached the end of the drive and indeed there was only a matter of two or three inches gap both front and back. The driver's window hummed down and Mr Sort-of-Smarmy gazed at me through his dark sunglasses, a smile twisting his thin mouth.

'You're Ingrid Clyde,' he said.

'No, I'm not,' I replied. 'Kindly let me through.'

'Oh, sorry, you *were* Ingrid Clyde. Married a cop by the name of Peter after chucking out and divorcing squaddie husband Patrick Gillard. Peter was shot in dodgy circumstances one night in a flat in Plymouth being rented by – guess who? – squaddie Patrick, who had somehow got himself blown up while supposedly serving his country. And before anyone could say can of worms he's back in your life and you've got his brother Laurence's kids as well as three of your own! I call that downright greedy, especially as poor old Larry was killed in dodgy circumstances as well. I've done a bit of poking around but everyone's clamming up on exactly how *that* happened. Never mind, all's very cosy again for you in deepest Somerset with the squaddie neatly invalided out. True?'

'Bald facts distorted into gutter journalism,' I said, determined to keep my cool.

'But that's what I do!' he crowed. 'As well as my detective agency I have a brand-new job with a local rag exposing all the phonies and tossers around here. The punters'll drink in every word. No actual names mentioned, of course. Just a few hints.'

'Move your car,' I said grittily.

'And now squaddie hubby's big chums with Jimmy Carrick who heads up our excellent city cop shop. Bet his newly-delivered-of-baby-daughter ex-sergeant doesn't know he's screwing a juicy little tart describing herself as an escort. Think I should tell her?'

I took a very deep breath. 'If you don't move this poser's

rust-bucket – you hadn't noticed all those brown frilly bits on the wheel arches that happened while you were inside, had you? – I shall call the police. You're deliberately causing an obstruction to private property.'

'You don't really know who I am, do you?' he sneered.

'Oh, yes,' I hissed at him. 'Your name's *filth*.'

This struck home for some reason and he started the car, deafeningly revved the engine for far too long, choking me with fumes, and then roared away, scraping a wing, I was delighted to notice, on a corner stone of the outer wall.

I went to meet the children, finding myself a little shaky.

SIX

Patrick made no mention of my failing to take his advice as he must have realized that I could not have allowed Matthew and Katie to come face-to-face with Cooper blocking the drive and risk him frightening them. His mind was fully occupied with what had occurred and, if I'm honest, was probably working out how he could make Cooper disappear without leaving a trace of evidence. I know he is fully capable of it, as his time in Northern Ireland and other countries proved, and it was probably only the existence of his family now that would prevent him from doing it again, words of wisdom to Carrick notwithstanding.

'We mustn't mention this to James,' I cautioned.

'Especially the bit about him having it away with some female,' Patrick grunted.

'Everything else Cooper said had an atom of truth in it.'

I was subjected to one of my partner's penetrating stares. 'You don't think this has, do you? Surely not!'

'Judging by their past behaviour the pair of them are perfectly capable of cooking up anything that would put him in a bad light.'

'What *is* Cooper's purpose in all this?' Patrick asked himself. 'Is it retaliation for James getting him banged up? A warning to the police to leave him alone? I did ring Carrick and ask if he had seen either of them since that night we went round, and he hasn't.'

'I'm worried that even if he might not be aware that you now work for the law he knows you and Carrick are friends.'

'I don't need to tell you how I hate people like that knowing *anything* about me.' The unsettling glint of murder was still in his eyes.

'Please don't do anything,' I was driven to say.

'As in?' he coldly queried.

'You know what I mean.'

He did not reply, back in his mental ops room.

Michael Greenway phoned Patrick just as I was preparing to serve dinner. Eavesdropping, I heard the commander saying that he would have preferred to be consulted before any leave was taken and that he had a small but urgent job for Patrick to do. Patrick told him the truth: that he had been unable to contact him but had left a note on his desk and that Cooper had been making a nuisance of himself outside our home. Whereupon the commander told him that we should have informed the local police and asked them to sort it out.

'Why couldn't you contact him?' I asked at the end of the call, having told the children that their meal was ready.

'He must have gone out in a hell of a rush as he'd left his mobile on his desk,' Patrick answered. 'I used it as a paperweight for my note. No doubt that's why he's in a strop.'

'Mike doesn't usually get in moods.'

'He's well overdue for a break.'

'Are you going back?'

'No, I told him I'll deal with it next week. I shall take two days off and try to track down this Raptor moron by asking low-life who might know.'

With this in mind Patrick turned himself into a fairly – no, fully – repulsive, down-and-out: hair tangled, some gel then smeared on it to make it look greasy, oldest gardening jeans and a holey plaid shirt with mower oil on it that had somehow escaped my eagle eye and been binned. Garden soil had then been rubbed into his face, hands and under his nails. The ensemble was completed with instant, if not very authentic, BO in the form of a bad onion from the compost heap which, Guides' Honour, he rubbed into his armpits. On that same night, quite late, I took the car about a quarter of a mile away and waited. Shortly afterwards he emerged from one of the many footpaths that interlace the village – having started off by entering the church-yard from the gate in our garden wall. I then drove him to one of the less salubrious outskirts of Bath where he slouched off into the gloom. You do not openly leave your own front door in disguise in case anyone is watching.

I had the windows of the car wide open and the fans on full blast all the way home.

I always worry but consoled myself with the thought that if everything went wrong and he found himself hunted down he could head for the Manvers Street nick, where if they failed to recognize him all he had to do was make such a thundering nuisance of himself they would lock him up.

The next morning at breakfast the children naturally asked where their father was, thinking his coming home the previous evening meant time off work. I explained that he was doing a job for James Carrick, which was perfectly true. We both felt that this Raptor character might be the key to finding out what was going on.

Patrick had no phone with him – nor, of course, credit cards or ID of any kind, just a small amount of cash, plus his knife, so I did not expect progress reports. It was unreasonable to expect much in the way of success either, as this would only be a hanging around in doorways near pubs, clubs and similar premises exercise, keeping his eyes and ears open and asking a few questions. But during his time away he also hoped to keep watch on Mallory and Cooper. To my knowledge neither had returned to the village.

Thursday came and went. By Friday afternoon I was restless again, feeling superfluous, moping around the garden. Mark was peacefully asleep in his pram just outside the conservatory, the three eldest children were at school and Vicky was at a toddlers' club held at a church hall down the road, and would be shortly collected by Carrie. She would take Mark with her. Elspeth and John were out for the day somewhere, in Bath, I thought, having time off from parish duties. Even the kittens, rescued and given a home after our old tortoisehell cat, Pirate, died, were asleep in their bed.

'All this splendid domestic organization and the wretched author can't write,' I said aloud to an apple tree, the newly-forming tiny fruit just visible between the leaves. Even that was engaged in a useful activity.

What was Patrick doing? For the first time I actually found myself wishing that he had retired.

The day's routines ground inexorably on. The family returned, John and Elspeth arriving shortly afterwards, and I went out to help them unload shopping from their car. Child care, cooking dinner, eating it, bedtime stories for Justin and Vicky, a little TV and a little reading followed, then bed.

Saturday. I went with Matthew and Katie to the livery stable and, with the former on George on a leading rein and Katie on her pony Fudge, took them around the perimeters of several nearby large fields that had just been harvested for hay. The children trotted their mounts, Katie venturing off on her own for a canter, only showing off to her brother a little, which meant I had to run with George. I almost forgot my worries: the sunshine was warm, the hedge bottoms full of wild flowers, and skylarks were singing high overhead. A full hour passed and by this time we were in the highest of the three fields. I paused; a superb view of Somerset spread out before us. The horses grazed but were increasingly troubled by flies so we moved off again, homewards.

My mobile rang.

'Hi, nothing to worry about but James and I have been in a spot of bother,' Patrick's voice said. 'Can you come to the nick and pick me up?' He sounded a bit strange. 'Please bring some of my clothes – I've chucked the others away.'

I told him that I was in the middle of the countryside with the children.

'When you can – no rush.'

'Right,' I said to Matthew, shoving my phone back in my pocket and seeing every reason to rush. 'Please hop off a minute.'

I mounted, altered the stirrups slightly, gave one to Matthew to enable him to get on again and told him that he was to hang on to me around my waist and NOT LET GO. If he thought he was about to fall off he was to SHOUT.

We set off, at quite a rush, George suddenly seeming to remember that he was a middle-weight hunter. I had no concerns about Katie; she has competed in pony club events and is a competent rider. We had to slow down through the open gateways but on the last slightly uphill field I leaned forward and stood in the stirrups so Matthew could have the saddle, letting George have his head. If I had not been agonizing over what might have happened in Bath I would have really enjoyed myself. The children and the horse did.

Their cover had been well and truly busted. Patrick had decided, after a second abortive night of trailing around the pubs and alleyways followed by watching Cooper's house, to make for Beckford Square to look out for Paul Mallory. There, as had I, he had come upon James Carrick engaged on the same mission. Staying well in character, they had shared a can of beer, behaved in rough but muted fashion and not seen a soul other than a few residents of the square, one of whom had finally ordered them to move, threatening to call the police if they did not. So they had, hanging around some time later in the car park to the rear of North Terrace. There they had suddenly been set upon by seven, or even eight, men.

'They seemed to know . . . at least the ones who went for James did . . . that we would put up some resistance,' he finished by saying at the end of his account of what had occurred, taking short breaths as though his chest hurt. 'They wouldn't have sent so many . . . just to sort out a couple of nosy drop-outs.'

'But this happened last night,' I said. 'Why didn't you ring me then?'

'Because James was taken to hospital with suspected broken ribs and possible internal injuries. I went with him. Despite my best efforts he got a real kicking.'

'What about you?'

'I'm all right. The odds were a bit high, that's all, and I only managed to floor four of them.'

Patrick had been waiting for me in the reception area, wearing someone's tracksuit and obviously having had a shower, and now, after not really answering my question, he prised himself out of the chair he had been sitting on and took the bundle of clothing I had brought with me. His knuckles were red and bruised and there was an emerging bruise on the side of his face. Limping a little and obviously in pain, he went off to change into his own clothes.

'The only good thing about it,' he resumed when he got back, 'is that the four I managed to deal with . . . were arrested. We may even find out who paid them to do the job. The other three, or four – difficult to tell in a badly lit area like that – got away.'

'You didn't have a phone with you, though.'

'James did.'

'The information to whoever organized it – this Raptor character? – had to have come from Cooper and/or Mallory.'

'Who else? But what proof do we have? How did they know? I've a nasty feeling James has taken this very badly and I can't say that I blame him. He was worried that he had broken his word to me, but I told him he had only promised to ignore all provocations, not refrain from doing a little undercover work.'

Elspeth was in the front garden when we arrived at the Rectory.

'You look as though you've been in a fight,' she said sternly to her son. In her seventies now, she is still an attractive, slim woman with an exceedingly sharp intellect.

'Indeed,' he agreed. 'Working undercover with your favourite copper.'

'Who, James?'

'Yes. I'm afraid he's in hospital for observation.' A wan smile to the pair of us. 'Would there be any invalid's nosh handy?'

'There's some soup in the fridge,' I told him.

'A piece of leftover steak and kidney pie?' said his mother. 'I can heat it up for you.'

Without a backward glance he followed her into the annexe.

James Carrick was kept in hospital for forty-eight hours and then sent home, the diagnosis two cracked ribs and severe bruising, including internally. He would be off work for at least a fortnight.

'And he'll get a hell of a bollocking,' Patrick added, having given me this latest news.

'But he hasn't actually done anything wrong,' I protested.

'Real cops aren't supposed to do things like that – especially DCIs.'

'So who the hell'll know what he was doing? Will he own up or are the pair of you going to use your imaginations and say that, as a chum, he was watching your back, *in his own time*, on an assignment for SOCA? That's not actually untrue.'

Patrick gazed at me tiredly and I could almost hear the cogs in his brain whirring.

'You used to be a hell of a lot more inventive when you worked for MI5,' I said crossly.

'As in cunning, if not an out and out liar, more like 007, successful in absolutely everything and better in bed?' Patrick queried with the ghost of a smile.

'No, you get better in bed all the time,' I retorted. 'Go and *phone* the man.'

Between them they concocted a story and, as far as Patrick and I know, Carrick did not hear another word about it. Patrick did, though, from Greenway, the grapevine obviously having gone into overdrive over the rest of the weekend, when he returned to work, a little bruised and battered, on Monday morning. I know, because I was there. When the commander had finished commenting on the general lapse in commitment to the job Patrick apologized, admitting that the entire episode had been a disaster and no one was any closer to finding out more about the mobster in question.

The commander then looked at me with every indication that he was aware I was not present in order merely to decorate my working partner's arm and pass the painkillers. 'You're not happy, Ingrid,' he said.

'I wasn't happy before I set off this morning,' I told him. 'This job of ours is rapidly turning into a complete waste of our time and effort.'

Out of the corner of my eye I saw Patrick shoot a quick glance of surprise in my direction.

'On account of our D12, MI5 experience we were recruited as advisers and consultants,' I went on. 'But now you're using my husband to do routine work. There are people in the main office who could have undertaken that assignment last week.'

'There are a lot away on leave,' Greenway observed.

I ignored the remark. 'To remind you: we *advised* you that there's a problem with this London criminal who appears to have extended, or be in the process of extending, his zone of operations to Bath. The man has proven connections with interfering in police cases. A Met CID officer working on one of those cases committed suicide – that was the official finding but it was disputed by his family. No one seems to have investigated that. Two newly released from prison criminals, Benny Cooper and his sidekick Paul Mallory, have been lurking outside DCI James

Carrick's house. Cooper is an associate of this mobster, they've been seen together, and he's been stationing himself outside our house too. Apparently he got his old job back at a local newspaper writing a gossip column and the latest development is that we all, Patrick, I and James Carrick, featured indirectly in it on Saturday. It wasn't as poisonous as the rant he delivered to me outside our house and no names were mentioned, but it was the old swipe at Bath CID and sundry friends those in charge there have – wealthy and dubious friends hiding behind the respectable facade of the church, a senior position in the army, etc. etc. *ad nauseam.*'

'Cooper sounds a great guy,' Greenway commented when I paused for breath.

I continued, 'I'll give you the story in case you aren't in possession of the full details. On Friday night when Carrick and Patrick were engaged in watching the area near Mallory's flat, working undercover – just about unrecognizable – as down-and-outs, they were waylaid and an attempt was made to do them serious injury. Carrick was quite badly hurt and will be on sick leave for at least a fortnight. You told Patrick that it was Avon and Somerset's problem. It isn't, it's very serious crime and this man, Raptor, or whatever he's calling himself right now, *is* based in London. You know most of this, but you're not even considering taking our advice and instead keep blethering on about Patrick's lack of commitment!'

Greenway's brow furrowed as if he was trying to remember if anyone had accused him of blethering before. Probably . . . not.

I went on, 'If there had been some kind of official support the so-called disaster probably wouldn't have happened and we would not have the situation whereby there's every chance that Carrick will now go and shred one or both of them into very small pieces.'

I had hazarded a lot in saying that, Carrick's reputation and career included.

'Is there a serious risk of that happening?' Greenway asked us both. 'I know you told me that Cooper was sent to prison for, among other things, masterminding an attack on Joanna Mackenzie, now Carrick's wife.'

'There was a touch and go situation recently when Mallory,

almost certainly under Cooper's orders, was parked outside his house, having turned up again after the crew of an area car had moved him on,' Patrick answered. 'That was when I promised to do all I could to help him sort it out.'

The commander does not have worry beads but a collection of brightly coloured paperclips which are either in a small antique china bowl on his desk or arrayed, as they were now, in complicated patterns on the leather blotter that, for some obscure reason, senior policemen never seem to be able to do without. Now, he impatiently swept the whole lot back into the bowl.

To Patrick, he said, 'How did these people know who you were?'

'God knows. As Ingrid said, we were in pretty heavy disguise. Even my parents didn't recognize me when they came upon me dozing on a bench in Victoria Park.'

This was a new one on me.

Patrick resumed, 'I'd hung around in the area close to Cooper's place the previous night but there'd been no sign of him. His car wasn't there either and he didn't come home. Carrick and I met up, quite by accident, in Beckford Square. He's very experienced in that kind of work as he used to go undercover when he was in the Met's Vice Squad. We shared a can of beer he'd brought with him – for authenticity's sake – two fingers, I'm afraid, up at Bath and north-east Somerset's No Alcohol in Public policy. A resident got highly annoyed and told us to leave so we spent an hour or so hanging around outside down-at-heel pubs and clubs. As I had previously, I whispered to a few guys that I was looking for someone calling himself Raptor in connection with a job for a friend of mine – I reckoned I was too filthy to get any job myself – but just got blank looks so gave up. We'd seen nothing of Mallory that night either, not even when we returned and went round the back of the terrace where he lives to a small private car park. That's where they jumped us.'

'Did anyone follow you back to the square?' Greenway wanted to know.

'We didn't see anyone but someone must have been watching our movements.'

'I take it this is being investigated.'

'Yes, DI Campbell's working on it. Several of these yobs were arrested so we might get a lead from them.'

There was silence for a few moments, broken by Greenway saying, 'You're beginning to convert me. Because now, if the local rumours are correct, Cooper has a powerful associate. From what you've told me, taking into account his job as a sort of newspaper hack, he must know everyone and everything about the city, especially anything on the illegal side. Perhaps this Raptor character is using him for that reason.'

Patrick said, 'Or if he just wants a place to enjoy quiet weekends away from the hard grind of serious criminal activities in London he could be using Cooper to sniff out and even deal with any bother from what he regards as the local plods or resident mobsters.'

'Does Bath have resident mobsters?' Greenway enquired.

'Right now, probably not. Not since the turf war when we cleared out those left standing or they disappeared or died from the effects of drink and drugs. What we don't want – and here I'm speaking both as a peripheral cop and someone who lives in the area – is an outsider to spot an opening and move in.'

The commander turned to me. 'Believe me, Ingrid, I do value what you both do here and I'm sorry if I've given you the impression that I don't.' And to Patrick, 'My concern having weighed all this up is that Carrick might take the law into his own hands and do his force untold harm. It's just as well he's out of it for a while. With Avon and Somerset's permission I'll send you back there with a remit to check up on the Raptor side of this – and I don't need to tell you not to tread on this DI Campbell's toes.'

We decided to start right where we were, in London.

'You really don't have to tolerate a carpeting from Greenway,' I said, still aggrieved, a little later. 'I know he's a commander but he did say a while back that he didn't want you to call him sir on account of your being a retired lieutenant colonel.'

'It's not a rank thing,' I was told. 'He has trouble at home, the usual kind that happens to policemen who work long hours, his wife fed up with hardly ever seeing him. She's threatening him with divorce.'

'Mike told you this himself?'

'No. Benedict, his son, still keeps in touch with Matthew. He told him and Matthew told me. I said it was a good idea to keep very quiet about it.'

'Even to keep it from your wife?'

'Ingrid, sometimes you're not very good at hiding your feelings. You might have displayed some kind of – well, sympathy that would have led Mike to realize we knew. I've only mentioned it now to explain what happened so please don't say anything.'

Sometimes women have to accept that men have their own laws of the jungle. And come to think of it, Patrick hadn't even looked mildly irritated at Greenway's diatribe.

The Metropolitan Police Detective Sergeant, Paul Smithson, who had supposedly committed suicide, had been living on his own at the time of his death as he was separated from his wife, Susan. The time lapse involved, getting on for a year, and the fact that the flat had been re-let meant that it was pointless for us to go there to talk to neighbours. We went instead to see his widow, who had moved from the family home in Ilford, but only a few streets away, to a terraced house in a street crammed into the area between the High Road and a large railway depot. We did not park outside.

The door was opened by a man, probably in his late twenties, with luxurious tattoos and a very generous paunch. When he saw us he prepared to shut it again but Patrick had already put his foot in the way, following this up with announcing who we were and that we wanted to talk to Mrs Smithson.

'Thought you were them religious nutters,' the man said sheepishly.

'I can do that as well when I've had a few pints,' Patrick told him in matey fashion.

He received a gap-toothed grin for this and we went in.

The place smelt like the pubs of yesteryear, of stale beer and cigarette smoke. It had that same look of time-worn nicotine-stained weariness of old hostelries too, and I found it hard to tell whether the beige-coloured soft furnishings in the room we were shown into had started life like that or had never been washed. The middle-aged woman sprawled on the sofa followed this trend, sporting a faded fake tan and a tight tracksuit – she was a large lady – that might have been one of the lucky ones but had been put into the washing machine with various garments from which the dye had run, the end result being a strange pinky-purply grey.

'Susan Smithson?' Patrick queried after introducing us.

'I don't call myself that now,' the woman replied.

'How would you like to be known?'

'Just call me Sue; it saves a lot of bother.'

'May we sit down?' Patrick went on to ask politely.

'God, you must be the first one to have asked that in here – ever,' she answered with a guffaw of laughter. 'Go on, sit. Cigarette?'

'No, thanks.'

'Is she allowed to have one?' Sue enquired, gazing at me dubiously. Well, as was our working habit I *had* merely been referred to as an assistant who would take a few notes.

'Thanks, but I don't smoke,' I said.

'We do, don't we, Jonno? He's my son,' she added with a wave of her hand in his direction.

They both lit up and there was a short silence before Sue said, 'You must want to talk about Paul.' She swung fiercely in Jonno's direction. 'Unless you've been up to something. Have yer?'

Her son twitched in alarm and almost dropped his cigarette. 'No, Mum. Would I?'

'I do wonder sometimes,' the woman remarked darkly. 'I just wish you'd go and get an effin' job.'

'I *have* tried, Mum,' was the faintly snivelling response.

'It is about your late husband,' Patrick confirmed. 'I understand you didn't agree with the inquest findings.'

'No, never in a million years. Someone killed him.'

'Look, I'm sorry to bring back unpleasant memories but he had taken a large overdose of sleeping tablets together with enough whisky to have rendered him in danger of dying from alcohol poisoning.'

'Paul never took sleeping tablets, never even 'ad one – he slept like something . . . well . . . dead.' A flicker of emotion crossed her face. 'Well, he did. And he never touched whisky either – didn't like spirits. Bitter was his drink. I told you lot that at the time.'

'In desperation, though?' Patrick prompted gently.

'Yeah, he was in trouble, wasn't he?' A big sigh. 'All I know is that he was working on this case involving some crime boss who the Met had been after for ages. Paul would have never taken money but someone might have threatened him to make him do something he shouldn't. I can't really help you as he never talked about his work. But he wasn't the sort of bloke just to chuck in living and top himself if he'd screwed up.'

'I shall have to ask you why you broke up.'

'That was my fault,' Sue said sadly. 'He was never around, working all the time, so I went out with someone else – just for a couple of meals, you understand – not an affair. Paul took it very badly when he found out, didn't believe me, and walked out. I was quite shocked, really. I thought we could have sorted it out.'

'Is that why you no longer use your married name?'

'No, not at all. I do on formal things, like at the bank. It made me feel a bit creepy after he died as I was sure it wasn't suicide. I thought there might be someone out there watching us, someone connected with this crook. So how did you find me, by the way?' she demanded to know.

'I asked your old immediate neighbours.'

'Oh.'

'Are you still worried about that – that you might be being watched?'

'Yes, I am.'

'I suggest you move farther away, this time without telling the neighbours where you're going.'

'I could afford a better area if *he* got a job,' said Sue witheringly, glaring at Jonno. 'I work most evenings at the Black Horse as it is.'

'Did you have any kind of communication with your husband just before he died that would lead you to think he was being threatened?'

'We weren't in touch at all for four or five months before it happened.'

'What about you, Jonno?' Patrick went on to enquire. 'No contact with your father at all?'

The man muttered, 'We did meet up for the occasional pint. But he said not to say a word to Mum about it.'

'Did you tell the police that at the time?'

'No. Dad had told me not to say anything, hadn't he?'

Patrick swore very, very quietly under his breath and then said, 'Well, now's the time to speak up, sonny. This is the Serious and Organised Crime Agency trying to put a mobster behind bars!'

Jonno jumped as though something had hit him, not surprising having been on the receiving end of Patrick's parade ground voice.

'How many times did you meet him?' Patrick went on to ask, albeit more quietly.

'What, altogether?'

'Yes.'

'A coupla dozen times, I suppose. P'raps a bit less.'

His mother turned an astonished gaze on him but said nothing.

'That sounds as though you met him quite regularly.'

'About every other Saturday evening, unless he was doing something else.'

'Such as? He can't have worked that much overtime, surely.'

'Dunno. Sometimes he'd just say he couldn't make it. Perhaps there was something on the telly he wanted to watch.'

'Where did you meet him?'

'The Swan most times. Or The Dog and Gun. They do good sausage, egg and chips there.'

'What kind of things did you talk about?'

'Football, mostly – he was a West Ham fan.'

'What else?'

'Dunno, really. This and that. He'd go on a bit like Mum does about me not having a job.' This with a worried look in Sue's direction. 'I know I'll have to do the work experience scheme soon or I'll lose benefits. But you don't get paid for that. Slavery, I call it.'

'But you're already getting paid!' I was forced to exclaim.

'Exactly!' Sue cried. 'Ta, love.'

I was not in a position to observe but had an idea that Patrick was giving Jonno a try-harder-to-remember-or-I'll-wring-your-neck look.

'And his motor,' Jonno said eagerly. 'He was for ever going on about that. It was always packing up on him.'

'Did you see him just before he died?' I asked.

'Yeah, I think it was a coupla days before.'

'And?' Patrick prompted.

'Well, nothing really.'

'Look,' Patrick said, ice-capped volcano style. 'This man was a suspect in an investigation because information about a certain criminal had gone missing, both from paper and computer files. Not only that, we know from subsequent events that personal details concerning witnesses, their addresses and so forth were leaked. That is a very serious matter. Did he not saying *anything* to you about it?'

'No, but the last time I saw him he said something about planning to take a holiday soon, that he was owed quite a bit of leave. Yeah, that's right, he thought he might go abroad somewhere, get right away.' Another sideways look at his mother. 'I got the idea he was going with someone.'

'No name was mentioned?'

Jonno shook his head.

'So, if anything, he seemed quite cheerful.'

'Yeah.'

It made no sense.

'Were you fond of him?' I enquired. Why this almost complete lack of interest? Or was this son of his emotionally, as well as brain, dead?

The man shrugged. 'Not really. I felt as though I hardly knew him. He'd never been around when I was a kid. Just a bloke I talked about football with.'

We left, Patrick having given Sue his card in the event of her remembering anything she might think useful.

SEVEN

'Surely Smithson must have known he was under investigation,' I said that evening at home. 'Had he been suspended from duty?'

'I've asked for the full info on the case but haven't yet received it,' Patrick replied. 'I'm guessing that he was informed and put on other duties, possibly at another station or unit. Under Project Riverside SOCA analysed five UK police operations where criminal interference was suspected and in four of them found examples of corrupt individuals including serving and former police officers. All had been used by private investigators to gain access to information. So Smithson wasn't the only one involved.'

'It can't have been Cooper who made contact with him as he was in prison.'

'No, I think we must assume that he's new on the scene, not remotely connected with that case, and someone who's small fry in what the criminal fraternity must regard as the sticks.'

'But a man with ambition.'

'Time to clip his wings.'

The information arrived by special courier the next morning and it transpired that Smithson, together with others under scrutiny, had not been informed that they were under investigation but allowed to carry on working under what was described as 'controlled conditions'. This had been to prevent them, if indeed the suspicions had any truth in them, from warning those for whom they were suspected of carrying out 'inappropriate actions'.

'So why did Smithson commit suicide?' I wondered aloud. 'Did he somehow find out that he was under investigation and was completely devastated because of being rumbled or because he was innocent and felt isolated?'

'Or was he murdered on account of having been forced somehow, blackmailed perhaps, into accessing files, had second thoughts and threatened to blow the lid off the scam?' Patrick mused.

'Nothing's for certain.'

'I agree. And according to his widow he didn't drink spirits and never needed sleeping pills. That's if she isn't trying to muddy the waters due to what she perceives to be the disgrace of it.'

This was not our immediate problem, however, and there was no point in working on it further. But I still had an unsettling feeling about Jonno.

'No, sorry, you can't interview the assault suspects – you're too close to the case as you were one of the victims and also must be aware that it's against the rules,' said Detective Inspector David Campbell when we found him in his office the following afternoon. He had been out all morning.

'I was assaulted on account of being close to the case,' Patrick countered. 'Not only that, I've been ordered to track down this man who likes to be called Raptor, or is using one of his aliases, who is rumoured to be an associate of Benny Cooper. These men were hired by someone and I want to know who that was.'

Campbell shook his head dismissively. 'There's nothing yet

to link the man you're looking for with this assault. The four men arrested in connection with it have been interviewed and remanded on police bail. You may listen to the recordings if you wish.'

Which we did, only to discover that two of them had only confirmed their names, refusing to answer any further questions other than to say they had been drunk at the time and could remember nothing. The third was already known to the police and his address was on file. The fourth man, who had provided an address, did not appear to have been in trouble before but had also refused to answer questions.

'How are you going to proceed with this?' Patrick asked Campbell afterwards, his anger apparent.

'We shall talk to them again – when they've realized the seriousness of the charges against them.'

I put a fleeting hold on Patrick's wrist on the arm nearest to me, hidden from Campbell, as a gentle reminder of his boss's instructions concerning treading on the toes of a certain DI in the sticks, and without another word he turned on his heel and we left.

'Thank you,' I said outside, having to raise my voice above the racket of adjacent roadworks.

Patrick threw his hands in the air in a gesture of acute frustration.

'We have their names and two addresses,' I reminded him, having written them down. 'And Campbell was perfectly correct: for you to interview the suspects is against the rules.'

'James might have a few ideas.'

'And we ought to go and see how he is.'

Carrick was not there and Joanna appeared deeply worried, their daughter bawling in her arms when she answered the door. I could see that her own tears were ready and waiting and took the infant from her, taking her for a little walk around the garden, as I do with Mark. This one was not so easily mollified but ended up producing a big burp and was then much happier. After checking that everything in the nappy area was all right I laid her in her pram and strolled with it in the drive until there was every chance that she would go to sleep. Finally, I wheeled her around to the back, where I knew Joanna left her on warm days by the opened French doors, and went inside.

Carrick's one-time strong and feisty sergeant was in pieces, Patrick on the big black leather sofa alongside her but not knowing what the hell to do. I seated myself on her other side.

'There's something terribly wrong with Iona,' Joanna wailed.

'No, it's called baby blues,' I said.

'And I don't know where James *is*,' she carried on as though not having heard me. 'He's supposed to be resting but he's gone off somewhere and I'm *sure* he's going to do something awful.'

Go and make some tea, I mouthed at Patrick behind the weeping woman's back.

He went and I put some paper tissues from my bag into Joanna's hands, she having wrung to soggy shreds the ones already in her possession.

'Baby blues?' she queried, turning red eyes to me.

'You must have heard of it,' I said a little too impatiently.

'Of course. But I'm not the sort of person to get silly things like that.'

'I had baby blues with all three of ours – only not quite so badly with Mark.' But I had still drenched my husband with abundant tears on several occasions. He hadn't known what to do with me either.

She actually gaped at me for a few seconds.

'You do get over it,' I told her. 'I discovered that it wasn't a good idea to take pills. Have you thought about going back to work?'

'I thought about it when I was pregnant and decided I'd quite like to rejoin the police,' she answered, smiling sadly. 'But now . . .'

'You could have a nanny.'

'James might say that I was, well . . . abandoning her or something.'

I too had entertained such pathetic lines of thinking, which I explained to Joanna. Baby blues. 'And yet he's said to me on more than one occasion how good Carrie, a professional, is with ours,' I finished by saying.

'It might be a good idea to sound him out about it, then.'

'Have you *no* idea where he's gone? I mean, he might just have gone out for a drive or a walk for some fresh air.' Not to mention getting away from the howling sprog for a while.

'No, he went very early this morning taking his car and said I wasn't to worry.'

Of course, how stupid of me – two cars are normally parked in the drive.

'Have you tried phoning him?'

'No, I hate the idea that he'll think I'm checking up on his movements.'

Ye gods. I took a deep breath. 'Joanna, you used to be a *cop*. You are *not* some air-head housewife who freaks out every time her husband goes out of the door. If this man who you used to work with closely on serious criminal cases can't weather a little checking up on for his own safety and welfare then he's not the James I know.'

Joanna stared at me for a few moments and then said, 'There's something else you ought to know – but you and Patrick must promise me that you won't tell anyone else.'

'Of course.'

'I had some photos through the post yesterday – you know, prints.' She uttered a slightly hysterical hiccupping sort of laugh. 'A bit odd these days with digital cameras and computers, isn't it? They're of James, with a woman in a night club. She's half naked and crawling all over him.' She burst into tears again and was still weeping, inconsolable, when Patrick reappeared with the tea.

I whispered the latest developments to him and for a few moments I think he was engaged in the same mental exercise as I was: inventing slow and excruciating methods of removing Cooper from the land of the living. Impalement on a red hot spike up his backside? Far too kind.

'Can we see them?' Patrick asked when Joanna had been persuaded to take a mug of tea.

'They're in the top drawer of that desk over there,' she mumbled.

'Did you have words about this?' I asked as Patrick fetched them.

'Well, yes, sort of. I showed them to James straight away – I did freak out a bit – and he was furious and said he remembered it but had no idea who she was. He'd been out with the team at Jingles, a night club in the city, on a regular outing they have, and this trollop, who was drunk, or acting drunk, just flung herself at him.' After a big sniff Joanna went on, 'I have to say I believe him. I used to go on these bashes myself when we worked together. We'd all have a meal somewhere and then go to a club. There were often little tarts who gave him go-to-bed eyes.'

'I take it the place was crowded,' I said. 'People wouldn't necessary have noticed anyone taking pictures with a mobile phone.' And after all, the man had once been described to me by a friend as 'wall-to-wall crumpet'.

'I'm sure it would have been. My real problem with it is that he seems to be enjoying himself.'

Patrick was looking at the three photos. 'And what man who had at least three whiskies inside him wouldn't laugh if something like this happened?' he enquired with a quirk to his lips. He handed them to me.

'At least four whiskies,' I decided. The girl looked about eighteen years old and had long dark hair. One of her breasts had fallen out of her dress, the southern end of which was so short it revealed, as she half lay across the DCI, a wisp of black lace not by any means covering her bottom.

'Was there a note with these?' Patrick wanted to know.

Joanna shook her head. 'No, nothing.'

'You've kept the envelope but unfortunately it's of the self-seal variety. There might still be some DNA on it, though.'

'Please don't show them to anyone. It's not as though anyone's trying to blackmail us. Perhaps Cooper, or Mallory, is just trying to break us up.'

'Joanna, we have to—'

'But I don't know what James is doing!' she cried. 'He was so angry he might be killing this man right now!'

'He isn't,' Patrick said. He replaced the photos in the envelope and gave it to her. 'But I respect your wishes. Will you keep us informed – as friends?'

She assured us that she would.

Shortly afterwards I received an email with the information that DNA taken from the body discovered in the ditch at Woolwich was a good match with that taken from several human hairs found on and inside Sulyn Li Grant's husband's rucksack. This fairly certain identification meant that work on the case could move forward. I emailed the sender to inform or remind him that a shooting had recently taken place at the deceased's business and that three officers from SOCA, including a commander, had been on the premises at the time.

'It doesn't get us very far, though,' Patrick commented. 'OK, he was murdered and his widow can be informed of the fact. Perhaps she'll tell the police a bit more now.'

'You think she's been withholding information?'

'I simply can't believe she's completely in the dark. But for now we shall have to let the Met get on with it.' He paused in what he was doing, staring at nothing.

'What is it?'

'The shooting at the café bar – they *must* have been after Greenway. The owner's wife gave you the strong impression that she was giving protection money to a Chinese outfit and her husband had insisted when she spoke to him about it that he wasn't paying anyone.'

'Yes, but he was involved with crime and she thought he was in some kind of trouble.'

'But he'd been dead for months by then. If anyone was after him they'd have gone in and hunted him out instead of firing from outside. If you start introducing *another* set of mobsters who didn't know he was dead it gets a bit far-fetched.'

'So you reckon he was murdered by whoever he'd upset in his own outfit and the attack was nothing to do with the café bar at all.'

'That's my theory.'

'It's possible but still a bit iffy. How could anyone have known Greenway would be at that particular place just then?'

'They couldn't. But by his own admission he goes there quite a bit as it's just around the corner from HQ and all someone had to do was put a casual watch on the premises during normal working hours, *his* working hours.'

'Perhaps we ought to call him.'

'I have already voiced my concerns. I can't tell him to stay away from anywhere.'

He contacted the Met instead, asking for an update on the case but the person in charge of it could tell him very little. Sulyn Li Grant had been told of the confirmation of her husband's death and she had remained outwardly unmoved, unable to offer any further information about him or his suspected criminal contacts.

I found myself unable to blame her if she was keeping anything she knew to herself.

DI Campbell was taking the assault on his boss very seriously and the whole car park was cordoned off with personnel doing an inch-by-inch search of the ground. He was not there personally but Lynn Outhwaite, Carrick's sergeant, dark-haired, petite and clever, was. She greeted us with a wary smile.

'Have you seen the DCI this morning?' Patrick asked her very quietly.

She looked surprised. 'No. I thought he was recovering at home.'

'He's supposed to be recovering at home. Lynn, when you recently had a team bash I understand you all had a meal and then went to Jingles night club.'

'Yes, we had a really good evening.'

'A little bird tells us that some tipsy dimbo draped herself all over him.'

'She did. Mind you, he's a good-looking guy. I have to say, though, he wasn't very amused about it even though he laughed at the time.'

'Any idea who she was?'

'No, none.'

'Or whether she worked at the club or was just a customer?'

'No, sorry. Why, has this any bearing on the case?'

'It *might* have. Found anything of interest here?'

'Just a shirt button and a tooth. I know who the latter belongs to as one of the suspects has a fresh gap where a front one used to be. The button is made of bone or horn and might belong to someone who got away, but it's hardly evidence.'

'It could be off the shirt I was wearing, which is in a bin somewhere at the nick.'

'I hadn't really pinned any hopes on it,' Lynn said with a sigh.

Patrick gazed around. 'As I said to the DI, it's worrying that those issuing the orders to these thugs must have known, despite our disguise, who we were. Up until now I've been at pains to hide my identity from both Benny Cooper and Paul Mallory, who are in the frame for this, mostly because of their past form for this kind of harassment. That cover's gone now – blown. Mallory lives on the first floor of this terrace and that's why we were here. Have any of the residents been interviewed?'

'They have and the people who aren't away, or were when it happened, all said they were asleep and didn't hear anything. Except for one, a Miss Braithewaite, who said she's a light sleeper and had thought she heard people running around in the car park some time during that night. She didn't get up to investigate further.' Lynn paused for a moment. 'I have to tell you that the DI doesn't go along with this London mobster connection. And as far as he's concerned Cooper's just a grubby local newspaper reporter with a criminal record. Glasgow's full of them, he said.'

'So what does he reckon was the reason for the attack on us?'

'Well, as you know they all said they'd all been drinking. He thinks that at the time they just felt like having a little fun with some drop-outs and it all went wrong for them.'

'It had to be premeditated, surely, as they all refused to answer questions other than to say they were too drunk to remember what had taken place. They'd cooked up that story *beforehand.*'

'I tend to agree with you. But Campbell's the boss right now.'

'And you? Have you heard any gossip about someone calling himself Raptor? He's also been known in the past as Nick Hamsworth, Craig Brown and Shane Lockyer. He likes the nickname Raptor because he was once in that gang.'

'Sorry, no again. They were a London mob, weren't they?'

'That's right.'

'You could try tracing the other members of it. One of them might know where he is now.'

'Carrick always says you're a real star,' Patrick said, blowing her a kiss.

She went bright pink.

'I should have thought of that,' Patrick said angrily when we had paused at a bistro to eat a light lunch. 'But it means hitting police records again, staring at yet more computer screens instead of breaking down Cooper's front door and—' He broke off abruptly, got his temper back under control and took a large, vengeful bite out of a beef sandwich.

'You'll get ulcers if you carry on like this,' I observed mildly.

'Please programme the oracle to make constructive remarks,' he retaliated through his mouthful.

'Well, actually, I think that's a really, really constructive opinion for me to air right now.'

'Look, those shits were out to half kill us!'

'Patrick—'

He got up and walked out, leaving the rest of his lunch on the plate.

Bloody hell, I thought. Cooper's winning, hands down.

This was not a time to report the latest state of affairs to Michael Greenway as he would no doubt see it as a silly domestic spat rather than his most dangerous operative having possibly raged off to chew the landscape and/or Cooper. Anyway, what could the commander, who really did not need someone else's domestic spat right now, do even if I wanted him to know what had happened?

Come to think of it, did I have the first idea what Patrick might do?

No.

I went home and Patrick wasn't there. I had been praying that he had cooled down and taken a taxi – the Range Rover was where we had left it in a car park – then seen sense and decided to work on the computer.

'I hope I'm not turning into one of those mothers-in-law who pops up every time their offspring have a bit of a problem,' Elspeth said, coming upon me in the garden where I had gone to see if Patrick was engaged on some kind of anger working-off project like sawing up the newly-felled dead ash tree into logs for winter fires. 'Only you look a bit worried and I was just about to make some tea. Would you like a cup?'

'Lovely,' I said truthfully, there being no sign of him.

'John's taking a funeral and they've asked him along to the village hall afterwards,' she continued chattily. 'I hope he doesn't eat too much or he won't want his dinner.' When we were in her kitchen she went on, 'A strange thing happened the other day when John and I were in Bath. We went for a walk in Victoria Park after lunch and there was a tramp – a homeless man, drop-out, whatever you call them now, dozing on a bench. Now even I can tell the difference between an unwashed body and . . .' She petered out when she perceived me nodding like one of those dreadful toy dogs people used to have in the back windows of cars. 'It *was* Patrick! I knew it!'

'As he said, working undercover to help your favourite copper.'

'And the pair of them were beaten up by horrible thugs.'

'Four were arrested, which was a good tally in the circumstances.'

'Ingrid, he shouldn't have to do things like that now!'

'James really needs his assistance.'

'Oh, so it is official. I do sometimes wonder with Patrick . . .'

'It wasn't, but is now,' I told her, realizing on reflection that that, at least, was one good thing to have come out of it.

Elspeth giggled. 'John gave him a ten-pound note.'

A little later domestic matters took over. Justin had one of his spectacular tantrums and I had to call on Elspeth's help because she and his father are the only ones who can deal with him when he gets like this – apparently she had plenty of practice with Patrick. Then Katie felt ill and was sick all over her quilt cover, and Matthew was sulking because he wanted to go riding on George and my hands were too full already. Even sweet little Vicky was crying, in between shrieking like a banshee, as Justin had broken one of her favourite toys by stamping on it.

The mother of most of this anarchy distinctly felt like a night on the tiles.

Jingles night club was situated in the basement of one of several quite large three-storey houses in a cul-de-sac at the bottom of Landsdown Road. It was not a disreputable area by any means, most of the premises in the rest of the short terrace given over to solicitors' and accountants' offices. There was also the headquarters of Ye Ancient Order of Ferret Masters, which to me sounded distinctly dodgy. (I found out at a later date that it was the jokey name for a real-ale-bangers-and-mash kind of dining club.) The end property, the one farthest away from the night club, was currently being converted into student flats. The entire arrangement, I felt, was satisfactory to all parties, that is, none of the office workers would be around to suffer the consequences of the other establishments.

I knew all this as Patrick and I had explored the area after speaking to Lynn Outhwaite during the morning. It looked quite different now, after dark, the narrow road with its original Georgian paving and 'heritage' street lamps resembling a film set for an historical TV drama. This visual impression was dispelled utterly by the racket – sorry, music – emanating from the slightly below ground level entrance to the club, the doors of which, I saw as I got closer, were wide open, probably on account of the sultry night air. The rest of the building above it was in darkness.

I had not even tried to phone Patrick as he was breaking our working rules by storming off without making subsequent contact and I thought silence might act as fair comment. I had called Joanna, however, and she had heard from James – she told me she had left a message on our phone at home – who had merely said that he was all right and she was not to worry.

Damn all men.

It was a little after nine thirty and I was not expecting the club to be busy – not yet, anyway. I had made enquiries and established that one had to pay a twenty-pounds-per-head entry fee, my preferred method of getting in to the place as I had no intention of going in waving my SOCA ID card.

Carefully, for I was wearing high-heeled shoes and the few steps were steep and worn, I made my way down towards the entrance. Just as I reached the doorway my mobile rang. I only knew this because it also vibrates and was in my evening clutch bag, at present under my left arm. Swearing, but glad that no one was near to hear me, I climbed the steps again and went a short distance away in order to be able to answer it.

'It's me,' said a voice I recognized. 'Where are you?'

'That's a bit rich seeing as you walked out on me this morning,' I snapped.

'Yes, sorry,' Patrick replied with not a hint of regret. 'But where *are* you – at a party? I can hear music.'

'No, I'm outside Jingles,' I told him. 'About to undertake a little sleuthing.'

'Ingrid, for God's sake don't go in there on your own! I know you've ignored my advice in the past and quite brilliant progress has been made in cases but please, this time, listen to me. Don't go in that club. I've been making enquiries about it this afternoon and the findings don't make it a safe place for you to be in alone.'

I counted up to five slowly and then said, 'My day's been pretty miserable so far. Perhaps if I just have a glass of wine and see if I can spot that girl who—'

'No! Look, don't go in there! I'll come straight over, but meanwhile please walk back to the end of that road, turn right and then right again at the next road junction and a little way along you'll find a restaurant called Dora's. Have your glass of wine in the bar and I'll meet you there. Have you eaten?'

'Just a poached egg on toast earlier.'

'We'll have a meal. The place is Italian and very good. Will you do that?'

I slowly counted up to ten this time.

'Ingrid!'

'Oh . . . all right,' I said, feigning reluctance.

'I really love you. You know that, don't you?'

'Yes,' I said.

I put my phone back in my bag and walked away. That had rattled his rivets a bit.

EIGHT

Patrick was still rattling somewhat when he came, quick march, into Dora's and looked around wildly as if half expecting a hail of bullets from all sides. Then, having caught sight of me, the tension in him visibly ebbed.

I beamed a big smile at him.

'You're a real cow sometimes,' he muttered, sinking into one of the big squashy orange armchairs opposite me.

'You can have squid with all the curly bits and suckers,' I soothed, and fetched a glass of Merlot from the bar for him. This was noble of me as it makes me feel queasy having to sit close to someone devouring a creature that's like a cross between a spider and a jellyfish, fried.

'Do you know if Joanna's heard from James?' Patrick went on to ask.

'Yes, she has. No details, though. What have you found out about the club?'

'I did some research on the registered owner. He has a criminal record – a British national originally from Newcastle-upon-Tyne, name of Nicholas Hamsworth.'

'You clever, clever man,' I whispered. 'But how did he get a licence?'

'Pass. There's an address, a council flat in Ealing, the one already in Records. That's why you couldn't find the name locally. But he's not there – no one is, the place is boarded up after what a bod from the local authority described as a small fire.'

'You asked the Met to take a look at the place, then?'

'I did.'

'Wasn't there an address in Glasgow?'

'Yes. Strathclyde Police are investigating that one. What we mustn't forget is that this character is reputed to move around all the time, which makes it very difficult for any one police force to keep tabs on him. That's where SOCA comes in.'

'So do we get the police here to raid the club?'

'I don't really have the authority to instigate that. My instincts tell me to report to Greenway and *then* inform DI Campbell. But I'll wait and see what our Scottish colleagues have to say first.' He picked up the menu. 'Yes, it has to be squid. Splendid, it's the pasta recipe using the ink.'

Ye gods, black pasta in black goo with things looking like entrails poking out of it. Perhaps I could eat my meal in the ladies' toilet. Or just have a brown paper bag.

I registered that Patrick was gazing at me over the top of the menu, eyes fizzing with amusement. Then he said, 'Actually, I'd already decided on the chicken on the specials' board.'

'You're a real pig sometimes,' I told him.

'We can go and have a drink in the club afterwards – just passing by.'

'Are you *serious*?'

'Why not? We might even bump into Cooper and Mallory there, and if we do I'll take a photo of them with my mobile.'

It turned out to be impossible to decide whether either man was present due to the gloom and the fact that most of the population of Bath now appeared to be on the premises. I was having second thoughts by this time as the bouncer on the door into where it all happened looked as though he had been fashioned by the JCB factory. But Patrick blithely showed him our entry tickets and we were waved within.

Sticking close I went with Patrick to the bar, which was in a far corner and constructed in a naff version of thirties Hollywood style. A blonde leaning on it gave him a wide smile which faded when she saw me, and then she turned her back to us. Just then the music started up again. From what I could see there was no live band, just a DJ kind of set-up in the other corner of this end of the room.

Patrick handed me my drink, a large bright pink creation with fruit, leaves and various inedible bits and bobs such as glittery twirly sticks and parasols, pointing as he did so – it saved shouting – at a notice promoting the 'house special cocktail'. I had an idea he was carrying on with his revenge for winding him up earlier as I hate sickly sweet drinks. He just had whisky and water.

Against all the odds we found a table in a corner, having with difficulty made our way around the people clutching at each other, swaying and stoned on heaven knew what, on what must be assumed to be the dance floor. There was no actual space to dance and the different coloured strobe lights gave the unsettling impression that everything was taking place in slow motion. And no, I have never been a fan of night clubs.

I removed the impedimenta from the top deck of my drink and employed one of the twirly glitter sticks to impale the fruit so I could eat it. The first strawberry was soggy and tasted stale, as though it had been reused, several times. My partner was meanwhile sipping his whisky, gazing around outwardly nonchalantly, but in reality highly alert and trying to get a glimpse of the girl photographed with James Carrick.

A couple of minutes later I noticed a closed circuit security camera tucked into a corner of the ceiling near where we were sitting, pointing directly at me. Surreptitiously looking about me I saw others, but no more than one might expect in similar establishments. It was the one almost above our heads that bothered me, staring like an accusing eye. Or perhaps I was getting neurotic.

It occurred to me that we had done nothing yet to investigate the two men who had given their names and addresses when interviewed in connection with the attack on Patrick and James. There was no reason why we could not question anyone else who lived near their addresses.

The pink drink was disgustingly super-sweet and probably meant for teenage girls with an IQ in direct proportions to the length of their skirts, I inwardly grumbled. Then I saw the girl for whom we were looking between a gap in the dancers. She appeared to have just entered, having emerged around a corner of the bar. Patrick's attention was elsewhere – she was probably not visible from where he was sitting – and my immediate problem was to draw her presence to his notice without making it obvious to whichever security wonk was watching his monitors somewhere behind the scenes. But at that moment – and I have a theory that telepathy really does happen – Patrick looked at me. Fortunately, just then the particular music track ended and I was able to whisper in his ear, also telling him of the existence of the camera, which was behind him. He nodded imperceptibly and a few moments later got up and went into the throng.

Almost immediately and somewhere out the back, a smoke alarm went off. This was followed in the next second by the wail of a fire alarm, rapidly cut off. A voice boomed into the room over a public address system.

'Ladies and gentlemen, will you please evacuate the club in an orderly manner. There is no cause for panic and the emergency exits will be opened. Your money will be refunded. Please do not run and risk people being hurt.'

Some people did run, knocking over chairs in their haste to get out; others slouched towards the exits. The rest, including me, stayed right where they were. You are far more likely to be trampled to death in these circumstances than die from smoke inhalation or burns. Besides which, I did not think there was a fire at all. They knew who we were and how to get rid of us. I could not see Patrick.

After a couple of minutes the room had mostly cleared and staff began to chivvy those remaining who were either too drunk to care or, like me, thought it all a Big Lie. The very large bouncer came in my direction and I rose from my chair and set off, definitely not running, on a course that, if he stayed on his, meant we would not meet. Somehow I knew that he would change tack and he did. Not liking the cut of his jib at all by now I performed a hard left turn, pushed my way into a group making their way out through a side door and, having climbed a few stairs, quickly found myself in the street, or rather an alleyway that sloped quite steeply downhill. Still imagining The Hulk right behind me I turned left again to see another door some yards away and tried the handle. It opened and, moving as quietly as possible, I went back into the building. There was a large lock on the inside with a key in it that would not have looked out of place in a church. I turned it, but doing so did not engender any warm feeling of security.

I was in some kind of utility area, a starkly-lit white-painted wide passageway in what must be a sort of cellar below what was already a basement. It was lined with shelves on the right-hand side which were filled with teetering stacks of mostly junk. A vacuum cleaner was stored there together with buckets and mops, a couple of broken chairs and other general rubbish, rather a lot of it. There was a bad smell of drains that appeared to be emanating from a sinister dark damp patch surrounding a rusting manhole cover in the floor.

At the far end of the 'room' was a door but, far more interesting, a narrow tightly-spiralled but quite short stone staircase was situated just to my left which, when I leaned around to look, had a heavy curtain drawn across at the top. Through it I could hear someone talking, a voice I thought I recognized.

Sliding my evening bag into the pocket of my silk jacket – I had already turned off my phone – I mounted the stairs, walking on tip-toe and glad there was a hand rail. Stopping just below the top I paused to listen, carefully moving my feet squarely on to the step in order not to lose my balance. I did not have the right kind of footwear for this kind of exercise.

I felt a stab of alarm as something cannoned into the outside door below and then again, as though a shoulder had been put to it. All the man, if it was the same one, had to do was go back inside the club and open the inner door, which had had no key or bolts on my side. How long would it take him? A minute at the most. Not having anticipated real problems this evening I had not come armed with the Smith and Wesson that Patrick has never quite got round to handing back to MI5. Besides which, it's too big to go in my evening bag.

Peeping around the edge of the curtain, I looked into a darkened area that appeared to be used as an office. A door on the far side was ajar and what light there was in the room was coming from the other side of it and tinged red, like the operational illumination in a submarine. Or perhaps a brothel.

'But it went wrong!' someone else suddenly exclaimed somewhere out of sight. 'And four of them got picked up.'

'They'll keep quiet,' said the first voice I had heard, almost certainly Benny Cooper. 'It's under control. They've been *paid* to keep quiet. They also know what will happen to them if they don't.'

'But he's been here tonight so it's gone wrong again! And we've had to shut the place. What kind of control d'you call that?'

Oh, yes, his winge-ship, Paul Mallory.

'Shut up and let me worry about it.'

'And when Nick or Raptor, or what the friggin' hell he's calling himself, comes back with his own private army, what are you going to say then, eh?'

'Nick does not have an army,' said Cooper grimly. 'Just a few handy blokes.'

'Yes, ex-squaddies with form and attitude. That's an army. Where is he, by the way?'

'Visiting his poor old mum, what else? Don't ask.'

There were heavy footsteps and a new, deep and robotic sort of voice said, 'I've lost her.'

'*Lost* her?' Cooper said. 'And what the hell were you going to do with her when you'd found her, Kev?'

'Well . . . I thought you'd want to scare her off like. Give her a smack or two . . . or something better.' A dirty snigger.

'You great shithead, that woman works for the Serious Organised Crime Agency!' Cooper bawled. 'Her husband, who was here with her tonight, is a one-man private army. I told you to make sure she was off the premises. You do not take it into your pin brain to do *anything* else unless I say so. Is that understood?'

There was a grunt.

'If there's any need to get rid of them it's going to be a proper job with Nick's permission.'

The curtain had been muffling any slight sounds behind me and I suddenly became aware that I was not alone on the steps.

Patrick kissed my ear.

'Did you hear any of that?' I breathed, holding the edge of the curtain tightly against the wall and trying to act cool, even though he had scared the living daylights out of me.

'I'll rely on you to relate every word to me later,' he whispered back.

'How did you get in?'

'The inner door was unlocked.'

I have known Patrick for a very long time now and had an idea what he was likely to do next. The form of it gave me another surprise as he flung the curtain aside and blew several very loud and juicy raspberries.

There were instant shouts and associated obscenities, and the bouncer came through the door on the far side of the office with more speed than one might have imagined possible.

I knew my role – to run like crazy. I skittered down the short flight of steps, unlocked the door and burst into the alley. It was not a moment too soon, for the hapless Kev came rolling head over heels down the stairs like a pole-axed bullock and slammed into the wall on the other side of the passageway, the impact dislodging an avalanche of rubbish from the shelves that cascaded down on him in a huge cloud of dust. Somehow, he righted himself and leapt at his tormentor, who was now tantalizingly just out of range at the bottom of the stairs. The manhole cover that he must have landed on then gave way under his weight and he travelled abruptly south, coming to a sudden stop at waist height. A dreadful stench belched upwards as a tidal wave of raw sewage flowed up past him and across the floor.

'Poor chap tripped,' said Patrick as he joined me outside, carefully closing the door.

The next morning Patrick received an email from Strathclyde Police to inform him that they had broken into the flat in the Broomielaw. The decision had been made as they had asked around among the other tenants of the block of flats, one of whom, who lived one floor above, had mentioned an unpleasant smell. There had been no furniture – nothing in the way of possessions at all, just a corpse that had been identified as that of a local mobster known as Jack 'The Pits' MacDonald, the nickname apparently a comment on his one-time job as a coal miner and general demeanour. He had been killed by a single shot to the head and reckoned to have been dead for around three weeks. This man was no loss to the community, added the author of the email with a Scot's characteristic realism, but they were very keen to find his killer.

'As he too has to be a serious criminal so it would mean two

of them would be out of circulation,' Patrick said after I had read
it. 'And talking of Scots . . .'

He did not mean the Scot-in-residence at Manvers Street. I
rang Joanna.

'He's gone to see his father,' Joanna reported in answer to my
question.

'What, in Scotland?' I asked.

'No, Robert's living in London now, with a woman he met on
the internet. I don't mind, honestly, as I know everything was
getting to him, especially with him getting hardly any sleep and
being attacked like that. And I do understand about the girl in
the night club and it was just that little bastard Cooper trying to
put pressure on him.'

'Come over tonight and we'll have a meal at the pub,' I said.
'Carrie won't mind another one to keep an eye on for a couple
of hours.'

Joyously, Joanna said she would and I resolved to give our
nanny an extra day off as a thank-you for that and helping me
cope with the previous day's domestic mayhem.

James Carrick, whose mother was not married when she gave
birth to him and changed her name after Robert Kennedy was
lost at sea from a private yacht and for years presumed dead,
has only been able to make contact with his father recently.
Before he retired Robert, a cousin of a one-time Earl of Carrick,
worked for F9, an undercover police unit based at an ostensibly
private house on the edge of Epping Forest, east of London.
Anonymity was vital and it was only now that the man was living
what could be regarded as a normal life. He had not even known
that he had a son.

One of the addresses held by Records for a suspect in the assault
on Patrick and James turned out to be very much out of date as
the house, together with several others nearby, had been demolished in connection with a road scheme, which meant that the
man had lied when asked to confirm where he lived. We had
only one other possible source of information – the address for
Nathan Forrester, the one who had no previous convictions. This
turned out to be a flat over a hairdresser's in Combe Down, to
the south of Bath.

A smartly dressed middle-aged woman opened the door. 'You

have him in custody,' she snapped, having given our IDs the briefest of glances and been informed of the reason for the visit.

'He gave the police this address,' Patrick said. 'Are you a relation of his?'

'I'm his aunt.'

'Then, if we may, we'd like to talk to you about him.'

'I know nothing about my nephew and his activities. He came to Bath to study for a degree at the university, got in with the wrong crowd and started taking drugs.'

'Nevertheless, if we could come in for a few minutes . . .' Patrick cajoled.

With ill grace she let us in.

'You must understand that he wasn't living with me,' the woman went on when we had seated ourselves in a bright and tidy living room and she had grumpily turned off the TV. 'I just allowed him to use the place as somewhere he could pop in for a chat and store a few of his things. But when it all started to go wrong . . .' She broke off with an angry shrug.

'And your name?' I requested, finding my notebook in my bag. Was it my imagination or could I detect the scented hot air smell of hairdressers coming in through the open window?

'Oh, Denise Blackwood. Mrs. My husband died last year. Nathan's my sister Joan's son. They live in Lancaster. I promised them I would keep an eye on him and provide him with some kind of base. But he didn't want to stay with me – found a flat or a bedsit after his first year in residence that he's sharing with someone. I don't know who. Frankly, after he started asking for money for drugs I ceased to take much interest.'

'D'you know where his digs are?' Patrick wanted to know.

'No.'

'Did he have a part-time job to pay the rent?'

'His parents send him an allowance but he does, or did, have a job. In a night club, I believe. I'm not really sure as it might be a restaurant. He did mention the name to me once but I can't remember it now.'

'Jingles?'

'That's it! How on earth did you know?'

'Because I'm a genius,' Patrick said with a big smile.

She did not smile in return. 'And now he's done something

stupid and got himself into real trouble. Will whoever it was they attacked press charges, do you know?'

'There's a complication in that the victims were two police officers working undercover,' Patrick informed her soberly. 'How well do you know your nephew? Before he started going wrong, I mean.'

'Not very well at all. They've always stayed up north and I've always lived in the West Country. There were various visits when Nathan and his sister were young, Christmas and so forth when our parents were alive, but that gradually stopped and I can't put them up here. And travel is so expensive these days, isn't it?'

'Did he ever mention any friends or acquaintances at the club? Or undertaking other jobs for them?'

Mrs Blackwood shook her head. 'No. You're thinking then that he agreed to take part in this crime for extra pay. That makes me feel very guilty after I'd refused to help him pay for drugs.'

'You mustn't blame yourself. Did he actually say that he wanted the money for drugs?'

'Yes, he said he was desperate. Perhaps he thought that might tug at my heart strings. It didn't but I did give him fifty pounds the first time he asked me as he promised he'd get some kind of treatment.'

'Would you say that Nathan is easily led?'

'Oh, yes, a real child in a way. His parents never prepared him for living independently.'

'So he's not exactly experienced in beating people up.'

'Not at all! Although of course I've no real idea what he's been getting up to lately.'

'What is he studying?'

'Engineering. But that's almost certainly gone right out of the window now.'

I asked her when she had last seen him.

'Quite recently. Around ten days ago, probably. He was listless and miserable and when I asked him what was wrong he said he couldn't tell me. I just assumed he wasn't enjoying his course – or it was the drugs.'

Patrick leaned forward and spoke intently. 'Mrs Blackwood, are you quite sure the drugs money he asked for *was* for him?'

She appeared taken aback. 'Who else could it have been for?

He gave every appearance of being extremely ill at ease but I've absolutely no experience of things like that. I don't come from that kind of background.' For some reason she accompanied this remark with a 'dear-oh-dear-the-very-idea' look in my direction.

'Has he been neglecting his appearance? Looking dirty, his clothes unwashed, his face gaunt, hands shaky?' Patrick went on.

'Well, no, but he looked untidy; his hair needing cutting. Quite scruffy, really.'

Patrick shook his head impatiently. 'Most male university students look like that. Can you describe him to me? I'm asking because although I was involved before the official arrests it's not actually my case so I can't match names to people.'

She thought for longer than might be expected, then said, 'He's twenty years old, tall and thin with brown eyes and fair hair that's had highlights put in it. Quite silly for a man, don't you think?'

Patrick didn't, I knew but, being a man of the world, he refrained from getting into an argument, saying instead, 'I know who he is now. Thank you.'

'Do you think he'll be sent to prison?'

'I can't answer that question. Are you sure you don't know the name or anything at all about the person he's sharing the flat with?'

'Only that he's crazy about some kind of experimental orchestral music that he plays very loudly. It drives Nathan mad as he's a jazz fan.'

'It *has* to be Paul Mallory,' I said heatedly when we were walking back to where we had left the car. 'He took in Nathan as a lodger for the rent money.'

'I agree it sounds possible.'

'Was Nathan one of those kicking James?'

'No, he was the one going through the motions of attacking me,' Patrick said reflectively. 'I didn't think his heart was in it and after I'd given him a hard smack around the head that wouldn't have really hurt him he flopped down on the pavement and played dead.'

'Surely the drugs must have been for Mallory and they were bought from Cooper. Mallory has no money and Cooper won't give him credit so he's forcing Nathan to buy them for him.'

'Whoa! You can't jump to conclusions like that. Nathan might be an addict and that's the hold they have over him. Damn the rules; I shall interview him at the remand centre. Tomorrow. Without asking Campbell's permission.'

We were not upset to learn that evening that Jingles was closed and would be for the foreseeable future due to what the media described as a 'sewage leak'. In reality the whole of the basement club was flooded as the blockage had been there for some time, backing up on Lansdown Hill.

NINE

The remand centre was on the outskirts of Bristol, a modern building of the brutish abandon-hope-all-ye-who-enter-here school of architecture, enough to make any approaching inmate's heart sink.

We had to wait for twenty minutes and then were shown into the interview room where Forrester was already seated. He eyed us both for a second or two and then dropped his gaze, having clearly not recognized Patrick. As Denise Blackwood, his aunt, had said, he was scruffy and his hair could do with a trim, although to my eye it had previously been well-cut professionally and the highlights had not been done at home. His clothes were grubby, as might be expected in the circumstances, but not cheap. His sullen expression, I felt, was to hide the fact that he was very nervous.

Having showed him our IDs Patrick explained who we were and then added, 'I'm not working on the assault case for which you've already been arrested and charged. I'm not arresting you for anything else either and you're not under caution – this is merely a chat.'

'About what?' Forrester said.

'Jingles, for a start.'

'Who told you I work there?'

'I just know.'

'I don't want to talk about that.'

'It's closed for the foreseeable future, by the way. The bouncer fell through a manhole in the cellar and the place was flooded with sewage.'

'Who, Kev?'

'Umm.'

Nathan could not prevent a smile creeping over his face.

'What were your duties there?' Patrick asked.

'I said I don't want to talk about it.'

'Look, I'm in the position of knowing more about the club than you do and have to tell you, if you didn't know already, that it's not on the level. Please answer the question.'

After a few mulish moments, Forrester said, 'I do just ordinary things. Clearing the tables, washing the glasses, serving behind the bar, but not the cocktails – Kit does that – a bit of behind-the-scenes cleaning. That's all really.'

'What's Kit's surname?'

'I don't know. He was just Kit.'

'Have you been asked to beat up people before?'

'No.'

'Sure?'

'Sure.'

'Yet you're knocking around with people with criminal records and that doesn't bode well for your career in engineering.'

'That's my business, isn't it? Besides, it's all gone now. I've got a criminal record.'

'Only if the victims of the assault continue to press charges and you're found guilty.'

'Fat chance of them changing their minds.'

'The men you attacked were cops working undercover.'

Forrester closed his eyes and mouthed something along the lines of 'Bloody hell.' Then he said, 'That would explain it.'

'What?'

'Why they didn't react like down-and-outs; one of them thumped the hell out of four of us and we got arrested.'

'Hadn't it occurred to you that seven, or even eight, against two was rather overkill if the opposition were a couple of drifters?'

'Yes, but basically I'm a coward because I've never been involved with rough stuff before and we didn't find out who we were supposed to sort out until we got there.'

'Sort out as in put in hospital, you mean. Or worse.'

The youth – and I could only think of him thus – flushed and mumbled, 'Kev just said they were bad boys.'

I wrote KEV in block letters in my notebook and underlined it but Patrick did not query about the doorman further, saying, 'It must have been the promise of money or threats that got you out on to the streets that night. Or both. By the way, how are you coping with being off drugs?'

'I'm not a drug addict.'

'That was the impression you gave your aunt when you asked her for money.'

'I didn't think she'd give me any unless I said I was desperate.'

'That's the stupidest bit of thinking I've heard for years. Aunts are far more likely to hand over money if you tell them that you're *hungry*. This bloke you're sharing the flat with . . . is his name Paul?'

A look of extreme wariness came over the other's face. 'No.'

'You're not a very good liar either.'

The thought that 'a chat' with the man in front of him might turn into something getting on for nasty, far worse than being arrested again for another crime, visibly flitted across Forrester's mobile features. I could not see Patrick's expression from where I was sitting but knew that the pressure, which so far had actually been just about non-existent, had gone up a notch, perhaps the hint of something darker showed in his eyes. I have been present during many such interviews and still do not know how he does it.

Patrick continued, 'As I said just now, there are several people connected with the club where you're working who have criminal records, including the registered owner. So was it money or threats?'

'I don't want to say any more.'

I said, 'It's always sad when young people get caught up in serious crime. If you go to prison you may well emerge a hardened criminal. All you have to do is tell the truth and we'll try to help you.'

'I've heard that one before,' Forrester snorted. 'In cop shows. It's not true, just a con.'

'This is *not* a cop show but it does actually represent the rest of your life,' Patrick told him. 'You see, I have first-hand information about what happened that night. The man you chose to attack with three others slapped you around the head and made you feel a bit sick and dizzy so you laid down on the ground and pretended to be unconscious as carrying on seemed a very bad idea. Meanwhile, your four other chums were kicking the other cop, who did end up in hospital.'

'I don't understand why you, or someone else, isn't pasting the hell out of me right now.'

'Because (a) this still isn't a cop show,' Patrick said grimly, 'And (b) I don't hit kids.'

Forrester swallowed hard. 'The others aren't my chums.'

'Your criminal associates, then. It won't really matter in court what they are. Is the name of the man you share a flat with Paul?'

Forrester hung his head for a moment, his eyes closed. Then he looked up and nodded.

'Mallory?'

'You knew already then!' Nathan cried. 'You have conned me!'

'I haven't. You told your aunt he played very loud experimental music. Mallory's connected with the club and has a criminal record. It was a guess as he's been bothering his neighbours with the racket for years. Yes?'

Another very reluctant nod.

'He's a drunkard and probably on drugs as well. Another man called Benny Cooper, who's a dealer, virtually controls him. I take it you know him too.'

'Sort of. He's a real creep so I stay away from him as much as possible.'

'Did you want the money you got from your aunt to buy drink or drugs for Mallory?'

'Yes.'

'Why?'

'He goes off his head, raving when he needs a fix, and after he came into my room one night with a carving knife I thought he might kill me to get what money I had.'

'Is Mallory the one threatening you to make you do out-of-hours jobs for them?'

'No.'

'Who, then? Cooper?'

'No, Kev.'

'Know where he lives?'

'No, you don't ask a man like that personal questions. He threw me against a wall once.'

'Why didn't you just leave?'

'He told me they'd find me wherever I went. And there's another bloke who I think is the boss . . .' He broke off and I saw that his hands were shaking.

'Who?'

'I didn't really mean to say that. I'm as good as dead if I tell you.'

'You'll get police protection.'

'No, I can't tell you. Not only that, the others arrested with me are here too. They'll find out and grass on me, I know they will.'

'How many of you were there altogether that night?'

'Eight.'

'So four were arrested and four escaped. Who are the others?'

'Dunno. They came in from outside and I don't know their names. That's the truth.'

'So they may have been the personal minders of this man, the boss, who you don't want to talk about.'

'Perhaps.'

That was a yes then.

'Have you met him?'

'Once. That was enough.'

'What does he look like?'

Forrester just sat there, avoiding Patrick's gaze, miserably shaking his head.

'OK, you four who were arrested are just blokes from the club.'

'Three including me are, plus a pal of one of them.'

Patrick turned to me. 'Cannon fodder threatened if they talked. You know, this mobster really is stupid. Why use ordinary employees at a club and set them against people they knew were cops when there's every likelihood of their being arrested?'

'You said it yourself,' I pointed out. 'Cannon fodder. He values his private army too much to lose them.'

'So he's nervous of losing his protection,' Patrick said under his breath. Then to Nathan, 'OK, this Raptor character . . .'

Forrester went white.

'That's what he calls himself and you've obviously heard the name. How did he know that two roughnecks were actually cops?'

'I can't answer that,' Forrester said hoarsely, then cleared his throat to add, 'As I said, we got our orders from Kev. Perhaps he got them from the boss.'

'Kev told you we were bad boys.'

'Yes. But he laughed as he said it.'

'No one could have known that two men dressed as down-and-outs were police officers. Unless, that is, one, or both of them had been followed from home – from a house where they already knew a policeman lived – by someone watching them. Now, being experienced in such things, I would never openly come out of my place in disguise, get in my car and go off to some kind of stakeout. But the other officer may well have done and been observed and followed. Was a watch put on a house, do you know?'

Forrester shook his head.

'You know that for sure then?'

'N-no, of course not. No one said anything about it, that's all.'

'Can you drive?'

'I've passed my test but don't have a car. I can't afford one.'

'I want you to tell me the truth.'

'I am telling you the truth!'

'What threats have been made against you?'

'Just that I'd get sorted out if I didn't do as I was told. I used my imagination.'

'When you applied in all innocence for the job at the club did you give your aunt's address as the place where you could be contacted?'

'Yes, I did.'

'This character who calls himself Raptor has been known to silence witnesses by making threats against their families. One police officer committed suicide, although it's beginning to look as though he might have been murdered. Nathan, you've got yourself in a hell of a mess and the only way out of it is by telling me the truth. Did they threaten to hurt your aunt?'

'No.'

Even I could tell that he was lying.

'It would have had to be something like that as I'm sure you've more sensitivity and intelligence than the whole lot put together. Most of them would probably boil down their own mothers for glue.'

'I'm not like that,' Forrester agreed with another small smile.

Patrick smiled back. 'No, and I believe you when you say that you didn't know the bloke you followed into Bath that night was a cop.'

'That's right, I didn't.'

One of the best interrogation techniques: charm, retreat and pounce.

There was a very long silence before Forrester blurted out, 'At-at-least . . .' and then floundered to a stop.

'And you still weren't told when you were given further orders after you phoned in to report what he was doing,' Patrick continued. 'But you know now. Tell the truth.'

More silence.

'Look,' Patrick continued, 'I want this man and because I'm a cop now and not working for special services I have to behave by arresting him, not put him into a sack and chuck him in the nearest river. But I assure you, I *shall* get him.'

'It's auntie, though,' Forrester whispered.

'She can be given police protection too – even taken to a safe house for a while. All the time you're dithering like this she's unprotected.'

'OK then, but . . .' There were tears in his eyes.

'All you have to do is give me your word that you'll make a full statement to the investigating officers.'

There was a muttered, 'OK.'

'What name is he calling himself now?'

'Hamsworth, Nick Hamsworth.'

'Thank you. Now tell me what he looks like.'

There was another endless pause and then Forrester mumbled, 'Just ordinary . . . I can't remember really . . . until you see his eyes . . . snakey . . . only with a person inside them . . . like sci-fi movies . . . sorry, that's the best I can do.'

I knew the look on his face. It's called terror.

'Carrick was damned careless,' Patrick said a little later when he was driving us back to Bath. 'To leave home looking like a heap of rags . . .'

I said, 'I'm surprised he hadn't noticed another car parked near his house after the trouble he had before.'

'Vehicles do get left in that road as, if you remember, there's a row of cottages nearby with no off-road parking. Or perhaps various bods had been taking it in turns to watch, had parked elsewhere and were on foot. Whatever happened, it must have been a lot more covert than before.'

'But you've checked what's going on at home?' I asked with a pang of alarm.

'Oh, yes, no sign of either of them. Dinna fret.'

'Will you write a report for David Campbell?'

'I shall have to as arrangements will have to be made to protect both Forrester and his aunt. What Forrester said was probably more helpful to him than to us anyway. At least we've confirmed that the order to ambush us came from the club and that Carrick was tailed to Bath. Jigsaw bits, that's all.'

'We have the name of one of the bartenders – Kit. Not to mention Kev. Kev could be questioned,' I suggested.

'I'll leave that up to Campbell – if he can find anyone big enough to have him picked up and they're up to date with their typhoid jabs.' This was followed by a cold-blooded chuckle.

'You don't think he's that important, then.'

Patrick took his gaze off the road for a moment to give me a surprised stare. 'Oh, come on! Do you?'

'No.'

'He's merely the club's in-house bone-head, follows orders and knows nothing.'

'Just testing,' I murmured.

We had been given a glimpse of Hamsworth and I did not like what I had seen.

Despite being presented with this evidence, together with what we had overheard at Jingles, DI Campbell was angry and told Patrick that he would be making an official complaint to SOCA. I gathered that Patrick was very polite, helpfully provided him with Commander Greenway's name and did not – I asked him – point out something along the lines of all police departments having their 'Life on Mars' moments. In truth, for him, he had handled Forrester extremely gently.

That evening, Joanna rang.

'You reminded me that I used to be a cop,' she began by saying to me. 'So I did a little investigating. I contacted Robert, James's father, to see if James was still there. He wasn't. I know it's terrible to doubt the word of someone you love but I'm sure something's going on. James only stayed for a few hours and was asking him questions about a London criminal – he didn't say who. If you remember Robert used to work for F9. Then he left and Robert has an idea he's gone to Scotland.'

'Any guesses as to why?' I asked.

'I can only think that it's in connection with this same person – although, obviously, he has friends there.'

'So the trail's gone cold, as the cliché goes.'

'Not necessarily. One of James's friends is a DI in Strathclyde Police – Neil Macpherson. I met him some time ago before James and I were married. *They* met at a course run by the drug squad when they were both in the Met. So I phoned him. At first he sort of stonewalled me and then might have remembered that I indirectly helped him by demolishing his best line of enquiry in connection with an attempted murder case he was working on – I won't bore you with the details – and told me that he had seen James and given him some information about a recent murder thought to be a gangland killing following the discovery of a body in a flat in the Broomielaw. That's all he'd say, other than he doesn't think James plans to stay in Glasgow for very long.'

'Is Macpherson leading the investigation, do you know?'

'He was cagey about that too – probably terrified I'll stick my nose in again – but I got the impression he is.'

'Do you know where this nick's situated?'

'Brig Street. It's near the river. The murder took place in Crimea Street.'

'You really *must* rejoin the police,' I fervently told her. 'How's the wee one?'

'Much more settled, thank God. I'm actually getting some sleep.'

'I'm not of a mind to go chasing after him,' Patrick said, albeit with a hint of regret. 'He must be checking on the Scottish wing, if indeed there is one, of Hamsworth's empire. Any thoughts?'

I said, 'It might be that as a body was found at a place where presumably this man used to live he's abandoned Scotland and brought any henchmen down south to re-establish the Raptors gang in either Bath or London, or even both. Travelling around to continually give the police the slip is all very well but it doesn't make for good control. But, now I think of it, the flat in Ealing had had what you said someone described as a small fire, so perhaps he's bailed out of there too. Wasn't there another address in Manchester?'

'Sorry, I forgot to tell you – it was repossessed recently after the rent hadn't been paid for ages.'

'So where the hell does he live now – above the club?'

'That's unlikely, too easy to trace.'

'Someone's going to have to get hold of Cooper and question him.'

Someone did, but cut his throat instead.

TEN

Cooper's body was discovered by a council worker three days later, dumped in a skip intended for scrap metal at a recycling site in the Lower Bristol Road, a hundred yards or so from his house. Early findings revealed that he had been dead for only a matter of hours, which meant that he had been killed during the early hours of that morning.

'He was of far more use to us alive than dead,' Patrick commented after we had received the news from Lynn Outhwaite.

Despite what had happened, I knew Patrick was not even indirectly involved with the killing. This was not just because he had spent the previous night securely tucked up in bed *avec moi* after a couple of days at HQ in London where he had worked on something else, the Bath assignment having temporarily hit the wall.

'Cutting throats isn't my style,' Patrick added, as though I needed convincing.

'Look, I know you didn't do it,' I exclaimed. 'Hamsworth has to be responsible.'

'Punishment after what happened at the club, perhaps. It being closed for the foreseeable future must have cut off a good source of income.'

'Why blame Cooper, though?'

'Possibly because he had been left in charge and was handy to inflict a filthy temper on.'

'Did you find out if David Campbell had made a complaint against you?'

'He hasn't so far. But Greenway was annoyed with me as well when I told him I'd spoken to Forrester. I asked him how the hell I was supposed to advance the investigation if I had to stick to all the rules and he told me to get Campbell on side. I just wish to God that Carrick would re-surface – if only to give me a bit of support.'

With this in mind it was a little weird when, a couple of hours later that morning, Patrick's mobile rang and it was DI Campbell. Would we both care to attend the Manvers Street police station with regard to his latest case?

He was in Carrick's office, understandable in the circumstances as his own had been hastily created out of a store room with only just enough space for a desk, filing cabinet and small set of shelves. If he had more than one visitor the door had to be left open with a chair placed in the space.

'We've found what is almost certainly the murder weapon,' was his opening remark after brusquely wishing us good day.

'Where?' Patrick wanted to know.

'In the same skip as the body. It presumably had been thrown in and being small had found its way to the bottom of the pile of scrap metal.' He took a specimen bag that had been lying in an open drawer and placed it on the top of the desk for us to see.

Patrick whistled softly.

It was a skene dhu, a *sgian dubh*, one of the small knives that Scotsmen wearing highland dress tuck into their hose, long socks. The blade was dark with blood.

'Have you seen this before?' the DI asked.

Patrick shook his head. 'No.'

'I know full well, as he told me himself, that Carrick sometimes wears the kilt and would have one of these. Also that the pair of you are friends of his and might be able to recognize it.'

Again, Patrick shook his head. 'This, to my certain knowledge, does not belong to James Carrick. His does not have a stag's antler handle – this one could even be made of plastic – but is plain polished horn. This blade is stainless steel and I think James's is not – you can get a better edge on hardened carbon steel.'

'You've seen it?'

'Yes, I have.'

The DI got to his feet and left the room with the exhibit, presumably to give it to someone to send off to the lab. When he returned, he said, 'You seem very sure. There's nothing to say that the man doesn't have two.'

'It's just not to his taste. There's some kind of phony jewel, a chunk of glass, set into the end of the handle. That's not James's style either.'

'But he and Cooper do have history.'

'Which Paul Mallory is more than aware of. I suggest you question him.'

'I was checking up on all that before you arrived.'

'I rather get the impression that you think Carrick could possibly have killed this man.'

'I'm only trying to eliminate him from the inquiry.'

'You *are* doubting your own boss!'

'Cooper did put Mallory up to almost killing the woman who is now Carrick's wife,' Campbell responded stubbornly.

We had agreed that we would say nothing, yet, to Campbell about the pair of them having taken it in turns to park outside Carrick's house. Nor the fact that Joanna had received photographs of James taken at Jingles night club with a semi-naked female in extremely close proximity. Had he finally snapped?

Patrick said, 'This has all been carefully orchestrated right from the beginning, but probably not by Cooper. He was used too, all of it as a war of attrition against the local senior policeman and to divert attention away from the fact that this mobster is moving his scene of operations to Bath. Cooper's murder is the latest development in an attempt to implicate Carrick in crime. No doubt he had served his purpose and they made further use of him by killing him.'

Campbell pondered.

'It appears from what Forrester said that he's gone back to calling himself Hamsworth,' Patrick added. 'Which is the name of the registered owner of the night club.'

'I wasn't aware of that.'

'That's because you haven't done any real work on it. Three of the four who were arrested work at the club; the other four, who got away, had been brought in from outside and *may* be

Hamsworth's minders – a bunch of thugs described as his private army.'

There was an awkward silence broken by the DI saying, 'We really need to find Carrick.'

'He went to Scotland, we think with the express purpose of talking to an old friend about a gangland killing in Glasgow. A mobster by the name of Jack MacDonald has been murdered and his body dumped in a flat once rented by Hamsworth.'

'Is he back?'

'No idea.'

Feeling about as useful as a stuffed mascot at a football match, I found my mobile and dialled Joanna's number in an effort to find out.

There was just the usual recorded request to leave a message.

The phone in Campbell's office across the corridor then rang and he hastened away to answer it. I heard him say, 'You've *what*?' and then there was silence for half a minute or so before he asked, 'So where is he now?' Then, presumably in receipt of an answer, he added, 'I want his clothes,' before crashing down the phone.

'It looks as though my suspicions may have been realized,' the DI was saying as he re-entered the room. 'Lynn Outhwaite and the team have just found Carrick. He was unconscious, his clothing bloodstained and lying in a space between one of the recycling bins and a wall. He started to come round as he was moved but appeared to be delirious. He's been taken to hospital.'

I found myself too shocked to say anything.

Campbell was flinging on his jacket.

'Are you going to the crime scene?' Patrick enquired, already on his feet.

'Yes. I was only waiting to ask you about the knife.'

'May we come along?'

'Officially?' the DI asked, pausing in snatching up a few possessions to give Patrick a hard stare.

'Any which way you like. And Greenway did ask me to get you on side.'

The nuances of this were not lost on Campbell, but he was in too much of a hurry right now to resent being part of a SOCA investigation. Besides, I felt, this was getting all a bit too much for him.

All I could do was ring Joanna's number again and leave a message asking her to call me.

We discovered that Cooper's body had had to be removed from the skip quite quickly, for although it had been fairly straight-forward to take his wallet from his jacket pocket and therefore find some form of identification, in this case his driving licence, the corpse had slowly started to slither, mainly on account of the blood, head first down into a crevice in the scrap metal. This consisted of old washing machines, fridges and the like. The decision to then carefully shift this stuff from the skip in an attempt to find more evidence had been Lynn Outhwaite's. It was she, 'nosing around' as she put it, who had subsequently found her boss behind a nearby container for recycling glass.

The municipal recycling centre had been closed to the public – police and incident tape were everywhere – which had resulted in a traffic jam of such record-breaking proportions that even Campbell's driver could not get through, blues and twos notwith-standing. We ended up having to walk back from a piece of waste ground destined for re-development a short distance away.

The council centre, the gates of which appeared to have been forced, was the usual desolate area, the city's dustcarts parked in an adjoining compound fenced off mostly with sheets of corrugated iron topped with rusting barbed wire. There was a notice board announcing that the area was shortly to be 'upgraded'.

Lynn was still upset about her discovery, a fact that she was desperately trying to hide behind a mask of super-efficiency. Campbell appeared not to notice, or was more tactful than I would have given him credit for, but I did and asked her if she was all right, fatuous in the circumstances, I knew, but I felt I had to say something.

'What was your immediate reaction on discovering him?' Patrick asked her quietly. 'Absolute first gut feelings.'

'That he'd been dumped there,' was her immediate reply.

'Did you think that way out of loyalty?'

'No,' she responded evenly. 'By the way he lay on the ground.'

'Not as though he'd crawled in and collapsed, you mean.'

'No, as though he'd been thrown in. He was lying on his back, feet this end.'

With Campbell we walked across to the place to see that the

gap between a wall and the container in question was quite narrow. Patrick got down on his hands and knees and slowly manoeuvred himself into the space – bugger forensics – gazing intently at the ground, which was covered in dead leaves and blown-in bits of plastic rubbish, as he did so. Then, with no regard for his clothes, he wriggled over on to his back.

'Carrick has broader shoulders than me,' he observed. 'So unless he travelled in backwards somehow, which is unlikely, he didn't get in here under his own steam. I reckon he was thrown in, at a guess by two people holding his hands and feet.' He wriggled out and then asked Lynn, 'Did he have any obvious injuries?'

'No, although his clothing had blood on it.'

'Where?'

'On the front of his sweatshirt and the cuffs and sleeves.'

'Smears, splashes, spots?'

'Smears and one more concentrated stain on his right shoulder.'

'Do you know if he's right- or left-handed?'

'He's right-handed.'

This was Patrick double-checking as I was sure he knew already.

'He was reported to be delirious,' I said to Lynn. 'Did he say anything to you?'

'He was mumbling something when I discovered him but nothing that I could understand, then seemed to become aware of his surroundings as he was being put into the ambulance. He definitely recognized me and started to speak but then appeared to lose consciousness again.' Her voice broke and she said, 'I hope to God he'll be all right.'

'Don't worry, I happen to know that the man has an ox-like constitution,' Patrick said.

'It's vital to retain a professional attitude,' Campbell insisted. 'We must be seen to be considering this from all angles. An intelligent man like James Carrick would think of something like backing himself into a small space to make it look as though he'd been put there. He felt ill – we all know he'd never given himself sufficient time to recover from being beaten up – and thought he might collapse at any moment.'

Patrick said, 'This was after he'd cut Cooper's throat and heaved him into the skip.'

'No, there was no blood on the ground. Cooper was killed in the skip.'

'So, weak, ill and feeling that he might collapse at any moment, he persuaded Cooper to climb into the skip where he killed him,' Patrick persisted derisively.

'He could have manhandled him in and the effort caused him to feel bad.'

'But why? Why bring him here?'

'To make it look as though he had been killed by this mobster you keep on about.'

'Why kill him at all? Eventually, Cooper would have been an important witness.'

'If Carrick was ill he could have been temporarily off his head. And, as you said yourself, the man had made life extremely difficult for him for years.'

Patrick made no further comment, doubtless thinking the argument not worth pursuing. There were no actual facts to support any theory right now and everyone would have to wait for forensic findings.

The DCI's car was soon discovered in a side road near to where Cooper had lived. It was immediately impounded by Campbell and sent away for testing. As for Carrick himself, he was found to have no injuries except for some fresh bruising to his body and arms and minor grazes. He did, however, have a dangerously high temperature due to a serious infection brought on by the earlier attack.

Joanna had contacted me shortly before we left the crime scene – it was necessary for us to get out of the way of the investigating team – and, in receipt of the news, had gone straight to the hospital having, at my suggestion, dropped off the baby at the rectory for Carrie to look after for however long was necessary. To lighten our nanny's workload I went straight home to take charge of my own children.

To say that Patrick was aggrieved at Campbell's over-professional, if not negative attitude was putting it mildly; perhaps inwardly ranting and raving was more accurate. But he had recognized that nothing could be gained by hanging around at Manvers Street, said I ought to have the car and headed off on foot along the Lower Bristol Road in the direction of the city centre.

He rang me during the afternoon with the news that although DNA testing would take longer it had been confirmed that although the smaller bloodstains on Carrick's shirt were the same blood group as his, the larger ones were not and in the meantime it was not unreasonable to suppose that it was Cooper's blood. Patrick was upbeat about this, saying that if anyone was going to go to the lengths of framing a cop for murder they would have to have a damned good try at doing it properly. Worse was to follow. Half an hour later he called me again to tell me that fingerprints on the handle of the knife were definitely those of the DCI, adding that it was perfectly possible that the weapon had been wiped, put into Carrick's hand while he was unconscious and then tossed into the skip.

All this made me think that Patrick had somehow got himself into the lab, a guess confirmed when he arrived back at home at around five-thirty.

'Scenes-of-crime people are at Cooper's house now,' he reported.

'Campbell should talk to Paul Mallory,' I said.

'That's the first place I went. He's not there.'

'Or not answering the door?'

'No, I got in and had a look round. The place is a real tip and I half expected to find him dead from a drugs overdose.'

'Is he bright enough to have hatched this plan to kill Cooper, implicating Carrick, on account of the humiliation he's been suffering for goodness knows how long?'

'And – or, Cooper wouldn't let him have any drugs, or pay him what he owed him?' Patrick mused. 'Yes, I think he's capable, especially after what Nathan Forrester said about him going into his bedroom armed with a knife. That has to be taken into consideration.'

'I don't think James did it, but what about you? If he had a sky-high temperature and finally cracked . . .'

'Of course he didn't do it. If you cut someone's throat and are not experienced, or received training in how to do it properly, neatly, you get covered in blood as the arteries are severed. James has never cut *anyone's* throat. The killer, or an accomplice, smeared Cooper's blood on Carrick's sweatshirt by wiping his hands and the blade of the knife on it. There might even be some of his own DNA on the garment.'

'But how on earth did they get hold of James in the first place?'

'We shall just have to wait until we can ask him.'

'I'm just hoping that Campbell doesn't arrest James without doing much more in the way of investigation.'

'I can't believe he'd take such a risk with his career and I shall inform Greenway if he does. SOCA can get seriously involved if we, meaning us two, can find a strong lead that shit-face Hamsworth's behind it. God, I need a drink. Shall we go to the pub?'

'There's an extra baby on board. Have a drink here and nurture your kids while I cook the dinner?'

I had a struggle to joint a couple of chickens without thinking about post-mortems.

DI Campbell, being the official investigating officer, wasted no time in talking to his immediate boss and as soon as the doctors looking after Carrick gave the go-ahead, the infection under control some forty-eight hours later, he went to the hospital with Lynn Outhwaite. This, according to the latter – she had opened what can only be called a hot-line to Patrick, probably because she regarded us as allies – had been a disaster as the two men had a blazing row and she and Campbell were asked to leave. Having carefully observed Greenway's orders not to tread on Campbell's toes, the reason he had stayed away from the hospital, this caused Patrick some grim amusement.

Lynn had gone on to say that the post-mortem on Cooper's body had revealed that he had received a severe blow to the head which would have rendered him deeply unconscious, and possibly brain-damaged had he lived. But it had not killed him as his heart had continued to beat, this resulting in the huge loss of blood following the deep knife wound in his neck. Other test results were irrelevant to the immediate investigations into the murder and a report still to come with regard to internal organs was not thought likely to throw further light on the investigation either.

Initial forensic findings on Carrick's car had revealed that the only fingerprints on the steering wheel, made from a plastic compound – James has never gone in for what he refers to as 'fancy' cars or accessories – were his. Joanna has her own car and doesn't like driving her husband's. There was smearing, destroying all but a thumb and index fingerprint, as though someone had lately handled the wheel wearing gloves with some kind of grease or oil on them, the precise nature of which was still being tested. It was when Campbell had put the suggestion to Carrick that he might have recently driven the car wearing gloves while eating fish and chips or some other kind of take-away meal that the DCI had lost his temper and called him a Lowland moron.

'I'd have lost my temper too if someone had said that to me,' Patrick declared after Lynn's call that evening, in the pub. 'For one thing, it's hardly been cold enough to wear gloves and for another, people who eat takeaways anywhere near their motors or even while they're driving, let alone with gloves on, usually have multiple piercings, ditto tattoos and a pile of tinnies on the seat beside them as well.'

'Not your average DCI or Range Rover driver then,' I said, straight-faced.

'No.' He then laughed. 'All right, I'm a snob. But you get my drift.'

'To be fair, Campbell *is* trying to be even-handed.'

'I think he's a complete arsehole.' Patrick got up to fetch himself another pint.

'That's completely unwarranted,' I said to his retreating back. No, actually, I reconsidered moments later, there are such concepts as people being innocent before proved guilty and sticking by your colleagues.

We had not been idle during the past two days and had every intention of talking to James ourselves. Following a suggestion from Joanna – I had not quizzed her about what, if anything, her husband had said to her in connection with what had happened – Patrick had contacted Carrick's one-time colleague, DI Neil Macpherson, whom he had already met, in Scotland. Mentioning that he was now working for SOCA, he had explained the situation, reminding the DI that he was a friend of James's. He had then requested details of any work-related conversations the two men had had, offering to fly up to Glasgow should Macpherson not wish to discuss anything over the phone or doubt his identity.

Macpherson had replied that he always remembered voices and then gone on to say that Carrick's main interest had been the investigation following the murder of Jack 'The Pits' MacDonald whose body had been found in the flat rented by

Nick Hamsworth, the tenant having helpfully used that name, and then, understandably, vanished. Macpherson related that he had pulled in a few local men, whom he had referred to as 'the usual suspects', two in particular having been known to act as heavies for a gang Hamsworth had been involved with but not run. Nothing really fruitful had come of this other than one of them saying that he had heard that the two men, Hamsworth and MacDonald, had fallen out over money the latter insisted the former owed him for a job.

In response to the next question the DI had said that the name Raptor had never been mentioned and he had no idea why Hamsworth had come up to Scotland in the first place, unless it was to distance himself from Metropolitan Police inquiries and earn himself more illegal money on the side.

The murder victim had been seen with Hamsworth – this information courtesy of an informer – in various pubs and drinking clubs and, there being no real evidence to the contrary, Macpherson could only suspect that there had been some kind of serious argument, sober or otherwise, and Hamsworth had shot him. 'There are always power struggles, you ken.' The murder weapon had not been found but, having received the bullet that had killed MacDonald, the ballistics laboratory report indicated that it had come from a Beretta of some kind. There was a warrant out for Hamsworth's arrest.

'Sulyn Li Grant had a Beretta of some kind,' I had commented on learning this.

'Thousands of them are knocking around the world's streets,' Patrick had muttered.

'I thought you'd kicked me into touch,' Carrick said when he first laid eyes on us the following morning. He was in a small side ward, the only occupant.

'Hardly, old son,' Patrick replied. 'Just doing as I was told and not upsetting your DI. Besides, I promised I'd help you sort this out.'

James was not placated. 'And when the hell did you start worrying about upsetting people?'

He still looked ill, his unshaven face gaunt and pale, and I wondered if he had in fact fully recovered from a gunshot wound he had received a couple of years previously, and whether it had been exacerbated by the recent injuries. Whatever the truth, he was being discharged the following day on condition that he went home to be looked after and stayed there.

I passed over some Scottish tablet, fudge, his favourite 'sweeties', that I had managed to track down for him, anything else that might cheer him up, and by that I mean single malt whisky, being absolutely and utterly banned while he was on strong medication.

'You realize the half-wit's about to charge me with murder!' Carrick went on heatedly, hardly noticing the gift.

We seated ourselves on a couple of chairs, Patrick exuding the slightly lofty and patient sympathy of a commanding officer visiting a wounded sapper. This had the opposite effect of what I feared: that the DCI would re-detonate, and he slumped back on his pillows and chuckled tiredly.

'OK,' he said. 'I'm right over the top.'

'Because you're on heaven knows what drugs,' Patrick pointed out. 'Did you give any kind of account of what happened to Campbell?'

'No, because he got my back up straight away by giving every impression that he thought I'd killed Cooper because I was found at the crime scene, my car was in a side road near his house and the murder weapon was a skene dhu with my fingerprints on it.'

'I've seen it and told him that it's not yours.'

'Anyone can have a spare in a drawer.'

'James, that knife is so naff you wouldn't even give it house room.'

'But I'm a clever cop, aren't I? I would have thought of that,' Carrick said bitterly.

'Suppose you tell us what happened,' I said bluntly, although his words uncannily echoed Campbell's thoughts.

'I can't remember much, but I know I left my car in the station car park,' Carrick began.

'Are you sure?' Patrick enquired.

'Of course. God, you don't imagine I drove all the way to Scotland, do you?'

'Campbell had it taken away for forensic testing.'

'He'd have to, I'll give him that,' Carrick conceded. 'Where were we? Oh, yes, what happened. I went to see Neil Macpherson. You've met him, Patrick.'

'Yes, I rang him,' Patrick said. 'This was about the "The Pits" MacDonald murder case.'

'Partly.' A sigh. 'I chickened out really. Had to get away from everything. I felt if I could go home, back to Scotland, for a bit . . .' He broke off.

'Lack of sleep's a real killer,' Patrick murmured. 'Not to mention the kicking you received.'

'But it didn't work,' Carrick continued. 'Glasgow wasn't home anyway and I knew I was running a temperature, but I travelled a little farther and went to see a few friends in Helensburgh. That was good but I was feeling pretty dreadful and knew I was a real bastard for abandoning Joanna like that. So I stayed the night with a couple I know and came back last Thursday. I can't actually remember the journey.'

'You should have gone to A and E *there*,' I scolded.

'I know that now. But at least I achieved something.'

'What's that?' Patrick asked.

'Neil had a fairly recent photo of Hamsworth, or a man who closely resembles much earlier mugshots of him, taken, believe it or not, by an off-duty cop at a football match as everyone was leaving, using his phone. This character was surrounded by heavies so trying to arrest him single-handed was out of the question. He called base but by the time help arrived the mobsters were lost in the crowd.'

'I take it you asked him to email it to the nick here,' Patrick said.

'Neil's more than a bit behind the times and gave me a print. I put it in my wallet – which appears to have been sent for forensic examination together with all my other stuff.'

'So this photo must have been taken just before or just after MacDonald was murdered.'

Carrick was getting tired. 'Yes, I suppose so.'

'What did you do when you got off the train at Bath?'

'I went round to the rear of the station where I'd left the car. Or at least, started to. I don't know what happened after that.'

'So it is conceivable that you drove your car to Cooper's.'

'I suppose so, but what the hell for?'

I recollected that in order to reach the car park one has to go through a tunnel under the railway. This is around fifty yards in

length, never very well illuminated and can be the haunt of
drifters and drop-outs.

'What time was this?' Patrick wanted to know.

'God knows – but it must have been late.'

Cooper had been killed early on the Friday morning.

'So everything until you woke up here, or in the ambulance,
is a complete blank?'

'No, not quite. I had . . . sort of dreams.'

'Lynn did say that you were delirious,' I told him.

'Nightmares,' Carrick continued, closing his eyes. 'In them I
killed Cooper – several times.'

ELEVEN

The photograph was not in Carrick's wallet. This did not
mean that it had never been there, having merely being a
figment of one of the DCI's 'dreams'. But Inspector
Macpherson had said nothing to Patrick about giving him any
photographs. Perhaps he had forgotten to mention it when they
spoke or had not bothered to, thinking he would find out soon
enough. On receipt of the news of the missing photo Patrick
immediately phoned Macpherson again, or tried to, the DI being
out of the office. The constable Patrick spoke to said he would
endeavour to contact him but could promise nothing, as although
Macpherson had a mobile phone he hated using it and kept
'forgetting' to recharge the batteries.

'James did say he was behind the times,' Patrick remarked
dismally.

'We're getting absolutely nowhere!' I raged. 'Hamsworth's
getting away with everything, even murder! I wish you could
take charge of this whole ghastly case.'

This seemed to bypass Patrick like the proverbial water off a
duck's back and he murmured, 'If a mobster finds a photo of
himself in a wallet he's idly looking through that belongs to a
cop he's going to remove it, instinctively, not thinking too clearly.
Will he keep it as a kind of memento or tear it up, pronto?'

'If he has a really big head he'll keep it,' I offered. 'As a sort of trophy. We've come across that with criminals before. Souvenirs of crime, to celebrate and gloat over.'

'Cooper was hit over the head with something,' Patrick continued, seemingly thinking aloud. 'But Lynn didn't say anything about any guesses as to what it might have been.'

He had another telephone conversation with DS Outhwaite and afterwards said, 'It was probably something like a hammer.'

It jangled in my memory. 'Sergeant Woods said something about a hammer being used as a weapon. Yes, I know. It was when a Mrs Pryce was killed in Beckworth Square some years ago. She lived in the terrace opposite. That was the case that James sorted out, the one that Cooper and Mallory were involved with when Joanna was hurt. A man – can't remember if Derek told me exactly who – had used the hammer to break the glass case at an art gallery in order to steal a valuable antiquity. Mrs Pryce grabbed it off him somehow – the hammer, that is – as they entered the terrace where he and Mallory lives. Perhaps she was going to bang on his door with it because of his loud music. Miss Braithewaite met her, thought she was being attacked, the women had a tussle and Mrs Pryce accidentally received a blow on the head. She had a very thin skull and died instantly.'

'The common denominators being Mallory and, unfortunately, still Carrick.'

Intensive forensic work was still being carried out at the murder scene and on Carrick's car. The tentative fish-and-chip or take-away-eating theory was soon thrown out as the grease on the steering wheel had been found to be actually new motor oil, the exact type to be verified by yet another, specialist, lab. A search was then made of the area adjacent to the recycling facility. As this was used for the council's garden waste collection as a general dump and dustcart parking zone, it entailed sorting through tons of waste in case the gloves, or cloth, the lab wasn't sure exactly what, had been thrown away after being worn to drive the car or used to wipe the wheel afterwards. This was still ongoing.

James Carrick was discharged from hospital as planned and went home. I told Joanna that we would look after Iona Flora for a few more days if she wanted us to but she said she had already benefitted from the advice that Carrie had given her and could manage. Not only that, the baby would help take James's mind off everything else.

OK, the domestic side was hunky-dory, I told myself, taking my turn at inwardly ranting and raving, but the murder investigation was drifting along like a ship with a broken rudder, the man in charge having seemingly settled on his main suspect, Carrick.

'You don't think those two could have any history?' I wildly burst out with that evening. 'Literally, I mean. Clans and so forth.'

Patrick started, deep in thought and in the process of taking a mouthful of beer. We seemed to be spending an awful lot of time in the village pub.

'You trying to drown me or something?' he asked when it was safe to speak.

'Sorry.'

'In answer to your question: no, I don't. Campbell's merely right out of his depth.' Then, no doubt in response to my continuing to glare balefully at him across the table, 'Patience. I know it feels as though we're doing nothing but it's sometimes a good idea to allow mobsters a little breathing space so they get cocky and start making mistakes. It's time someone went to find Kev. I shall. Later tonight.' With a big smile, he added, 'You're welcome to come if you're feeling particularly strong.'

I soon discovered that the strong bit was going to have to be my stomach as the first thing he wanted to do was to break into Jingles to look for anything useful to the case. Patrick had concluded, probably rightly, that Campbell would not give him a search warrant as there was no real evidence to support such a request.

Lynn Outhwaite had passed on the information that the club only rented the basement and lower cellars and that the owner of the premises, a businessman and property developer, was in the process of restoring the upper floors with a view to renting them out as offices. He was at present in Australia and had been for several months, which had meant that contact with him had to be made by phone. He had confirmed that there was no proper access between the lower and upper floors at present, a woodworm-riddled staircase having had to be removed, just a temporary doorway – the building was rambling and not on 'conventional' levels, he had said – that he, the owner, had made, which was double-locked and bolted from his side.

We gave a miss to the subterranean area where we had exited the previous occasion. While there was every indication from outside that sewage was no longer swilling about – everywhere appeared to have been hosed down – the stench was still enough to floor a horse of delicate constitution. Travelling a little farther along a wide sideway we found ourselves at a rear door that was obviously used for deliveries with the usual lidded plastic rubbish containers crammed up nearby against the outer wall. I did not think this was likely to offer much in the way of a sewage-free environment as, if anything, it was lower than the other level.

It was a little after one-thirty in the morning and, not for the first time while engaged in night-time surveillance – all right, MI5-style breaking and entering – I felt distinctly nervous. We were clad in our usual 'invisible' clothing: dark-blue tracksuits with matching hoods and black trainers. We also possessed bala-clavas, which were in our pockets, and we would use them if necessary. The problem with them is that they muffle sound – not useful if there is a possibility of being surprised by unwelcome angry someones.

The night was muggy with intermittent drizzle and I felt hot and itchy in my winter-weight clothing. I thought there might be every possibility that this door we were standing by would be bolted and barred from the inside so no amount of wrangling with Patrick's 'burglar's' keys would be of any use. But there was a hefty click – the lock looked old enough to be the original – and the door opened at the first turn of the ornate cast-iron knob.

I gathered that we would be looking for employees' records, if such a thing existed, and any other useful information. It seemed logical that the location of such items would be in the office at the top of the stone staircase, if we went in the way I had. Even entering by a different route, the staircase should not be too hard to find.

'What about alarms?' I whispered in Patrick's ear.

'Well, there's nothing on this door,' was his totally infuriating response.

I then recollected that he has a 'gizmo', a device he calls his sonic screwdriver – a little electronic masterpiece designed to silence and de-activate alarm systems that have comprehensively failed when nothing else will. It also works very satisfactorily on equipment that is functioning perfectly. It was given to him by a man once under his command who now works as a security engineer. He felt that he owed Patrick a favour, on account, I seemed to remember, of his actions in preventing him from getting into serious trouble for some misdemeanour or other. I know there are others with whom Patrick still keeps in contact, mostly those who served with and under him, continuing comradeship.

Our small torches illuminated a surprisingly cavernous interior and we quickly went inside and closed the door, no key on the inside. The smell caught at my throat and I heard Patrick retch. The whole interior, the walls and floor constructed of stone, was soaking wet but looked fairly clean and had obviously been sluiced out as well, turning what must have been curtains of cobwebs overhead into a revolting black slimy-looking mess. Below, the space was empty but for a set of aluminium step-ladders, logical as anything stored down here would have been ruined. No stairs led off from this room but it had three doors, one in the end wall opposite the entrance and another two, close together, on the left-hand side. The latter proved to be old lavatories, hosed down but still unspeakable, as in full to the brim with brown. There was nothing visible in the way of closed circuit cameras or infra-red movement detectors in the main room.

'This door has to lead somewhere,' Patrick said under his breath, going over to it. Perceptibly, he shivered. 'God, it's cold down here.'

I didn't think it was.

In the lamplight there was only one shiny narrow strip of metal visible in the space between the door and its frame, suggesting that it was held only by the catch and not locked. Patrick shone his torch right around the door and then wordlessly shook his head: no visible electrical contacts either. He turned the handle and opened the door just an inch or so.

No alarms shrilled into the silence, just a tiny squeak from the hinges.

He opened it wider, quickly, and a short wooden staircase rose before us. This too was soaking wet, water trickling in little runnels reflecting the light from our torches as it drained from above. The smell, wafting towards us on a cold, clammy draught, was even worse here. It was not so quiet, though; the persistent drip, drip of liquid travelling downwards. The owner of the place had mentioned that it was on unconventional levels, probably on account of it being on the side of a steep hill.

'Don't walk too closely behind me,' Patrick warned and set off up the stairs.

I never do. For one thing, my reactions are a lot slower than his.

When he was near the top I started to follow. The stairs did not creak, probably because the wood was saturated and swollen. Would this place ever re-open? was the inconsequential thought that flitted through my mind. Moments later I saw Patrick's torch beam illuminating a smallish space above me and reckoned that he was in some kind of corridor.

It was, and wet up here as well with a dirty tidemark about a foot up the walls. I kept right back as I saw two open doorways yawning blackly, one on each side, and through the nearest of which the draught seemed to be emanating. Patrick, who had drawn his Glock, went into each in turn, giving whatever lay within a swift reconnoitre and then emerged with a further shake of his head. Nothing to be found there, perhaps with the exception of an open window. I glanced in as I passed and saw that it was in fact broken.

'Don't flash the light around,' Patrick scolded.

Yet another door, closed, was situated at the end of the passage. We stepped over the heap of filthy, oozing carpet that someone had begun to wrench up and then abandoned and made our way towards it. It was modern and well-fitting. Patrick shrugged in fatalistic fashion and tried the handle. It opened.

I was beginning to worry about all these inner doors being unlocked but then again, who the hell would want to get in here?

The police, that's who.

'I do urge extreme caution,' I said under my breath. 'You were once almost blown up in a mobster's flat in London.'

Patrick, who can be overly gung-ho at times, usually takes these kind of utterances by his oracle seriously. 'Does he have the expertise?'

'We did hear someone say, in this building, that he employs ex-service people.'

He nodded in acknowledgement and shone his light through

the opened doorway, illuminating a room with an untidy muddle of chairs and a table roughly in the centre loaded with used crockery and drinks glasses. The curtains across the small window were closed. No one had attempted to lift this soaking carpet and our feet squelched on it as we cautiously went forward into what, I was sure, was the room where we had heard the men talking. Next door, then, must be the office.

Patrick was being extremely careful, shining his torch low in order to see any trip wires. We had both already noted the infrared motion detectors in two corners of the ceiling but they were not working, which suggested that all power in the building had been turned off or had tripped – I guessed the former. Thinking along the same lines as I was, Patrick flipped down a light switch: nothing.

The door into the office was ajar and my nerves twitched as my cursed writer's imagination trotted out all kinds of scenarios of the bloodbath variety. Giving my partner plenty of room I fingered the Smith and Wesson in the pocket of my jacket, finding myself taking a deep breath, not having been aware of holding it. I could taste the stench at the back of my throat.

The office appeared to be roughly as we had seen it before. It possessed a couple of tall built-in cupboards, a filing cabinet, a few chairs and a desk with a computer on it surrounded by a jumble of dirty polystyrene cups. Discounting another soggy carpet, it looked just like any ordinary office. Patrick went first to look behind the curtain that covered the opening at the top of the stone stairs, wrenching it to one side and shining his light into the dark void beyond. He then went from sight for half a minute or so, checking the area below. Returning, he investigated the cupboards which were wooden and old and may well have been put in when the building was constructed. They appeared to be locked.

With no power in the premises it was pointless to investigate the computer, so we first turned our attention to the filing cabinet. This looked promising as there was so much jammed into the drawers they would not shut properly, never mind lock.

'We'll be here for a week,' Patrick muttered, rifling through the stuff in the top drawer. He hefted out a whole armful of files and loose sheets of paper and dumped them on the desk, sweeping all the rubbish already on it on to the floor. 'See what you can find. Did you bring spare torch batteries?'

I had.

I went through it all, initially carefully but then more quickly. None of the paperwork before me appeared to refer to the club at all but to a fashion shop in the city, in Union Street, with letters, bills and so forth dating as far back as thirty years. I did not recognize the name of it. Further down the pile were even older photocopied documents and correspondence that referred to another business in Trowbridge, a town fairly close by.

'Just junk,' I said. 'Nothing to do with anything here.'

'Same here,' Patrick grunted, working on the second of the three drawers. 'I reckon they inherited this thing with the building.'

'What's behind it?'

'I'll have a look in a minute.'

Concealed by the filing cabinet was a wall safe. It was open, the door just pushed to, the interior empty.

Wasting no time, we went back to the desk. The middle and two top side drawers were locked but yielded to the skeleton keys and a strong wrist. The former contained several A4 files, the top ones of which appeared to refer to the club but only to drinks and other similar orders from suppliers.

'Ah,' Patrick exclaimed quietly, having flipped though the last of them. 'Staff rotas, salary records and other stuff.' He removed all the papers from the file, folded them in half lengthways and handed them to me without further comment. Routine, this; I stuffed them into the back of the waistbands of my tracksuit and knickers, and pulled my top down to cover them.

The other top drawers contained a small amount of drugs, at a guess cocaine, a loaded Colt revolver and ammunition for it. Those lower down held a muddle of rubbish, pornographic magazines and chocolate bars, one deep bottom drawer jammed with spirits bottles, some half-full, some empty and one obviously having been spilt, the smell of booze penetrating even the room's resident stench for a moment.

One could describe this as a collection reflecting a misspent life, I thought.

This conclusion was further enhanced when the first cupboard we looked in was found to contain a jumble of costumes, bondage gear and whips. We exchanged glances and I giggled. There is a daft and irresponsible part of me that always makes me want to laugh in such otherwise nerve-racking circumstances.

'If they're running a brothel here, where is it?' he wondered.

'Somewhere on the other side of this other cupboard?' I suggested.

I could not really tell in the gloom away from the torch beams but had an idea I was then given a look that commented generally on the freakishness of authors' imaginations. So it was gratifying when, after the lock was forced and it broke, we discovered that we had before us yet another doorway.

'If anyone's living here . . .' I murmured.

This door was alarmed, Patrick's gizmo beeping excitedly, and proved to have an electronic lock connected to it as there was a series of clicks and clunks and the door swung very slightly in our direction. I did not have to be told to stand to one side as Patrick opened it as wide as the outer cupboard door permitted, he on the other. Regrettably, I wanted to giggle a lot more, a legacy of watching Hammer House of Horror-style movies when I was younger, picturing a stone-dead Kev toppling like a wardrobe through the opening.

Mister I-know-your-every-foible's gaze was on me, a thousand-watt stare, in fact. I bit my lower lip hard and then noticed a sheen of sweat on his face.

There was some kind of dim illumination within and when we cautiously entered we saw that it was coming from a side room where the door was ajar. The rest of the doors in a short corridor were closed and there were three stairs with a door at the top at the other end of it. The flooding did not appear to have penetrated this far, perhaps because we had had to step up to go through the cupboard. Surely, now we were somewhere to the rear of the main room of the night club.

This was not Narnia.

Patrick was bow-taut; we had entered a potential death-trap with any number of hidden and sophisticated surveillance gadgets watching our every move. And here, we could assume, there was a separate electrical network which might power a security system in the rest of the building. It seemed inconceivable that a mobster like Hamsworth would not thus protect himself.

The fact that Patrick's reactions are a lot faster than mine was then forcefully demonstrated when the door at the end of the corridor was flung open and a powerful flashlamp was beamed directly on us. He went for the only option and shot it out, then dived to the floor, taking me with him. In the next few moments when men burst through the doors on either side he scrambled the short distance along the floor and shot out the lamp in the side room too. The men – several of them – shouted obscenities while kicking around on the floor, trying to find us. One boot made painful contact with my side and another must have been grabbed by Patrick as the owner was precipitantly upended, hitting his head hard on the wall by the sound of it.

'Get hold of *him*!' someone yelled, perhaps whoever had been holding the flashlamp, as the voice did not come from immediately nearby.

Someone else tripped over me and thumped down on to the floor, and I took the opportunity to do a swift crawl between various legs in the opposite direction, back towards the cupboard entrance. One of my feet was grabbed and hauled rapidly backwards. Praying fervently that it wasn't Patrick I kicked out with the other, high-ish, and my shoe crunched into what felt like a face and nose. There was a yell of pain. Offering thanks – wrong voice – I scuttled off on all fours, only to cannon into the side of the wall in the dark, seeing stars. At that moment an overhead light was switched on and I immediately rolled over and pulled the Smith and Wesson from my pocket.

They had Patrick on the floor: four, no five, of the most bottom-clenchingly ghastly yobs I had ever had the misfortune to come upon. One of them kicked Patrick in the chest but he managed to squirm over on to his face.

'Drop the gun or he's dead!' shouted one of the men. He and another man were holding guns to Patrick's head.

'Kill the bastard!' Patrick shouted to me.

They kicked him again, several times.

I bent down and put the revolver on the floor. The risk of trying to disable them both and failing was too great. And the light was poor, the same strange red illumination we had seen the first time we had come here.

The one who had spoken came over to me.

Snake eyes. This was Hamsworth, and he was gazing at me with scorn.

'I expected something tougher-looking,' he said with a smile that was quite brave considering the number of bad teeth it displayed. 'But you're quite a girl.'

'You're all under arrest,' I told him.

He laughed out loud, turned to his henchmen and they obediently guffawed as well. Then he said, 'Surely you don't expect us to take any notice of that.'

'No, not at all,' I replied. 'It just means that a charge of resisting arrest gets added to the final tally. Not that it will make much difference with several murders at the top of the list.'

He looked far older than his criminal records would suggest. In a word, raddled, his face pock-marked and, even in the strange light, an unhealthy putty colour. His eyes had a yellow tinge and were really reptilian; I was almost expecting his tongue to be forked and flick in and out of his mouth like a snake's.

'Who then, duckie?' he mocked. 'Do tell.'

'Benny Cooper, for a start.' Could I kick this man where it hurt most, grab the gun from the floor where the moron had left it and shoot the other openly armed mobster before he killed Patrick? Each of the unsavoury quartet, one trying to staunch a nosebleed with a bloodstained handkerchief, had a foot on Patrick as though he was a big-game trophy.

'Oh, no. Very, very sadly, Cooper was killed by a copper,' Hamsworth drawled.

'How about Bob Downton, then?'

'The little shit who ran a coffee bar with the Chinese woman in London? SOCA *has* been busy. Nah, wrong again. He got mixed up with some very nasty folk – I do know them, mind – and thought he could keep some of the proceeds for himself.' He glanced around quickly to check on what was going on behind him – not enough time for me to do anything. 'You know what you read sometimes in the papers? "Their mutilated bodies were found on waste ground?" Well, duckie, that's what's going to happen to you. Right now. But we're going to have a little fun first, aren't we, boys?' Again he turned and there was general sniggering.

I risked everything and gave him a violent shove while he wasn't looking at me, followed him down, scooped up the Smith and Wesson and fired it, fairly high. The bullet found a target and one of the men went down like a skittle. Then, the wrist of the hand holding the gun received a blow from somewhere to the rear of me and a couple of arms like steel bars grasped me and hoisted me into the air as though I was made of feathers. The gun dropped from utterly numbed fingers. It felt as though my arm was broken.

'Good old Kev!' one of the men roared.

I was dumped back on my feet but still restrained so tightly I could hardly breathe. Hamsworth had already picked himself up and now came over. I braced myself.

'We want you in fairly good condition or you won't be able to play, will you?' he grated, visibly controlling the urge to lash out. 'Now listen, duckie, the length of time your screwing-mate here takes to die depends on your being a good girl.' He regarded the group. 'Get him up.' Turning back to me, he added, 'It's a pity you are going to die really, because you won't be able to remember that Raptor was better than even a so-called top-class cop outfit.'

I forced myself to eye Patrick with clinical detachment, having realized with a shock that he was not well and might have been far more badly hurt when he and James were attacked than everyone had thought.

Hamsworth jerked his head at Kev and I was forced-marched towards the nearest doorway on the right and literally tossed within. I landed half-on, half-off something soft, an unmade bed I saw when the light was switched on.

'No, get rid of him before you draw lots,' Hamsworth said.

The door slammed.

TWELVE

Several truths jumped into my mind. I was sure that whatever happened next they would kill us, Hamsworth raping me last so he would have the added pleasure of killing me. Although I was still in possession of my mobile phone there was no time to call for help. My right arm was still just about useless.

Desperately, I cast about the room. There was an old wooden sash window but it was immovable. The only other item of furniture was a dilapidated cupboard – empty, I discovered. A curtained-off hanging space that contained a few flimsy garments, an ironing board, an iron and a few other bits and pieces was in a corner next to a washbasin.

Someone who must have won first turn, Nosebleed, burst into the room and kicked it shut. By great good fortune he placed himself perfectly for a kick in the groin and as he folded up I hit him, left-handed, as hard as I could with the iron, getting him on the nape of the neck.

I supplied a few graphic sound effects, screams and shrieks of, 'Get your filthy hands off me!' to cover the sound of him thundering to the floor and then jumped on to the bed, bounced around quite a few times, screamed again, jumped off and turned out the light.

To produce the sound of heavy breathing was no bother at all.

Half a lifetime went by while I tried to work out the odds. I was fairly sure I had shot one of them in the shoulder so he could reasonably be regarded as one less. Another was unconscious, or at least I prayed he was, a yard or so away from me. That left three counting Kev, plus Hamsworth.

Finally, the door opened a crack. 'Shane, you gone to sleep in there? We let you have first go because she buggered up your hooter but reckon you've had long enough and we're all coming in for our share. The boss is getting impatient.'

Another little eternity went by, during which time I hid behind the door. What the hell had they done to, and with, Patrick?

There was no more time to think; the door was flung open and two of them jostled in, laughing and making pig-sty noises. The time-honoured shove caught the last off-balance and he cannoned into the man in front of him. I did not wait to see any more, threw the iron in their general direction, provoking a howl of pain, ran out and slammed the door, leaving them in the dark.

Unbelievably, the Smith and Wesson had been kicked into a corner in the corridor. I had only seconds to get to it before everyone reacted. The first reaction took me completely by surprise – Kev hurtling, sideways, out of the room where the light had been on, bouncing off the wall and reeling back in again only to re-emerge in the same fashion, followed by Patrick. He gave the man a cracking blow to the jaw that must have rendered him unconscious before he hit the floor.

'Thank God you're OK . . . Hamsworth's mobile rang,' Patrick gasped, heading in my direction. 'He's gone outside to get a signal. Go, I'm done . . . can't shoot 'em all.'

I asked no questions and we headed back the way we had come, with me firing a warning shot, still left-handed, down the corridor as I heard the bedroom, or rather brothel room, door open.

'Where's your Glock?' I asked as we crossed the office.

'Got it,' Patrick grunted.

Once outside – there was no sign of Hamsworth – it became obvious that he had suffered further punishment when he practically collapsed, leaning against a wall.

I got him away for a short distance, knowing it was not far enough, and then called an ambulance and the police – in that order.

The tally was, like Carrick, two cracked ribs, one having been on the mend from the previous attack but re-damaged, and internal bruising. Also, like James, there was some sign of infection, source unknown, again in connection with the first attack as he had a temperature. I railed against the nursing staff in A and E for not examining him when he went there with James on the first occasion but then apologized as it was different staff.

By the time the police had arrived – not very promptly according to someone interviewed on local radio who lived nearby, heard shooting and also dialled 999 – the whole building was deserted. The premises were searched and a quantity of drugs and weapons were found – some of which, of course, Patrick and I already knew about. A call was put out to local hospitals requesting information about any men treated for bullet wounds, broken noses or possible concussion. Next day, the place was boarded up pending enquiries into it having been an illegal brothel, and descriptions had been put out of the men we had come across. As far as we were concerned this, and my spending a little time at Manvers Street helping to create a photofit image of Hamsworth, were the only positive developments.

Patrick was at home, seething at what he regarded as his failure to protect me and for 'messing up on the job', quote, in general.

'You're not admitting that one of them did rape you to save me from feeling worse, are you?' he said, not for the first time.

I knelt at his side and kissed his cheek as he sprawled, up to the hilt with antibiotics like the DCI, on the sofa. 'No, absolutely not.'

'When I heard you screaming . . .' Head back, he closed his eyes.

I have a good line in screams.

'And your arm?' he went on to ask.

'Just bruised.' Assuming all shades of black and blue under the sleeve of my top, actually. 'Constructive thinking,' I encouraged. I was refusing to allow the nightmares of Hamsworth, crawling, scaley, lizard-fashion, pursuing me through an endless darkened building, to get to me.

'They got away,' said Patrick bitterly.

'And they'd broken through into that part of the building they weren't supposed to be in, through that door they came through, so they could hide away in part of the upper floors. We weren't to know that and nor, obviously, was Lynn.'

'And I'm no nearer to helping James.'

'You're not being constructive.'

'No, but we almost had the man in our hands!'

I went away to make some coffee and when I returned Vicky was on the sofa with him, having given him her new teddy bear to cuddle. She and Justin had been told that 'Daddy has hurt his chest so you mustn't jump on him,' the two older ones using their eyes but being assured that there was nothing to worry about.

'Very good medicine, this,' Patrick said, smiling down at his little daughter.

Further results on samples taken during the post-mortem on Cooper showed that he had eaten very well shortly before his death, having consumed oysters, steak and asparagus. He had probably enjoyed fine wines with his meal as well, as he would have been twice over the legal limit had he driven his car.

'Which means that Carrick, feeling ill, took him out to dinner just before he killed him,' Patrick, still not feeling well, said.

DI Campbell, who had just imparted this information to us, was already regretting having asked us 'to attend' the nick in connection with our nocturnal visit to Jingles and clearly hating the fact that Patrick was armed, although he was probably ignorant of the existence of the Smith and Wesson. Patrick, who had duly handed over the staff records and other information we had found – having copied them to peruse later – had brushed off his reservations about our activities. He had gone on to tell him that he had his orders to arrest Hamsworth and as the local police were attaching no importance to his mission then he would act alone. I did not mind being omitted from this remark as Campbell appeared to attach little importance to my input either and, anyway, there was a head-to-head man thing going on here, into which Patrick would not want to drag me.

Campbell said, 'As I've reminded everyone more than once it's important to act professionally and stick to the evidence. We have a murder weapon with the DCI's fingerprints on it. He was found at the crime scene. And, yesterday, a pair of leather gloves was discovered on top of a pile of garden waste at the recycling site that Carrick has identified as his. They have the name of a Glasgow mens' outfitters on a label inside. There are traces of the same grease on them, or motor oil as we now know it is, as we found on the steering wheel of his car. The forensic people think the wheel was wiped with them, not just worn while driving. He can't explain that *although* he remembers putting some oil in his wife's car recently.'

'Wearing his leather gloves?' Patrick queried. 'Really? It's been very warm lately.'

'Perhaps he didn't want to get his hands dirty.'

'Oh, come on! What man would do that to decent gloves?'

'They're by no means new,' Campbell responded urbanely.

'Let's try to re-create this,' Patrick persisted. 'He gets in his car in the station car park and absent-mindedly puts on the greasy gloves but takes them off and then wipes the wheel with them. That makes no sense at all.'

'But he was ill. I'm not saying for one moment that the man did any of this while being in what I'll describe as his right mind.'

'I suggest to you that someone else put on the gloves because he didn't want his fingerprints to be found inside the vehicle. His hands were greasy as he had been fiddling around with his car and without thinking he had tried to clean them on the gloves as he got behind the wheel, then realized that he ought to wear them. Before he threw them on the tip he wiped the wheel with them just to be on the safe side.'

'That could be one theory,' the DI agreed.

'Have you found the weapon with which Cooper was struck on the head before his throat was cut?'

Campbell shook his head. 'No. It's likely to be some kind of heavy, blunt object, possibly metal, as it did a lot of damage to his skull.'

'Just the one blow?'

'Yes. And delivered to the top of his head, so whoever did it must have been quite tall.'

Carrick happens to be quite tall. I could see where he was leading with this. So, too, could Patrick. 'Or Cooper was on his knees having already been knocked over.'

'Carrick's just over six feet in height,' Campbell persisted.

'Kev,' I said to Patrick, ignoring the remark.

'The bouncer at the club,' Patrick explained to the DI. 'Outgrew his intellect before he was born.'

'Who you say you came across at the club.'

'We came across quite a few of Hamsworth's retinue. They must have all been living there.'

'Pity you didn't arrest him.'

I held my breath, waiting for Patrick to boil over but he merely said, 'Would you have given me a search warrant? Backup?' Into the subsequent silence, he added, 'Thought not. Can we go now?'

'You've both made statements?'

'We have. Are you going to arrest Carrick?'

'I'm not prepared to discuss it with you, and would prefer it if you stayed away from him until he's well enough to be interviewed.'

Patrick's response to this was unrepeatable.

'Right now Campbell has to get through me in order to talk to James,' Joanna stated robustly. 'And as far as I'm concerned he's not well enough yet. Does the wretched man have any other lines of enquiry?'

Patrick said, 'All I know is that as many people as possible are working on it. And, as you've probably realized, nothing's gone out to the media other than the finding of a body at the council tip. The biggest problem as far as we're concerned – that is, Ingrid and I – is that he resents what he regards as SOCA's interference. I can understand his point of view but seeing as both cases, his and mine, seriously overlap . . .' He stopped speaking with an angry shrug.

'Did I hear friendly voices?' said James Carrick, descending the stairs into the hallway where we were standing.

There followed, in the adjoining living room, a detailed de-briefing, both men – and here Joanna and I exchanged little smiles – demonstrating exactly how good they are at what they do, covering everything that was, officially and otherwise, currently existing or missing.

'If he doesn't arrest me I shall go back to work,' Carrick said after Patrick had related what had been said at the police station earlier. 'Not that I shall be able to work on the case, of course.'

'How the hell can he arrest you?' Joanna demanded to know. 'Any fool can see that you've been set up.'

'But you've told me that Hamsworth denied that he'd been involved in Cooper's death,' Carrick said.

'Well, he would, wouldn't he?' replied his wife furiously.

'And that he wasn't involved with the murder of the café bar owner in London, which may well be true,' Carrick added. 'I'm only making the point that, although, Patrick, you were duty-bound to report as closely as possible everything that was said in the club the other night, it does give Campbell more leverage in writing that mobster out of the equation.'

'Yes, and it'll look good on his report into the case even when you've either been found not guilty or the case never comes to court due to new evidence,' Patrick said contemptuously. 'He's covering his back and, as I originally thought, is right out of his depth. His thinking is that he has Suspect A, and B *might* follow. If not . . .'

'Perhaps I did kill him.'

'I'd stake my entire reputation on your not having done so. You've never cut anyone's throat.'

'Perhaps I battered him over the head and someone else finished the job.'

'OK, what with? They haven't found it yet.'

'God knows.'

'Any hammers, mauls or medieval bludgeons normally kept in the boot of your car?'

'I always keep a few tools in a vehicle as you never know when you might need them.'

'So do I. But a hammer?'

'Yes.'

Patrick found his mobile and dialled Lynn Outhwaite's work number. She promised to look out the list of contents of the car in the case file and, a couple of minutes later, rang him back.

'Several tools in a polythene carrier bag but no hammer,' Patrick reported.

'Bloody hell,' Carrick muttered.

'Right,' I said briskly. 'I suggest we work on the theory that, under orders, Kev struck Cooper down. A thicko like him might have chucked the weapon as far as possible before anyone could stop him. It's likely that Cooper was taken to the tip with a view to killing him, as perhaps for some reason or other he'd become a nuisance to them. Or they might just have felt like murdering someone as a jolly thing to do. The tip area's been searched but what about adjoining properties and gardens?'

Patrick contacted Lynn again and it emerged that, once knowing the full PM findings, she had taken the initiative in extending the search, which was still ongoing. Complicated by the existence of surrounding warehouses with extensive yards, one of which had been partly demolished and the rubble left lying there, even examining an area within what might be regarded as the distance a man might throw something small and heavy would take at least another two days.

'She'll make DI, easily,' Carrick said quietly.

'You mustn't forget Paul Mallory,' I reminded them. 'Has he done a runner thinking he might be a suspect? *Is* he a suspect, in fact?'

This last remark of mine became academic because, the following morning, James called in to the police station at Manvers Street with a view to talking to Campbell and agreed to be officially interviewed. Again the men had a serious argument, really serious according to Lynn, which ended with the DI arresting Carrick for Cooper's murder and releasing him on police bail pending further enquiries.

'Greenway says it's none of our business unless it gets in the way of my brief,' Patrick told me, having called the commander to keep him up to date. 'That's what he has to say, of course, but I thought he might have been a bit more helpful under the counter in view of the fact that he knows Carrick quite well. But he's under huge pressures at work due to the merging of SOCA into the National Crime Agency.'

Restlessly, he paced the room, trying to excuse his boss, act in a cool professional manner and keep his promise to Carrick, not to mention being a good, as in responsible, husband and family man.

And failing utterly.

'Ingrid . . .' he began.

'I know,' I said when he stopped speaking.

'I shall have to forget that I'm a cop in order to sort this out.'

'Please be careful,' I implored.

He left the room, perhaps not having heard me, already working on tactics.

The dark side.

I was praying that Patrick would not embark on anything just yet as he was distinctly unwell. The cracked ribs would take a few weeks to heal properly but he would not wait that long and as soon as he felt better he would proceed. None of this had been discussed and I have known him long enough now for such a conversation to be unnecessary. Therefore, with difficulty, the oracle shut up shop and waited.

This was not to say that I was excluded, for while it was true that, over the next couple of days, a weekend, he spent quite a lot of time at the Carricks' home, the pair of us worked during the evenings going over the case files, looking for more weak links. It went without saying that the DCI would be excluded from whatever Patrick intended to do as, physical fitness apart, he would severely risk his career if he was involved. As far as weak links went there was already one: Hamsworth's conceit; his being the all-powerful Raptor. The files were courtesy of Lynn Outhwaite, perhaps going against Campbell's instructions, although nothing was said. She seemed to be prepared to risk her own future prospects in order to get to the truth.

They – Lynn's team – had also examined the copies of the contents of the file we had found at Jingles: staff rotas, salary records and time sheets, but there were no personal details or addresses listed. Not a lot of use, then.

We were thus brainstorming on the second evening, having

decided to target Hamsworth's oafish retinue who had ambushed us at the night club – if they were the mobster's ex-services retinue Patrick swore to eat every hat in the house – and had written down as detailed descriptions of them as we could remember when Patrick's work mobile rang. It immediately became clear to me that the person on the other end of the line was Susan Smithson, the widow of the Met CID officer who had, supposedly, committed suicide.

'She wants to talk,' Patrick said at the end of the call, having promised to ring her straight back. 'As soon as possible. A trip to London would fit in nicely. I'm sure that's where Hamsworth and Co. have gone. Coming?'

'You're not fit enough yet,' I told him.

'This is only about talking to Mrs Smithson and looking at mugshots at HQ.'

We both knew it would not end there.

'Of course,' I said.

Mrs Smithson had asked us to meet her at the Black Horse in Ilford, the public house where she worked five nights a week, and it had been arranged that we would be there at twelve-thirty the following day. We decided to drive as the Range Rover, otherwise referred to as the battle bus for good reason, is very useful as a miniature HQ. Firearms can be kept in a secret compartment only accessible by us, the security code needed to open it changed every month, and we keep spare clothing, over-night bags and other equipment in the car at all times. There is also the added advantage of a designated space in SOCA's under-ground car park together with an official pass exempting the vehicle from the city's congestion charge.

The woman had arrived before us and was sitting in a corner of the saloon bar. This, she immediately explained, was because she did not want to have to get into conversation with the regulars who usually patronized the public bar. She seemed ill at ease and not just, I thought, because of this. If my memory was as good as everyone keeps telling me it is, she was wearing exactly the same outfit as when we had first met her.

'Hope I haven't dragged you here for nothing,' she continued. 'The traffic's horrible round here on Monday mornings.'

Patrick's natural caution – when interviewing anyone with

even the most tenuous connection with crime never allow them to get a glimpse of your private transport – had, as before, caused him to park at least a quarter of a mile away and we had walked from there. Although the M4 had been very quiet when we had left at just after four-thirty that morning she was quite correct: the road outside the pub was gridlocked.

Patrick bought a round of drinks, having to forego the East Anglian bitter on offer on account of his medication and suffering fruit juice instead.

'You know when we last spoke I hinted that I sometimes wondered what Jonno got up to?' Mrs Smithson went on hesitantly.

We both obediently nodded.

'Well, this is terrible seeing I'm his mother and all that, but I'm beginning to think he *really* is up to no good. It made me furious, and quite upset actually, when he came out as bold as brass that he'd been seeing his dad like that. And without telling me! I mean, I'd have given him a message to take to him, saying that I wished he'd come back and how sorry I was and how much I missed him. But the little toad didn't and I'd like to know why. The problem – my problem – is that Jonno has money, quite a lot of it. I found it in the wardrobe when I was cleaning his room and putting stuff away the other day – he chucks his clothes all over the floor. There it was on a shelf right in front of my eyes: a wad of notes, more money than I've ever had in my entire life. And he never—' Here she broke off, struggling with tears.

'But with no job?' I asked quietly, aware that I should be the one to speak here.

'Nothing that I know of,' she replied after wiping her eyes and taking a sip of her half of shandy. 'But he goes out more now and comes in at all hours, drunk sometimes by the way he bangs about. I don't ask – I don't dare to now as he's recently changed from the Jonno he used to be. Treats me as though I'm just his landlady. Wants his meals at times to suit him even when I'm working. It's actually very upsetting.'

And here she did burst into tears, sobbing silently into a paper handkerchief.

'D'you know where he is now?' Patrick enquired when the worst was over.

She shook her head. 'Sorry, no, he went out at around ten this morning.'

'Does he have any kind of routine?'

'No, just comes and goes. He seems to just use the back way now, sneaky-fashion. I suppose I should have expected something like this as he bunked off school whenever he could and didn't do any good at exams. I did warn him but he still seemed to spend most of his time hanging around on street corners with the kind of yobbos who make me want to scream.'

'Is there anything else in connection with this that's adding to your fears? Strangers calling for him? Phone calls that he's secretive about?'

'He spends a lot of time in his room talking on his mobile now and if it rings when I'm around he takes it somewhere else. Haven't had any odd bods calling round, though.'

'Can he drive?' I asked.

'No, he's never had the money for lessons – not until now, anyway – and neither have I since Paul and I split up. After he died his car was only fit for scrap.'

'Has he ever dealt in drugs, do you know?' Patrick asked.

'Not that I know of. But I was just coming to that as it crossed my mind when I saw the money and I remembered from police programmes on the telly that notes can be tested for drugs. So I pinched one of the tenners to give you. He won't miss it out of that lot.'

She took out her purse, removed it from a compartment that appeared to have nothing else in it and gave it to him. It was folded into four and Patrick, holding it by one corner, dropped it into a small plastic evidence envelope, a few of which I always have in the pockets of my 'working' jacket, together with plastic gloves.

Patrick thanked her and said, 'This alone probably couldn't be used in court as evidence as it's been handled too much, but if there are traces of drugs on it then it might act as a pointer while we're working on a couple of cases. It goes without saying, of course, that there's absolutely no evidence that your son is involved in crime.'

'But he's keeping it very secret, isn't he?' Sue protested. 'Surely if he'd won the lottery or done well on a horse he'd tell his mum and share some of it with her.' Again, tears threatened.

'Strictly speaking, I should give you a receipt for this,' Patrick

continued. 'But under the circumstances I think it will be safer
if I don't. You'll have to trust me.'

'Oh, I trust you all right. Paul was a cop too, wasn't he?'

Had we travelled over a hundred miles merely to learn that a
lazy and uncouth man who was beastly to his mother had money
stashed away in his wardrobe?

THIRTEEN

We had checked into the rather good hotel we often
use when in town, the thinking being that there is no
harm in projecting a tourist image when engaged in
undercover crime-fighting. After dinner, Patrick went out.
Continuing to play the successful novelist living the high life –
hey, it meant I could wear my long black dress with glittery bits
– and waiting for my husband to return, I sat in the lobby, flicking
through magazines and making a glass of Chablis last a long
time. As writers do, I find people-watching entertaining as well
as valuable and was able to store away a few details for future
use, including a woman having either a very bad hair day or
whose wig was askew, who arrived so drunk that she required
two others to keep her more or less upright. They, grim of visage,
steered their squirm-factor fifty companion towards the lifts.

We had spent the rest of the morning and the afternoon looking
at mugshots at HQ, and would have to carry on the next day,
trying to identify the four men at Jingles with Hamsworth and
Kev. We had two possible matches, one who had a squint and
another a long scar running down his face from the outside
corner of his left eye to his chin. The former was known for
grievous bodily harm and drug dealing, had been released from
prison within the past six months; the latter had been outside
for three years but had form for affray, robbery with violence
and burglary..The remaining two would be more difficult to try
to put a name to.

I had a long wait but was not unduly concerned, and was
forced to have another glass of wine. Patrick arrived at just after
eleven-thirty, by which time I was seriously considering going

to bed. He looked the same as when he had gone out, very elegant in his black suit, matching shirt and pearl-grey tie, betraying no hint that he had driven out to Ilford with the express purpose of mugging Jonno Smithson – having got changed and worn his balaclava, of course. He went to the adjoining bar to get himself a tot of single malt and then joined me on the long leather sofa.

'And?' I queried as our eyes met.

'Got his phone, his wallet with a small wad of money, and believe it or not a debit card of his mother's was in it – and a knife. I left him his wristwatch.'

'A *knife*?'

'One of those nasty cheap things that's sold as a hunters' knife.'

'What did you do with him?'

'Put him where he belonged, in someone's wheelie bin.'

I knew that these items – Patrick would have been wearing gloves – were now in evidence bags and, the following morning, the phone would be taken to SOCA's HQ, where he has a contact who would 'dissect' it for information and arrange traces on past calls. The other items would go to the lab, although unless the knife could be connected with other crimes it was not likely to be useful. Also, more than aware that the man in my life carries such a weapon, an Italian throwing knife, for added self-defence which has saved our lives on more than one occasion, I very much doubted that he had threatened Jonno with it, as he would regard that as bringing himself down to the level of common criminals, and besides, he does not need to.

'It was as Mrs Smithson said,' Patrick recollected. 'He used the alley to the rear of the houses. No mistaking that rotund outline against the street lamp in the adjoining road and I could smell him, just like the house, as you said pubs used to, of stale beer and cigarette smoke, almost before he appeared – which was quite something seeing as the whole place stank of tom cats.'

I made a play of moving a little farther away from him. 'No one saw you?'

'No. And what was interesting was what he said. When I surprised him, grabbed him, he started blubbing about doing what he was told and now being part of what he referred to as "it". But he clammed up when he realized that I was just after his personal possessions. I could hardly question him any further.'

'Part of a gang?' I guessed.

'It would follow.'

'It's horrible that a policeman's son has gone that way.'

'As we both know, Ingrid, it's not a cosy world.' Having said that Patrick paused just before taking a sip of whisky. 'You don't suppose they could have got to his father through him? If, as his mother said, he's been knocking around with the unemployable since he was a teenager perhaps he could have gone from there to what he might regard as bigger, better things.'

'Surely gangs wouldn't want to involve themselves with someone who had a relative in the Met?'

'It would depend on the gang. Those involved in trying to bribe policemen might.' Again he broke off and then said, 'It's not a good idea to bring him in for questioning – not yet anyway. And there's Mrs Smithson's safety to think of.'

'At least he's unlikely to report what happened tonight.'

'Not to the police, anyway.'

'There's one thing I'm sure of,' Patrick said after we had spent a fruitless morning looking at hundreds more photographs on the official Records website, and it goes without saying that you can't just Google this. 'And that is that the men who jumped Carrick and me at the back of Beckford Square – barring the bar staff from the night club – were not the same as those we happened upon that night at the club. The first lot, I'm convinced, were pros, possibly the ex-services bods Cooper was on about.'

'We shall just have to concentrate on following up Squint and Scar from our club night,' I murmured, massaging my aching temples.

'I shall email our DI friend in Bath with our suspicions. Never let it be said that SOCA doesn't cooperate.'

'Do these two have last known addresses?'

'One was thought to live in a caravan on a farm near Frome. I've noted down the name of it. The other inhabits various squats in Bristol.'

'Better and better,' I said grumpily.

'At least they were likely to have been in the Bath area,' Patrick countered, sounding offended. 'Anyway, Avon and Somerset can check it out.'

'Then tell Lynn Outhwaite. You can always say that it was too thin a clue to bother Campbell with.'

Patrick made no response but must have taken up my suggestion because half an hour later he received a call from the DS with the news that both men were known to her and her colleagues. The squint, Terry – or sometimes Gerry – Baker, had been forced to leave his last squat as the building was about to be demolished. He had been glimpsed around Bath and was perhaps sleeping rough. The other man, known as Sid Byles but whose real name was anyone's guess, had, according to an informer, also been forced to leave where he was living as he had managed to set fire to his caravan during a drunken binge and it had been completely destroyed. His whereabouts were not now known and neither man had been spotted for at least a fortnight.

'No, they're here,' Patrick said to himself. 'Right here in the capital.'

Later, as we silently consumed sandwiches in the canteen, Patrick no doubt working on his next move and I wondering whether I ought to be involved in whatever it was, his phone rang. He quickly handed it to me as he had a mouthful.

It was a DS in the Met reporting that two men had been arrested in connection with the murder of Bob Downton, Sulyn Li Grant's husband. They were members of a gang that operated in east London and their names had been mentioned by another gang member who was 'helping with enquiries' after the death of a local drugs dealer. A raid on a house in Ilford, the home of one of those in custody, had resulted in the discovery of a handgun, ammunition, assorted drugs with a street value of several thousand pounds and, among other almost certainly stolen items, a wallet containing credit cards and a driving licence in Bob Downton's name. Both men were now wildly blaming each other for his murder.

'It's not far to travel if they used the Woolwich ferry in order to dispose of the body,' Patrick commented. 'That's good news insofar as we can write off that line of enquiry.' He re-acquired his phone and, knowing that the commander was out of the building, rang him to tell him the news and remind him to be careful in case he was still in danger.

Greenway listened carefully, as is his habit, then told Patrick that he would bear it in mind but did not say he would put in place any personal safeguards. Patrick gave me this reaction and then glumly finished his lunch.

'Back to plan A?' I queried over coffee.

'I don't have a lot of choice, do I? But it's a distraction and wastes time.'

'Shall I go home?'

'You may as well.'

As the wife of a serving soldier I had learned to cope with Patrick's absences, not with a smile on my face, just cope. Perhaps wrongly, I had refused to live in army married quarters as I had my own home at Lydtor, Devon, bought with money my father had left me and the meagre royalties I had squirrelled away from my first few novels. Writing had been a good way of blotting out the loneliness and it was my own fault that I had rather selfishly shut myself away, preferring this to what I had regarded as the boring chatter of other women. Until our relationship had started to go wrong, at least I had had his letters to look forward to.

Years later this present situation was worse as there would be no contact at all until he either had to give up or completed his mission. As had happened before, he had left all personal possessions with me, including his gold watch and wallet containing his driving licence and credit cards, carrying only some cash and a mobile phone kept especially for the purpose that has only three contact numbers in the memory. Two are bogus, the third is an emergency one that is only put through after a code number has also been keyed in. Otherwise any caller has to listen to 'Auntie Mabel' – me – wittering on endlessly.

I had a feeling, no, a fear, that once undercover and James's reputation – not to mention career – at stake, Patrick would go after Hamsworth alone and I might not hear from him for what could be quite a long time. When I had first joined MI5, my role initially that of 'female companion', there had been no reason why I should not gallivant off into all kinds of hazardous situations with him. Then, once pregnant with Justin, everything had changed and because Patrick had been told that following his injuries it was unlikely he could father children, 'only firing blanks' as he had so characteristically put it, the news had been a real shock.

Now we were responsible for five young people.

Several days went by, during which, again as on previous occasions, I tried to bury myself in domesticity and my family. I could not concentrate on writing. I told the children and Patrick's parents that he was working 'away' – perfectly true and the latter were aware that I could not go into details, even if I knew any. This was not to say that I did not keep abreast with local developments and on the fifth morning, after arriving back home and having heard that he was now a lot better, I went to see James Carrick.

'There have been no real developments,' he replied in answer to what was inevitably my first query. 'Lynn keeps me informed and I understand that a senior officer from Complaints, no name yet, is going to bless us with his presence in order to interview me. Which, joking apart, is a good idea as even Campbell has admitted that there's been a clash of personalities. The sooner it happens the better as far as I'm concerned, as I'm desperate to put all this behind me.'

'Campbell has no real evidence against you,' I reminded him. 'Anyone could have put that knife in your hand.'

'It's just the dreams, though, hen,' he said, imitating a Glasgow accent. 'In them I killed Cooper several times. Perhaps they weren't dreams.'

'How did you kill him?' I asked baldly.

'Oh, shot him, stamped on his face, threw acid over him and watched him melt away into a revolting puddle . . .' The DCI stopped speaking, not wanting to evoke any more memories.

'But you didn't hit him over the head with the hammer from your car and then cut his throat?'

'No.'

'Funny old thing then, as that's the way he was killed. Haven't they found the hammer yet?'

'Lynn told me this morning that they've sifted through everything within throwing distance with no success.'

'Then the gang, or just Kev, got rid of it another way. Haven't they traced *any* of these men?'

'Not yet. And I'd be the last to say that Campbell isn't trying.'

'What's happening about the night club?'

'There's been some progress as they've traced a couple of the girls who worked there, including the one who was told to throw herself at me that night so someone could get a couple of pictures. But that's only one small bit of bother out of the way.'

'It's made Joanna happy, though,' I said with a smile at her. She was seated on the sofa, cradling a sleeping Iona.

Carrick smiled in her direction too and then said, 'The place is still boarded up and likely to remain so even if it hadn't been flooded.'

Joanna said, 'So shall *we* go and look for this damned hammer then, Ingrid? My first instincts are to give Campbell a black eye but . . .' She shook her head in mock regret.

'That's a very good idea,' I replied, really meaning it.

'Was the club searched for the murder weapon?' Joanna went on to ask.

The DCI was not sure and phoned Lynn Outhwaite. It appeared that the answer was that it was searched but not specifically for that. He was about to end the call when Joanna impatiently signalled that she wanted to talk to her.

'Hi, Lynn. I don't think we've met but I used to have your job and was so damned good at it my boss married me so he would have sex and a thinking woman on tap. Ingrid wants me to help SOCA search the club for the murder weapon. Are the keys available or do we break in?'

James was staring at her in total disbelief but she forestalled any comments after the call by saying, 'This is your wife reverting to cop. You can swap to mother.' And to me, 'She'll meet us for coffee at Mario's in about an hour. With the keys. Coming?'

It must be said that since travelling from her native Cumbria some years previously Lynn Outhwaite, once rather straight-faced, has developed a sense of humour and had difficulty, when first spotting us, Joanna's remarks still fresh in her mind, in repressing a smile.

'The place *was* searched,' she was at pains to point out. 'And as you know we found drugs plus a firearm and ammunition. Counterfeit fifty-pound notes were hidden behind a drawer in another part of the building. But I can't say that we tore the club apart looking for the murder weapon in the Cooper case as the

DI was still reluctant at that time to connect that death with the gang leader who appears to have been running it. I have to say that, personally, I find it hard to believe that the killer would have kept anything connected with the crime where we must assume he was hiding out.'

'And Campbell's *thinking now*?' Joanna enquired, stirring her coffee, the two words dripping with scorn.

'He's like an oyster with regard to communication but at the same time a committed and professional policeman. And you mustn't forget that although we have a strong suspect we still have another ongoing murder inquiry: the woman whose body was found near Oldfield Park station,' Lynn responded diplomatically. 'You know my position on this and also the fact I can't let you have the keys is the reason why I'm coming with you.'

Which, thought about for a couple of moments, was another very good idea. I glanced at Joanna and saw my own conclusions mirrored in her expression.

'Thank you,' she said.

Mario's was right opposite the police station so all we had to do was cross the busy road and make our way to the parking area at the side of it where Lynn had left her car. A few minutes later we had arrived at the club.

There was a new metal bar secured by two padlocks across the main door and, judging by the number of keys on the bunch that the DS was wielding, the same standard of security on the other entrances. It was good to know that Hamsworth and Co. could not have sneaked back in.

'This Kev character,' Joanna mused. 'Who the hell is he?'

'God knows,' Lynn muttered, lifting off the bar and starting on the original door locks. 'He doesn't appear to have any local form – and by that I mean in this force – and if you key in Kev, or Kevin, on the national database you get around two million of them. Those staff records you forwarded to us, Ingrid, weren't much use in that direction either.'

'It doesn't pay to keep records if you're involved in anything illegal,' I said.

The place still smelt horrible but at least some form of temporary lighting had been restored on the floor that housed the club itself, at the request of the police, Lynn went on to inform us, in order to search it. At the time the lower cellars had been deemed too dangerously unhealthy to enter. I did not remind her that SOCA had already trawled through them.

After putting on the gloves that Lynn handed out we crossed the so-called dance floor and had a quick look behind the bar. This possessed all the miscellaneous items and gadgets one might expect together with a few left-behind coats, gloves and scarves, plus a couple of umbrellas and someone's dry cleaning.

'Oh, we found a couple of knives here that had probably been confiscated from punters,' Lynn remembered. 'They're at the nick.'

After quickly searching a kitchen of sorts and a tiny room where the staff must have hung their coats we progressed into the office where, judging by the mess, the searching team had hauled out everything from the filing cabinet and desk drawers on to the floor. The computer had disappeared so presumably had been requisitioned. The contents of the cupboard had been similarly treated and my companions paused momentarily when they caught sight of the contents.

'You know, I reckon James would just *adore* me in these black corsets and fishnet stockings – I don't think,' Joanna muttered. 'Handcuffs for that special *Fifty Shades of Grey* session, ladies?'

She found no takers and I kept very quiet about my 'tart rig' bra.

Going through the door concealed by the cupboard still seemed to be the only way to enter the rest of the complex and I could not control a shudder when we started to walk along the corridor beyond. At Lynn's suggestion, playing very safe, one of us stayed in the corridor while the other two took it in turns to search the four rooms on either side. I took the first on the left, where the light had been switched on. It was very small and closely resembled the one into which I had been tossed on the other side of the corridor, just housing a dishevelled bed, a washbasin and a curtained-off corner for hanging clothes. The police had searched here too but I looked beneath the bed and yanked the soiled sheets from it in order to lift the mattress. I found nothing and the three other rooms were similarly unproductive.

'Patrick and I didn't get this far,' I said as we reached the three stairs with the door at the top.

'As we already know those renting the premises shouldn't have either,' Lynn said. 'But they broke through and replaced the door with this one and used this part of the building they weren't paying rent for as a sort of doss-house and hide-away. There's no power in here at all as the owner had it all disconnected for safety's sake before he started work.'

We entered a very large room, with a couple of doors on the left-hand side, that was strangely bright after the previous gloom. The windows here had not been boarded up – there had been no reason to do so. The restoration project was manifest as the whole area had been stripped out, including the interior partitions, the joists overhead supported by steel props. Old electricity cables and water pipes dangled down everywhere and the plaster had all been knocked off the walls. The floors were bare boards – where you could see them for rubbish, that is – plus clothing and sleeping bags left by the intruders. An ancient sofa stood in one corner, perhaps brought in from the club.

Methodically, and although we knew it had already been searched, we worked our way through the piles of stuff, going through all the pockets of clothing – they had left in an awful hurry – before putting it all in a large heap at one side of the room. We must have been more thorough than the police team as we discovered another handgun and a wad of fifty-pound notes, counterfeit like the others, possibly, in the pockets of an anorak in one corner. Lynn placed these items in evidence bags while no doubt composing a suitable rocket for those who had missed them.

'I think those are just a loo and a bathroom,' she said when we were finishing around fifteen minutes later, having even tipped out and re-examined the bags of rubbish, and were regarding the two remaining doorways. 'But I wasn't present when the first search was made.' She opened the first one, which did indeed reveal a revolting lavatory.

The second would not open, the handle immovable. In response to her silent gestures we followed her to the other side of the room.

'I'm a bit worried about this as even if it's somehow locked from the outside the handle should still move, shouldn't it?' she hissed. 'And if it's locked from the inside it might mean someone's in there holding it.'

'Anyone could have got in through the windows,' Joanna whispered, looking out of the one by which she was standing. 'Look, there's a fire escape on the next one. And that anorak we've just found might not have been here when it was first searched.'

'It hardly warrants calling up help,' Lynn fretted. 'The beastly thing's probably just jammed and I'd be the laughing stock of the nick.'

'It's a very large anorak,' I pointed out.

They just looked at me, rather round-eyed.

'Shall I shoot the lock off?' I went on to offer, knowing that was exactly what my working partner would have done right now.

'What, with the weapon we've just found?' Lynn responded, askance.

'Of course not. I have my own.'

I could almost hear her thinking. Finally, she whispered, 'We ought to give a warning first.'

'Don't be silly.'

'OK, SOCA's doing it without my permission.'

I took the Smith and Wesson from my jacket pocket and went back to the door, leaving the two slight cases of heebie-jeebies where they were. This threatened to become three when I heard a slight sound of movement on the other side of the door.

I stood well clear and the shot cracked out, the cheap lock smashed in a cloud of wood splinters. There was a howl of alarm from within and Kev burst out, a tsunami of unshaven oaf, saw the gun and then me, jinked and made for the exit.

'Get him!' I yelled to my two apparently transfixed companions.

'Police! You're under arrest!' Lynn gabbled as she led the chase after him, getting the regulation bits out of the way.

We got him.

Comprehensively.

Three women, vengeful for three different reasons, all with some training in self-defence that came gloriously back to us, arrested him.

Better than that, we pulverized him into submission.

First.

FOURTEEN

'Apparently he could hardly wait to get into the custody suite and they're getting a medic to look him over,' James Carrick said, eyeing Joanna and me when I dropped her back at home. The pair of us had made a point of tidying our hair and repaired any flaws with regard to make-up before we left the nick. Lynn had not bothered to address her dishevelled state and I really hoped she would receive all the credit for the arrest.

'There was no food there,' Joanna commented in off-hand fashion. 'He'd have had to emerge soon anyway.'

'Did he resist arrest then?' her husband persevered.

'Of course he did! Tried to kick, punch and even bite us. We had to get quite rough with him.' Perceiving suspicion – I had an idea he was actually worried that his wife might be had up for assault – she added, 'James, you've never even clapped eyes on this man. He's an eighteen, or even twenty, stone thug with a brain the size of a pea.'

'OK, OK,' he soothed.

We were both concealing reddened and potentially bruised knuckles but I felt quite pleased with myself for not having yielded to temptation and floored him by hitting him with the gun butt. Patrick always tells me that my merciful streak will be the death of me one day.

Carrick continued, 'And on the grapevine Lynn heard just as she got back that someone's taken a shot at Commander Greenway again. That's what she actually rang to tell me.'

'They didn't hit him, I hope,' I said.

'No, but it was a very near miss this time and the same method as last time – two blokes on a motorbike, presumably stolen. The bike drew alongside and the pillion passenger took a shot at him as he was walking back to the office after having had a coffee break at a local café.'

'Surely he's not still going to the one where the shooting took place last time!' I exclaimed.

'Dunno,' he replied tiredly.

Kev, whose full name was Kevin Hopkins – someone at the police station recognized him – was pronounced to be merely bruised and a little frayed at the edges and fit for questioning. I had to admire DI Campbell for dismissing out of hand his claim that he had been savagely beaten up by the crew of the area car who had answered Lynn's request to help her take her prisoner away. The DI had then charged him with assault and resisting arrest and being in possession of a firearm and counterfeit currency, for a start, the anorak we had found being his property. Campbell had also made no comment at all about any assistance the DS might have received, official or otherwise, both of which small enigmas I asked James about when he had forwarded these titbits of information to me over the phone later that same day.

'It's the Scotland thing,' he said. 'If you get burgled out in the sticks near big cities the crime prevention officer usually tells you to get yourself a shotgun. It's a different country. We don't pander to criminals up there.'

'I hope Campbell will interview Hopkins himself.'

'No news on that yet. But at least he's been charged in connection with Patrick and I being beaten up. Is he there, by the way?'

'No, he thinks Hamsworth's bolted to London so that's where he is.'

'It would figure if they were responsible for both attacks on Greenway. I just hope the man gets himself a minder now. And I have to tell you, I admire Patrick's courage in carrying on with this.'

I too hoped Greenway was getting armed protection. I also wanted to be at the nick, right now, with Patrick, interrogating Hopkins about Cooper's murder. It seemed to me that there was no official urgency to do this.

I thought the most natural thing to do in the circumstances would be to contact the commander about his narrow escape.

'News travels fast,' he commented wryly.

'James Carrick heard it through official sources,' I explained and then went on to inform him about the arrest of the club bouncer. 'But we didn't find the other murder weapon – probably a hammer,' I added. Desperate for him to get involved with the peripheral investigations into Hamsworth and his gang, I then said, 'Sorry, I know it's not for me to say this but everything's in a state of paralysis here in Bath. James Carrick can't take charge because he's still not fit and has been charged with Cooper's murder and Patrick's God knows where looking for Hamsworth. Can't SOCA give it a bit more priority?'

I felt I could not have put it more tactfully. *And* I had left out the bit about Patrick not yet being fit. This fact was gnawing at me.

'It's perfectly all right for you to say that kind of thing,' the commander hastened to assure me. 'But believe me I'm right up to my ears here with at least two other vital investigations that need my personal attention as well as the National Crime Agency thing. I'm sure what you have is only a temporary glitch. But please keep me right in the picture.'

I felt like raging at him that he could easily spare half a day, and was perfectly entitled to question a man suspected of murder in order to try to tie up an important end in one of his own inquiries. He would thus possibly save a lot of work and expensive man hours, if one really was going to talk about money, and ensure the personal safety of one of his staff, not to mention that of several other police officers who were working on various aspects of the case.

'You've gone quiet, Ingrid,' Greenway remarked.

So I said it, but not raging.

He went quiet.

On a gusty sigh he finally said, 'OK. I'll come down on an early train. Tomorrow. I'll phone Campbell and tell him I'm coming in case he's planning on sending that muscle-bound lout away on remand. You'll have to brief me and, if you want to, can assist at the interview.'

I found myself staring at my mobile after he had rung off. I had said nothing to him about Hopkins' personal appearance, only that he was the door man, the bouncer. So who had Greenway been talking to?

Sticking firmly to the rules, Commander Greenway first arrested Hopkins on behalf of SOCA, the charge that of grievous bodily harm relating to the assaults on Patrick and me at the club. I was cautiously congratulating myself on succeeding in getting him to come as it meant that for the first time since his arrival at Manvers Street Hopkins was encountering someone as big as he was, albeit not mostly blubber.

Apparently David Campbell had been staggered when Greenway had announced his intention but when we turned up was obviously not happy about my involvement. Greenway pointed out that I was acting as his assistant and would take a few notes as he would leave all the recorded evidence in Bath. He went on to say that he had no problem with the DI being present as an observer if he so wished and would be interested in having the same role when Campbell interviewed the suspect in connection with other charges at a later date. This, again, was all very right and proper but I thought it would be impossible for matters to proceed along any tidy demarcation lines. However, the DI found himself hardly in a position to argue.

I had put Arnica on my hands to alleviate the bruising and the first thing Hopkins said when he had been cautioned and the interview recording machine switched on was, 'That woman beat hell out of me! With the others! And I didn't do nothin' to deserve it!'

Urbanely, Greenway said, 'You resisted arrest with violence. And I would like to point out that the three ladies who apprehended you are slightly built, one being only just over five feet four inches in height. So I would keep quiet if I were you – unless you want to be laughed at.'

Hopkins lapsed into a sullen silence. He had a hatching black eye and there was a big bruise on the side of his jaw that I was fairly sure was where Patrick had hit him. Other than that his face had a few livid marks and both lips were swollen, one with a small split. We had kicked his backside rather a lot – I didn't want to know about the state of that – and he was sitting rather uncomfortably in his chair.

'I understand that you worked at Jingles, the night club,' Greenway began by saying.

Hopkins grunted.

'As well as your official duties as doorman did you act as some kind of bodyguard for a man using the name, among others, of Nick Hamsworth when he was on the premises?'

'No.'

'No?'

'I've never been nobody's bodyguard.'

'You do know him, though.'

'No.'

'He was there, in charge, that night at the club when you seriously assaulted two of my operatives.'

'We didn't know they was the law. There was a buzz goin' round that a mobster from Bristol was goin' to try to take over the club.'

'Answer the question. Do you know this man?'

'S'pose I do, then,' Hopkins muttered.

'And because of this rumour the decision had been made to

break into a part of the building that wasn't included in the rental agreement – in order perhaps that you could remain on the premises at night to guard it and use it as a hideaway.'

'I don't know about rental agreements and stuff like that.'

'I think you're lying. Were you aware that the club was being run as an illegal brothel?'

'I don't know nothin' about that either. I just did as I was told.'

'Orders issued by Hamsworth – who also liked to be known as Raptor.'

The man just shrugged.

'Where is he, by the way?'

'God knows.'

'It looks as though he's done a runner and left you to take the blame.'

'No.'

'So what were you doing there? Hiding in a bathroom, wasn't it?'

'I haven't got nowhere else to go, have I?'

'No home or digs?'

'I got chucked out for not payin' the rent.'

'So as well as leaving you to take the rap, Hamsworth hasn't paid you.'

Again, Hopkins shrugged.

'Left behind like all the rubbish,' Greenway murmured.

'Who are you callin' rubbish?' Kev shouted.

'I'm not. But it's the way you were treated. Abandoned with no money, no food and every prospect of soon being arrested for serious assault.'

'It's only their word against mine,' Hopkins said with a hint of triumph and a jerk of his head in my direction.

I caught Greenway's eye and said, 'According to one of the men arrested when two undercover officers were set upon by a group of thugs previously to the rear of Beckford Square, it was you who issued the orders, passed down from the boss. You've already been charged in connection with that. Like all of them, no doubt, this man had suffered violence from you and his relatives had been threatened if he didn't do as he was told. It's going to end up being several people's word against yours. And here you are, the one left behind to serve a long prison sentence. They always made fun of you too, didn't they, Kev?'

He glowered at me and I was glad that two other men were with me in the room.

'They being Hamsworth and what Benny Cooper referred to as his private army, I mean,' I went on. 'The ex-servicemen, not those in the club that night. Those were just the local hangers-on and odd-job boys, weren't they? And now they've *all* high-tailed it to London, leaving what they regard as stupid old Kev behind.'

Perhaps thinking that he might have to act as my minder if I carried on in this vein, Greenway quickly said, 'So here you are charged with GBH and another charge of murder soon to follow.'

'Murder?' Hopkins echoed, his small eyes popping.

'Cooper. You were obeying orders just like you said and bludgeoned him with a hammer before finishing him off by cutting his throat.'

I had been thinking that the interview was not going at all well, without any proper structure, but it appeared that Greenway had his methods.

'I wasn't involved with that!' the big man protested. 'I wasn't even there that night they grabbed the cop and . . .'

'Keep talking,' the commander ordered.

Hopkins leaned forward in his chair, winced and sat back again. 'Look, I wasn't there. I was ill. I got a horrible bug after fallin' in the drain. It was just after that I got kicked out of the digs. Honest, I wasn't *there*.'

'OK. They grabbed the cop, and then what?'

'I'm not sayin' no more.'

'But if you weren't there and completely innocent it's a good idea to provide a bit more information. That way I *might* believe you.'

Gazing at the ceiling for a moment, the man appeared to come to a decision. 'All right. Cooper was making a real nuisance of himself. Right bumptious little sod he was. And then, when he started ordering everyone around when the boss wasn't there . . .'

'Hamsworth decided to get rid of him,' Greenway said when the big man stopped talking.

'Nah, he wasn't there then either.'

'Oh?'

After a long pause, Hopkins said, 'They all got a bit drunk.'

'Who's all?'

'The blokes at the club the other night. But not the boss.'

'Names?' the commander demanded to know.

With the eagerness of a man endeavouring to save his own skin, Hopkins said, 'There was Dave MacTavish and Ned Freeman.' With a furtive glance in my direction he added, 'And Squinty Baker – the one with the funny eyes.'

'Is his first name Terry or Jerry?' I asked.

'Dunno. Everyone just calls him Squinty.'

'Tell us what happened,' Greenway said.

'Look,' Hopkins pleaded. 'If I tell you how it was, how they told it to me, will you get me off the murder charge?'

'Only if you're found to be telling the truth. I can't do anything until we know for sure.'

'That's not good enough.'

Greenway thumped a big fist down on the table and DI Campbell, standing over by the door, was the only one who jumped. 'But they might have been giving you a stack of lies, mightn't they? Just give us the story and then everyone can get on with investigating to see if there's any truth in what you say!'

'OK,' Hopkins said reluctantly. Then, after another long pause, continued, 'They decided to cart him off to the tip and chuck him in a skip or something like that – to teach him a lesson, like. But it went wrong. They went to Cooper's in Dave's car and he'd got this can of motor oil that he'd pinched from work – he works at that place that sells and services posh motorbikes. It wasn't quite full and he hadn't put the top back on right – it fell over and spilled all over the back seat. So they had to clear that up a bit and Dave was furious as the oil was posh too and he already had a buyer for it. When they got to Cooper's Mallory was there. He's a real creep, a junkie. Cooper treated him like a doormat, made him run errands all the time. They was in the middle of a row as Mallory wanted money, and a fix, and Cooper was saying no. He was horrible to that man and hit him several times and—' Here Hopkins broke off and actually seemed distressed.

'Please continue,' Greenway urged quietly.

'The boys all took exception to this as . . . Well, OK, Mallory's a creep but he's weak and pathetic and no one likes to see a man kicked when he's down.'

I put a large exclamation mark on my notepad but made no comment.

'They got hold of Cooper, really keen to take him to the tip now and chuck him into something he couldn't get out of in a hurry. Then this cop rolled up. The boys didn't know he was a cop but Cooper and Mallory did. The bloke was drunk, stoned out of his mind and was raving that he was going to get Cooper if it killed him. Then he collapsed. Went down like a ninepin. And he was burning hot, perhaps sick as a parrot rather than been on the booze.'

I looked at Campbell, who dropped his gaze.

'Anyway,' Hopkins went on, really getting into his stride now. 'They looked in his wallet for some kind of identification, to double-check, like, and as well as finding out that he was a DCI Dave found a photograph of the boss so they knew the cop was on to him too. He kept it. Then they used the cop's car – he'd left it nearby on the double yellows – as they couldn't all get into one. They didn't know what to do with him really but took him along and Dave drove it to the tip with the others following in his, Ned driving it. God knows how, Ned could hardly walk he was so pissed, let alone drive. Mallory wouldn't be left out and went along as well. They couldn't stop him.'

'And?' I said.

'Mallory killed Cooper. He went mad when they'd broken into the tip. Hunted through Dave's and the cop's car boots – they didn't know what the hell he was after until he found the hammer – and shoved Cooper over before bashing him over the head with it. He was crazy, insane, right off his rocker and threatened all the guys with it, demanding some kind of knife. Dave had one, a Scottish thing which he said was a good luck charm but he didn't want it no more as it hadn't brought him any. Someone helped Mallory heave Cooper – they all thought he was dead, actually – into a skip where Mallory used the knife on him. God knows what he did – we couldn't see and didn't want to. Then everyone scarpered before Mallory could climb out and start on them too.'

'They took both cars?' Greenway asked sharply.

'Too right. Didn't want to leave the lunatic with any transport.'

'So wasn't Mallory's car parked near Cooper's place?'

'God knows. Perhaps they'd both arrived together.'

'They didn't see where the man went or what he did with the hammer and the knife?'

'No, and they shoved the cop out of sight somewhere. No one wanted that madman to get him as well.'

'*Really?*' Greenway enquired in utter disbelief.

'Not bloody likely. It would have made them accessories, or whatever you lot call it, to murdering a cop. Not only that, Dave said it would've been like leavin' a baby to drown.' And, on an afterthought, 'They *was* stoned, of course.'

'But they'd found the photo,' I said, needing to get one small detail right in my mind. 'And as you said, that meant the cop was on to Hamsworth. Wasn't that an unwise thing to do, to just leave him there, a danger to the boss?'

Hopkins frowned deeply. 'Look, lady, I wasn't there, and as I keep sayin', they *was stoned.* There had been talk of us all gettin' out and leavin' him with his London boys, a right dodgy lot. Too much trouble, too many risks of us gettin' blamed for anything *they* did out of line. As it was, Dave told him the cop went off his head and killed Cooper in case he got mad at us for not stoppin' Mallory. We wanted out and to hell with him.'

'But they've gone off, presumably with him, now,' Greenway pointed out.

'Yeah, well, he offered them more money, didn't he?'

'But not you?' the commander went on to ask, I'm sure also from the need for absolute accuracy.

'No, not me,' Kev muttered.

I didn't *quite* feel sorry for him.

'He's far too unimaginative and stupid to be able to make all that up,' Greenway said a little later. 'And so probably are the rest of them, come to think of it. My only slight reservation is that they remembered afterwards what had happened.'

He and I were in Campbell's office, the DI having arranged coffee and biscuits.

'I reckon he'll plead guilty to the lesser charges if a deal's done with him and he's told he'll probably be out of the frame for Cooper's murder,' the commander went on. 'That story is so perfect, so absolutely believable I think I could write the screenplay if Hollywood ever wanted to film it. What say you, Ingrid?'

'Likewise,' I replied.

'So what's it to be, Detective Inspector?' Greenway continued. 'Do I go and pay a quick call on your DCI to admire the new baby and tell him he's no longer charged with murder and free to come back to work as soon as he's well enough?'

'I've already put out a warrant for Paul Mallory's arrest and Lynn Outhwaite's gone round, with backup, to his address,' Campbell hastened to say. 'It's likely that Mallory did see where they put Carrick and was rational enough by that time to think it might save his skin if he wiped the knife and then got Carrick's fingerprints on it before tossing it into the skip. We don't yet know what he did with the hammer. And yes, sir, by all means.' He added, ruefully, 'I'd better go and pack my bags.'

The commander got to his feet. 'I hardly think that'll be necessary if you make suitably regretful noises. I won't be able to come down again but I'd like Patrick Gillard to interview Hopkins if we can't manage to track down this Raptor character. Just to see if he can give us any leads, however small, as to his possible whereabouts. I suggest you don't release him on police bail – partly for his own safety but mostly to prevent him from communicating with anyone.' When we had left the room Greenway said to me, 'There was a bank raid last week in Ascot that the Met thinks was Hamsworth's doing. Very efficient and run on military lines, according to witnesses.'

But Patrick Gillard remained off the map.

FIFTEEN

I had established, from Carrick, that Lynn Outhwaite was still keeping in contact with the girl at the club who had been ordered to compromise him that night. Other than saying that it was Kev who had told her what to do she was continuing to refuse to answer any more questions about the club or the people who had worked there, out of fear, Lynn knew. The DS rang me while Greenway and I were at the Carrick's to tell me that Mallory had not been at home, and, according to others questioned who lived in the same terrace, his car had disappeared two or three days previously.

An obviously delighted James, in a mood to get in his car and head for Bath on the receipt of the news, had merely smiled broadly when informed that Campbell was all ready to pack his bags. Then he had said, 'I'll take him out and we'll get drunk together.'

'How did you know about Hopkins?' I asked the commander as I gave him a lift back to the station.

'From your husband. Before he went undercover he called me and said the same kind of thing that you did – that I ought to get my head out of the sand and take more responsibility over this.'

'I didn't put it quite so rudely as that,' I demurred.

'No, but you two have a way of speaking politely that's actually like a kick in the pants.'

I had thought long and hard about what I was about to say next. 'There's something I think you ought to know.'

'That he's going to get Hamsworth, whatever it takes?'

'Yes.'

'Even though Carrick's off the hook?'

'Oh, yes.'

'I'm learning, aren't I? He's hard-wired like that. It was one of the reasons Richard Daws hired him.'

As we parted, the commander said, 'Don't worry – even if he brings me the man's head par-boiled on a silver platter I'll think of something.'

Not for the first time, I found myself admiring him enormously.

I wanted to contact Patrick for several reasons, not least because of the strong likelihood now that Mallory had murdered Cooper and Patrick no longer had his promise to James as one of his priorities. But none of my reasons could be regarded as emergencies, unless my going off the rails with worry counted for anything. So, as usual, and again unable to concentrate on writing, I plunged myself into domesticity and motherhood, taking down and sending to the cleaners the living-room curtains that we had 'inherited' from Elspeth when we bought the rectory, unpacking the last of the boxes of our move and lugging most of the contents off to charity shops, and taking the two eldest children riding, the last, of course, a joy.

'You don't think Mark might be gay?' Carrie said out of the blue the morning after yet another day engaged in a housework maelstrom not included in the cleaner's brief when I was hunting around for something else to do. 'I mean, he's so downright *sweet.*'

I was actually glad of any interruption. 'He's always been a bit sort of girlie, hasn't he?' I replied thoughtfully.

'Vicky's given him one of her dolls as he likes it so much. Don't worry, it's a soft toy and I've checked, he can't swallow any of it.'

'Better not mention it to Patrick. We won't really know for sure for ages and if it's true it'll take a while for him to get used to the idea.'

'Military men are often like that though, aren't they?' she observed thoughtfully and went away again.

It was just after midnight when my mobile phone rang, jerking me from sleep.

'Hi,' said a familiar voice. 'Everything all right?'

I told him what Kev had said. There was no need to point out the implications.

Patrick is not a man to go in for cowboy whoops of joy but after saying he was really pleased for James's sake he went on, 'Word has it that Hamsworth has a small chain of clubs, mostly in the east of the city and a high-end hush-hush one in a big private house on the edge of South Woodford. There's a chance that it's his actual home so my next job is to pin-point the place.'

'And then arrange a raid?'

'Only if he's guaranteed to be there. Otherwise he'd disappear to somewhere like Equador for ever. Did Greenway mention the shooting?'

'No.'

'Nothing at all? Nothing about now having armed protection?'

'Not a word, and I didn't quite like to ask.'

'Perhaps I should have winged him.'

'Who helped you?'

'Someone in the Diplomatic Protection team. He just removed the plates from his bike, no bother.'

'Where are you now?'

'Sitting under a bridge on the towpath of a disused canal. The rats are as big as ponies.'

'Do you want me to do anything?'

'Yes, stay right where you are. I can't talk any more now. I love ya, kid.'

And he had gone.

I could not sleep for the rest of that night.

At ten-thirty the next morning I had a call from the person at SOCA HQ to whom Patrick had given Jonno's mobile phone for examination. He wanted to know how he could contact Patrick as he did not wish to consign the information to an ordinary email. I had to tell him that he would have to give a message to me, for forwarding if possible, and I would instigate any immediate action necessary. What he told me, deliberately vaguely, ultra cautious over an open line, was absolutely staggering. Finally, he promised to send a full report via Recorded Delivery.

In short, the information gleaned, several voice messages that for some reason had not been deleted, gave every indication that Jonno had been begging for help from a person calling himself Nick who had told him – my caller saying he had censored the language – to stop wingeing, grow up and never to contact him again. Jonno, it would appear, had been responsible in some way for the death of someone referred to as 'your old man'.

That would be his father, Paul Smithson, the police officer.

I was in a real quandary now as I would have to contact the Met immediately about this but had no idea who was handling the case, if indeed there was one, the man in question being deemed to have committed suicide. And in view of the illicit manner in which the evidence had been obtained . . .

'With regard to our previous conversation,' I began when Greenway answered his phone.

'Anything fairly concrete about anything right now would make my day,' he admitted briskly.

I gave him the story.

'That's great news and sounds very much like our friend Hamsworth. I shall arrange to listen to the recordings, get them copied and pass them on. We have a way round this even though the evidence might not be presented in court. The line to Jonno will be that a mugging suspect was stopped, searched, and stolen items were found in his possession. Jonno *was* mugged, end of story.'

'Do you know if there have been any test results on that ten-pound note Mrs Smithson gave Patrick?'

'No, that hasn't come my way yet.'

'Is Patrick keeping in touch with you?'

'Not really because, as you know, it's too dangerous. The only information I have is that he's helping out in exchange for dossing down in a Salvation Army hostel somewhere in the East End.' Obviously in a hurry Greenway ended the call with, 'Thanks for the info. Good work.'

Not really? What the hell did that mean?

Quite oblivious until Elspeth told me that she too had done exactly the same when upset and angry, I went into the garden and, with vicious stabs, dug all the dandelions out of the lawn using an old chisel.

'You're sitting there as though you want me to do something,' James Carrick said.

'Are you back at work yet?' I enquired from the comfort of a brand-new leather sofa and really feeling the effects of lack of sleep, not just the previous night either.

'I went in for a couple of hours this morning with a view to catching up and mending a few fences with David Campbell. But to answer the question, I'm officially back next week, providing the doc says it's OK.'

'And the fences?'

He pulled a face. 'It'll take a while but we'll have to cobble something together. If only Lynn was promoted . . .' He waved his hands around orchestra conductor-style. 'And?'

'Has Mallory been found yet?'

'He hasn't even been sighted. A watch on railway stations and airports and all that kind of thing's in place but, unfortunately, no sign of him.'

'Will you help me find him?'

He gazed into space thoughtfully for a few moments and then said, 'Personally, I think that because of the state that he must have been in after he killed Cooper – assuming of course that the story we've been given is the correct one – it's very likely his body will be found jammed against a weir somewhere on the River Avon.'

'He wouldn't necessarily need a car to do that – and it's not at his place.'

'But if he hasn't killed himself?'

'We could play detectives,' I suggested jokingly.

'I suppose I'd be easing myself back into the job.'

'You would.'

'Is this official SOCA-wise?'

I shook my head. 'He's regarded as being Avon and Somerset's business.'

'I'd go along with that. But I can understand your wanting to do something to take your mind off worrying about Patrick.'

'I'll admit that but Mallory is, or was, indirectly part of Hamsworth's empire and if we find him . . .' I shrugged and left the rest unsaid.

'His flat's been thoroughly searched,' James went on to say. 'He doesn't have a computer and nothing in the way of paperwork, mostly unpaid bills, gave any clue as to where he might go if he needed to make a fast exit. No pictures of family or friends, no letters, nothing. Obviously, there are people working on it.'

'We should still have a look around,' I told him. 'I'm very good at finding things that the police have missed.'

'Are you now?'

'You might have to swallow your professional pride a bit,' I pointed out.

'We've worked together before,' he recollected. 'D'you still wave guns around?'

I gave him the wrong kind of victory sign.

Aware that Patrick had also searched Paul Mallory's flat and despite what I had said, I was not optimistic that we would find anything useful. Carrick told me that the police had had to break in to conduct their search and the front door was now secured with a makeshift padlocked contrivance. Not being in possession of Patrick's 'burglar's' keys, I asked Lynn Outhwaite for the key, promising to return it shortly. I left James's name unmentioned as understandably, he did not want Campbell to think him interfering. She said she was glad of any additions to the team – but that was not quite what I had in mind.

As Patrick had said, the whole flat was filthy and I did not have to be told that the homes of drug addicts and those who drink suicidal amounts of alcohol usually are. Bearing in mind Carrick's warning about the possible presence of used needles, I wandered into the very large and lofty living room while he tackled the bedrooms.

At one time the decor must have been at the height of modernist chic, in my view out of place in this setting but nevertheless worth looking at – if you were a man and enjoyed more than slightly pornographic posters of women, that is. Stained from having God knows what thrown at them over the years and with tattered edges they bared just about everything, pouting, from all walls. I could imagine Mallory in here, at night, his 'music' blaring, on his own private death slide into oblivion.

'Strobe lights, too,' James said, pointing towards the ceiling, having come in when I had been contemplating all this rather than searching for far longer than I ought to have done. 'I can remember being here one night as I wanted to talk to Mallory in connection with the Mrs Pryce murder case and Cooper was here as well and tried to get me drinking. It was like that scene in *The Ipcress File* where Harry Palmer's tortured with noise and crazy lights and only holds out by sticking a nail in his palm. As it was I threw up when I managed to get away.' He added, 'I'd been drinking too much already you see. My life seemed over after Catherine died.'

She had been his first wife and had succumbed to a rare form of bone cancer.

Carefully, we went through the contents of a chest of drawers, some open shelving, a brimming wastepaper basket that contained old newspapers and pornographic magazines, empty drinks bottles and the mouldy remains of convenience meals, including used plastic cutlery. Nothing about the man emerged, nothing but what was in front of our eyes in this room: his drug and drink addiction, his music, his obsession with sex.

'He's destroyed himself,' I whispered when we had come across absolutely nothing to give us a lead as to his whereabouts and had had a quick look at the kitchen. 'There's nothing left. It's horrible.'

'I think you'll find it was Cooper who destroyed him,' James said soberly. 'Shall we go?'

'Before we do I'd quite like to talk to Miss Braithewaite who lives in the flat upstairs. Or would that be an unpleasant reminder of her unfortunate connection with Mrs Pryce's death?'

'We parted the best of friends but I really can't see that it'll be of any use,' Carrick replied. 'And it's not every copper who's had to arrest his English teacher for murder. Thank God it turned out to have been a complete accident.'

'The Serious Organised Crime Agency again!' exclaimed the lady in response to my introducing myself, having released any number of bolts and chains on her front door in order to open it. 'Do come in. D'you know Patrick? He finished cleaning my windows for me.'

It did no harm to tell her that he was my husband.

'Even better. And James, lovely to see you again. I hope you can both stay for a cup of tea.'

She was immaculately dressed in a lilac linen suit and very sprightly for her years, although obviously getting frail, and the contrast between her home and the one below could not have been more stark. Here were cherished antique furniture, faded Chinese rugs, soft watercolours and embroidered pictures of flowers on the walls, the latter perhaps of her own creation.

'We're looking for Paul Mallory,' Carrick said when we had been presented with our tea in fine bone china cups and I was busy munching on a biscuit, having forgotten all about lunch. 'And in case, Miss Braithewaite, you're wondering why I'm not wearing my usual suit and tie it's because I've been off work and am not officially on duty again until next week. Ingrid is a friend and I'm giving her a hand.'

'I had noticed,' said the lady, who had indeed been eyeing his jeans, sweatshirt and trainers. 'Well, as you know, I had all the floors soundproofed when he started making that ghastly noise but I *can* just hear it sometimes, especially in the summer if the windows are open. I have to say it was lovely and quiet while he was in prison. But over the past few days it's gone completely silent again, which made me think he wasn't there. The police have been asking about him and someone said his car wasn't parked at the back but I don't know – I wouldn't even know which one is his.'

'Have you spoken to him at all? Do you know anything about him that might give us a clue as to where he's gone?'

'I was asked that. No, I don't come face-to-face with the man to be able to say anything to him – not even good morning. He does have that friend, Cooper, who I'm sure you know about. I could hear them, or at least someone, having dreadful rows occasionally and I fear drink was involved.'

'He's not at Cooper's place,' Carrick said. The identity of the murder victim had still not been released.

'I fancy he's not a person to come to a good end, if you see what I mean,' said Miss Braithewaite tentatively.

'You once told me that you could pick out the children who might go wrong,' Carrick recollected.

'I said that when we were doing the play? When you were playing Wimsey?'

'That's right, and the boy you cast as the arch-villain went on to become one in real life.'

'Oh, no, did he? I sincerely hope he didn't hear me and I gave him the idea.'

'Not a chance.'

Frowning, Miss Braithewaite said, 'You know, there's a place where Mallory *might* have gone but you simply mustn't go rushing off there as I'm sure I'm quite wrong. That music that he's really enthusiastic about was written by Karl Humpleschlacht. I absolutely hate it but can remember listening to a programme once on Radio Three about him and other so-called progressive or fringe composers. I didn't listen for very long, I have to confess. Apparently he was living in London – this was in the fifties, you understand – went mad and in the end threw himself off a bridge into the Thames. Hammersmith, I *think*. But he knew he was going mad and used to spend more and more time away from his composing in what he regarded as his sanctuary. If Mallory's following in his hero's footsteps . . .' She took a breath – more a disapproving sniff, really. 'It can't have done him much good, though, can it?'

'I've never heard of private asylums,' James said a little later.

'Think of it as an exclusive clinic,' I suggested. 'Asylum isn't a word that's used in connection with mental illness these days.'

We had left the car at the rear of North Terrace for a short while and hunted out a café that had wi-fi to enable me to ask my smart phone about Buckington Hall, Surrey. As the name suggested it had once been a stately home and had belonged to the Heaton family. After the place had to be sold to cover death duties it had variously been a girls' boarding school, a hospital during the First World War, a military command centre during the Second and lastly, a treatment centre, no doubt vastly expensive, for the titled and wealthy who had drink, drug and/ or mental problems. Some really disturbed, and deemed to be dangerous, clients had been permanent residents. There was no further information following its closure in 1961.

'Something tells me I shouldn't ask Surrey Police to make enquiries,' Carrick said. 'It's just too flimsy.'

I made no further comments concerning professional pride, saying instead, 'If we call at the nick you can listen to the radio while I email them through official channels and ask them to contact me on my mobile.'

Information was forthcoming and I received a call amazingly quickly. I was told that the hall and grounds were now derelict after several attempts by the local historical society to save the property, a venture complicated by lead being stolen from the roof and marble fireplaces, carved panelling and even a staircase ripped out from within. Since then vandals had started fires on several occasions. Efforts were being made to trace the present owner, an eccentric nonagenarian who lived in the United States, with a view to the place being sold to a developer. It was most unlikely that anyone could be in the house, the police spokesman continued as, since the attacks by vandals, it had been surrounded by security fencing topped by razor wire.

I reminded him that the man in question was regarded as desperate and the main suspect in a murder investigation, and finished by asking if someone could check. Apologies followed that nothing could be done in the very near future as they had what he described as a 'major incident' on their hands.

'The canteen coffee machine just blew up. And it's raining,' Carrick commented dourly.

I looked at my watch. 'It'll be almost dark by the time we get there.'

My companion registered horror. 'Hen, you're not going to set off and go looking for that maniac in a derelict building at *night*!'

No, perhaps not.

'Tomorrow,' James said decidedly.

He was quite right; it was flimsy and I was grateful to him for being willing to accompany me. Joanna, I knew, would have relished such a venture but in the present circumstances for her to come with me would have been most unwise and I would not have allowed her to. If she was injured . . . To her credit, she seemed not to mind her husband setting off with me early the next morning on what I was beginning to think was a fool's errand, a woman clutching at anything to keep herself busy when she ought to be concentrating on writing a novel that had already been far too long in the creating.

'If he's there, or we think he is, we call out the local cops,' Carrick said as he got in the Range Rover. 'Not only that, the place is almost certainly going to be hellishly secured.'

'I do have bolt-cutters,' I said.

'Why didn't I know you would?' he muttered.

'There's a Smith and Wesson in the safe by your right knee should you want to carry it.'

'Look, I'm not nervous!' he protested, his Scottish accent a little more pronounced than usual.

'I know you're not, I'm just telling you it's there,' I assured him. He was, a purely temporary state of affairs due to having recently been savagely beaten up.

'Patrick has the Glock?'

'Plus his knife. He always has his knife.'

And is more dangerous with that than most men armed with a meat cleaver.

'I sincerely hope he's not going to try to take this Raptor character and his retinue single-handed.'

'The idea's only to locate him, hopefully somewhere where he's likely to stay for long enough to enable Patrick to call in and get the Met to arrest him.'

He gave me a 'I've-heard-that-one-before' kind of look and then said, 'I felt I should tell Lynn what we were doing.'

'I'm glad you did.'

'Then they'll know exactly where to look for us, or rather where our decomposing bodies will be – under tons of fallen masonry,' he gloomily added.

'James, did you sleep last night?'

'No, I couldn't get off for some reason.'

'Then for heaven's sake have a snooze now!'

He did, sleeping as if dead. I got some breakfast inside him too when we stopped for fuel on the motorway, something else that had not quite happened.

*   *   *

Buckington Hall was situated near Virginia Water and set among trees, most of which were in Windsor Great Park. It proved to be quite hard to find, even with the satnav, and after bouncing down sundry tracks and unmade roads – yes, it was raining – we ended up in a lane that appeared to be the service road to a golf club. And, suddenly, there it was, the huge gates chained up, warning notices about alarms and guard dogs everywhere and, as we already knew, razor wire.

'I think I watched one of those ghost hunting programmes that was filmed here,' Carrick said, gazing at what was before us. 'They said it was a nightmare – it looks like one.'

I could not blame lack of food and sleep this time because he happened to be right.

Quickly, James went on to add, 'It's Joanna who likes watching them – but I have to sit and hold her hand.'

Even though the drive was overgrown the house was visible, little more than a blackened ruin with vegetation growing on the chimneys and what remained of the roof. The windows were just rectangular holes and like sightless eyes but still, somehow, looking at us.

SIXTEEN

There was no question of entering through the main gates – it was too well secured. I pulled off the lane and parked in a nearby clearing, just off a forest track. Another car was there already, but it wasn't Mallory's. We had seen several people either jogging or walking dogs so I was content that our presence was not conspicuous.

We set off, walking along the lane, following the boundary wall of the house and one-time gardens until we reached its extremity in that direction and underwent a right-angled turn. There we discovered a narrow winding path that branched off the lane, running roughly parallel with the new direction of the wall, well-worn as though the route was regularly used by walkers or deer. Unfortunately, from the point of view of climbing over it, the wall appeared to be in very good condition and in places was swathed in ivy and brambles trying to gain access and other climbers growing on the inside endeavouring to escape. After about ten minutes we came to a door set in it. It was almost invisible due to the vegetation and, I thought, had been intended for the use of garden and estate workers for maintenance purposes. It proved to be well and truly locked and probably bolted as well, so we carried on walking.

'Supposing he's here,' Carrick said. 'Where has he parked his car?'

'There must be at least one other entrance to a place like this,' I replied. 'And for all we know he may have been here before, in the footsteps of his hero kind of thing, and be familiar with the layout.'

'Not a bad day for a walk anyway, now the rain's eased off a bit.'

'I know you don't think he's here.'

'Do you?'

'No, not for one minute. I'm just telling myself we're eliminating it from enquiries.'

'You're learning all the jargon.'

'If you were fully fit I'd hit you.'

We carried on. But for the cooing of pigeons and the occasional sudden burst of birdsong – wrens, I thought – it was quiet, the drone of the endless procession of airliners heading to and leaving Heathrow muffled by the leaf canopy. The path began to curve to the right, away from the wall and, after pausing for a short discussion, we carried on in as straight a line as possible, picking our way through the ferns and long grass. Small fallen branches lying hidden in the leaf litter were a trip hazard but at least there was no obvious reason for us to progress in silent, stealthy fashion.

After another ten minutes or so we arrived at a second doorway, identical to the first, traces of the original green paint still adhering to it. It was equally well-secured, the thick ivy growing across it as good as several added padlocks. Without comment, we walked on.

Finally we arrived at the limit of this side of the wall, which predictably turned ninety degrees to the left. After further progress, slower as the trees were farther apart here, the grass much coarser and growing in tall tussocks, we came to another entrance. Through the wrought-iron gates, smaller and less ornate than the ones at the front, the view was of little more than an English jungle, the traces of what must have been a gravelled carriage drive just discernible for a short distance before disappearing into the greenery. On our side of the gates the drive merged with another lane, which, judging by the sound of traffic, then joined a road not far away. A group of cars was parked nearby.

'That's Mallory's,' I said as we approached. 'The black hatchback.'

'Bravo, Miss Braithewaite,' said Carrick.

'There are now good grounds for calling out the local force,' I observed.

'Or SOCA and Avon and Somerset Police could decide not to trouble them due to their doubtless ongoing major incident.'

'Sure?'

'Sure.'

We high-fived and then turned our attention to the gates. These were as well secured as just about everything else with, if anything, even more razor wire, so we decided to carry on walking around the boundary wall with a view to climbing over it, somehow, when out of view of the lane and anyone who might return to their cars. This proved to be a good idea as, after passing another of the small side doors, we came to an oak tree growing fairly close to the wall, its branches having grown right over the top.

'I'm not that good in trees,' I said.

'And I'm thinking I'm not that good right *now*,' Carrick muttered.

'You shouldn't climb it with dodgy ribs,' I told him.

'Perhaps not, but then again I want Mallory, badly.' He flexed his shoulders and, going to one side of the tree, went up it like a monkey until he was level with the lowest branch. 'There are all kinds of holes and bumps you can use as steps,' he called down.

I scrambled up, trying not to think about the coming down bit. James moved across and a little higher to a branch that stretched over the wall where he waited for me, holding on to the branch above. Not being all that thick, the one taking his weight swayed and dipped under him and I decided not to add mine to it as well.

'No, you're all right,' Carrick said after I had voiced my caution. 'We could do with it being a bit lower.'

'It might break,' I fretted.

'No, oak won't. It'll only come to rest on the top of the wall.'

Which it did, surprisingly gently, as I edged along it and we both carefully sat down, feet hanging, to survey the ground about eight feet below us. This appeared to be roughly the same as on the side of the wall we had just come from, long grass and ferns with a gone wild fruit tree of some kind, perhaps a pear, growing against the wall itself.

'I suggest we both drop off simultaneously,' Carrick said. 'Otherwise the branch will flip up and possibly unseat who's still on it.'

OK, they sometimes failed to sleep or have breakfast but sometimes men can be really, really useful.

We dropped off and I landed in a heap in a flurry of leaves and bits of twig.

'Are you all right?' I enquired urgently, noticing that James looked a bit white.

'Aye, just jarred myself a bit,' he gasped.

'I'll never forgive myself if you're hurt again.'

'Och, no bother, I'll just have more sick leave.'

We paused for a couple of minutes while he recovered and then made our way towards the carriage drive, or rather where its route should be as, surely, that would make for slightly easier walking and lead us directly to the house. After floundering for a while as there were a lot of bramble thickets that had to be navigated around, we finally emerged from a small copse of birches to find our feet on harder ground. To the right, the house could be seen as a dark rectangle through the greenery.

Trees and shrubs had seeded themselves in the drive but we made good progress and a few minutes later we found ourselves near to what must have originally been the carriage house and stables. The house lay beyond a short distance away. From this angle the state of the building did not seem too bad as the roof, although sagging in places, was mostly intact on this side. But the blackened stonework and missing window frames spoke of a serious fire. Now, this hideous relic of another age seemed to intrude on its peaceful garden that had returned to nature and I found myself thinking that it ought to be demolished. Soon.

In contrast, the stables and coach house were in quite good condition, perhaps because nothing valuable had been deemed to be within by those who had first broken into the house itself. We checked all the windows and the locks on the doors, all of which seemed to be original, none of them forced. Mallory wasn't here. There were no sinister ghostly vibes either but it was not difficult to imagine all these doors open and hear the clatter of shod hooves on a stone floor, the jingle of harness, the deep-throated sound horses make, like a chuckle, when they see a feed being brought or someone they recognize and like. It was quite possible that the last on these premises had been requisitioned by the army during the First World War and died horribly in the mud of the hell that was the Somme. The gardeners and other workers on the estate may well have been called up, as had happened at the Lost Garden of Heligan in Cornwall, and also never returned.

'You OK?' Carrick suddenly asked, startling me slightly.

'There are memories here,' I said.

'Of nightmares?'

'No. But it's sad, very, very sad.'

It was then that we heard music. Of a sort. It sounded like the kind of background music hell might have.

'He's in the house!' Carrick exclaimed, automatically speaking quietly even though if we could detect it from around fifty yards away the din indoors must be stupendous.

Feeling no need for a covert approach, we followed the drive. Ahead of us, it curved around the side of the house towards the front entrance. Here, at the rear, there appeared to be at least three entrances, one into what must have been the kitchens and another being a side door into the wreck of a large conservatory. Fleetingly, I mourned the dead plants among the shattered glass that I could see even from a distance, thinking of all those thousands of man-hours that had been spent cherishing orchids, tropical ferns and other exotics when it had been a private house. A third access was through a porch, a Victorian add-on that had survived more or less intact – mostly, I reckoned, on account of its extreme ugliness. As at the main gates there were warning notices everywhere but no sign of the security fencing about which we had been told. Perhaps, like every other damned thing of any value, it had been stolen.

'Is that Humpleschlacht?' I asked, the sound ever louder with each of our footsteps and, right now, sounding akin to a percussion instrument factory collapsing during an earthquake. Flocks of birds, no doubt disturbed by the noise, were wheeling restlessly around the rooftops.

'It has all the . . . characteristics,' Carrick responded and then stopped in his tracks. 'I have to tell you that this bloody racket has bad memories for me.'

'When you were ill that time after calling on Cooper?'

'Aye. That and . . . Catherine's death.'

'Did you get home all right?'

He brightened a little. 'Ah, well, it was in the days when Joanna had resigned from the force and had a private investigator's business in Milsom Street with a guy by the name of Lance Tyler. Tyler was killed in a road accident shortly afterwards but that's beside the point. She had a case that had also taken her to the square that night and we sort of met.'

'You mean you almost threw up over her, don't you?' I said, glad that he was talking about it.

'Well, actually . . .' He smiled. 'Almost.'

'She took you home and looked after you?'

'Not a chance. She told me she knew what men looked like who lived on just whisky, followed me home in her car, stood over me while I cooked us both dinner, we ate it – I can't remember exchanging a word the whole time – and then she went off, leaving me with all the washing up.'

'You're a very lucky man.'

'I know.'

We carried on.

The outside door of the porch was hanging off its hinges as though an attempt had been made to wrench it right off, perhaps to steal it for the heavy and ornate cast-iron knocker and letter box. Judging by the rusting state of these items now it had been an historic event and the thieves had moved on elsewhere. The inner door, a cheap, modern replacement, had however been forced open recently and stood ajar, the wood freshly splintered, every indication being that the attack on it had been a frenzied one. I then noticed a crowbar thrown down nearby.

'I urge extreme caution,' the DCI said very close to my ear, the noise at such volume now that it was an attack on the senses. He pushed the shattered door and it swung wide.

The place was little more than a shell, I realized with a shock. I could see right through to the front of the house. Not all that long ago there had been another fire, a serious one, as tiny wisps of smoke were still emanating from a pile of charcoal-black beams a few yards to our left. Some distance away, towards the front of the house, large pillars were still standing but supported nothing in what must have been an imposing entrance hall. The ground – it could no longer be called a floor – was covered in inches, or even feet in places, of roofing slates, masonry and more charred wood. From where we stood I could see right up to the remains of the roof and through the holes in it to the sky. The rest only seemed to be held up by a prayer. It occurred to me that the vibration of this appalling noise could bring it all down.

But we had to go in.

On this ground floor some of the interior walls were still standing, where the kitchen had been possibly off to our left. It was possible to imagine, approaching the front and looking at the gaps where they had been, the doors, left and right, that would have led into a library, dining and withdrawing rooms, and, at one side, the elegant staircase in place before it was plundered and sold, together with the fireplaces and other fittings, to a reclamation yard.

Carrick touched my arm and gestured to the nearest doorway on our left, obviously of the opinion that that was where the music was coming from. It was actually just about impossible to tell as the cacophony was everywhere, the noise booming around, echoing in what was in effect an empty box. But Mallory could not be far away.

And then, there was an abrupt silence. The end of a track or had he spotted us somehow?

We froze and I held my breath for a few moments, listening. Then, in the direction Carrick had indicated there were a couple of clicking sounds and it started up again. This drove him into action and, not being at all careful where he put his feet, he ran over to the doorway. Slipping, sliding and nearly falling on some slates, I followed.

It's the details you notice first. In a way that reminded me inexorably of Patrick when emotionally affected, Carrick, icy, his body stiff with self-restraint, went over to the CD player, bent down and, after trying several buttons, switched it off. It had started to rain lightly again, a fine coolness that drifted down through the holes in the roof to glisten on the remnants of what had once been beautiful and were now ruined or destroyed forever. Mallory, ruined and destroyed forever, was already wet – soaked – he had clearly been here for several days and was staring up, pop-eyed, at Carrick from where he huddled, shaking, on the floor like a beaten dog, his sodden clothing like so many rags. Everything he was wearing appeared to be bloodstained.

'I know who you are, you know,' he croaked. 'Have you got a drink?'

'Sorry, no,' Carrick replied quietly, and somewhat kindly. 'But we can soon get help for you.'

'Karl came here, you know. He wrote my music. It was his refuge. His spirit's here, so I brought the music so he could hear it again. And then Cooper spoilt everything and came along too.' Staring right through the DCI as though he wasn't there, Mallory went on, 'I hit the bastard on the head with the hammer and he just laughed at me. So I cut his throat and the blood ran out but he was still smiling.' His voice was slowly rising to a wail. 'And now he's here, too. I've seen him looking in at me through the windows and the only way I can keep him away from me is with Karl's music. He never really liked Karl. And now you've switched it off he'll come back!'

'He won't come back,' Carrick assured him. 'As you know, he didn't like me either.'

Mallory cheered up a little. 'Yes, you're right.'

'What did you do with the hammer?'

The man shook his head. 'Can't remember. Might have chucked it in the river.'

In the end, an air ambulance was called to take Mallory away, apparently collecting quite a crowd of onlookers, and, because of the overgrown conditions within the garden walls and the surrounding woodland, he had to be winched out.

The room, perhaps once a parlour, was the smallest enclosed space in what remained of the manor house, and for this reason I am sure Paul Mallory had chosen it for his sanctuary. Carrick and I and those members of Surrey Police who attended gravitated to it for a debriefing. Also, this part of the house was the most protected from the elements by what roof was left – the rain was heavy now.

The inspector, whose name was Brian Hough, was a square chunk of a man with dark hair that badly needed cutting and dark, worried-looking eyes. I wondered whether he had come purely out of curiosity or had been concerned that his staff might be bullied by a stroppy DCI from the sticks. He was not pleased about the considerable brute force, plus bolt cutters, that there had been no choice but to apply to the main gates in order to gain entry, the keys being God knew where. Carrick, all smiles, had made the point that it would be a waste of time anyone sending the bill in Avon and Somerset's direction.

The usual proof of identity requirements having been dealt with, followed by a few answers to pertinent questions, Carrick went on to say that someone in his team would need to arrest Mallory at some stage for murder, if and when he was thought fit to plead. I then told Hough that I would leave it up to Commander Greenway to decide whether the suspect was thought sufficiently connected with Nick Hamsworth to charge him with also being an accessory to serious crime. Privately, I thought not.

'Isn't that the character who calls himself Raptor?' Hough queried. And on receiving an answer in the affirmative, said, 'We saw there was a warrant out for his arrest, of course. He fancies an upmarket lifestyle does that one, according to a reliable source of information we have in Guildford. The whisper is that he runs several clubs in the east of London and one for his chums and the nobs, as it was described to me, somewhere in the Woodford area.'

'We already knew that,' I said, not relishing the leery way he was looking at me. At all. 'Does Hamsworth's manor really extend as far south as Guildford?'

'No, but my source's manor extends as far north as London.'

'Do you think he would have any idea where Hamsworth actually lives?'

'He might tell me something if I send him your smiling photo and say it's for you,' he replied with a wink, waggling his mobile in my direction in a frankly dirty fashion.

'And I might send him your photo with your bloody brains blown out if you try it,' I retorted, omitting the colourful additions with which Patrick would have lavishly sprinkled the reply had he been present. I do try to behave like a lady.

'Only joking,' he blustered, having also been on the receiving end of a don't-mess-with-SOCA look from Carrick. He went away from us, miming that the reception was better outside and those of us remaining, together with a sergeant and a uniformed constable, maintained extremely straight faces.

My irritation was partly caused by an overwhelming desire to leave. Scepticism about 'ghost-hunting programmes' apart, this was a horrible place to spend any time and I think I shall never be able to dispel from my mind how Paul Mallory had looked, crouched down, reduced to a state little better than an animal. He had remained where he was, on the floor, shuddering uncontrollably, even with Carrick's jacket around his shoulders, during the wait for medical help and the police to arrive, occasionally giving his surroundings baffled looks, as though he had forgotten what he was doing there.

Hough returned, shaking his head. 'Sorry, no, he said he has no idea.'

'What's his name?' Carrick wanted to know.

'I really can't tell you that,' the DI told him. 'He's very useful sometimes with bits of info and I don't want him upset.'

'Look, I'm not the kind of bloke to pull rank . . .' Carrick continued, succeeding in giving every impression that he was.

He received the information, with the addition of a couple of 'sirs' and we left, this author especially glad of the added luxury of not having to climb back over the wall. If anything, the rain was heavier now but I turned my face up to the soft grey sky for a few moments, the cool wetness a benediction after that house.

'How the hell did he get over the wall carrying a CD player and a crowbar?' Carrick mused.

'Like a man from a nightmare,' I muttered, picturing a creeping, dark, Gollum-like *something*. Truly, I needed to get out of here.

James put an arm around my shoulders. 'I have you to thank for this, Ingrid. I'm enjoying the prospect of no longer being charged with murder.'

'Honestly though, d'you reckon you would have been capable of killing Cooper in the fevered state you were in?'

'Oh, aye.'

*   *   *

'This business of someone in Guildford with information about Hamsworth is odd,' James said, 'if not downright dodgy.'

A hot meal in an Italian restaurant had done us both a lot of good.

I said, 'Are there professional informers?'

'Yes, there are.'

'Perhaps whoever it is has a network of spies but lives a safe distance away, as Hough said.'

'That's been known too but it's usually as a sideline to inform on rival mobsters. But according to Hough this character can usually be found in the Blue Boar in the town centre. He's hardly keeping a low profile, is he?'

'He's made himself untouchable, then.'

Carrick stared at me. 'How?'

'I don't know. And even if we find him there's no guarantee he'll give us any more info face-to-face than he did Hough over the phone. He might even have been telling the truth.'

In the end we decided that it was worth a try before we headed home.

As we had some while to wait before the Blue Boar opened for evening trade, we parted company, Carrick saying he would like to search out a computer store, while I headed off intending to browse around the fashion shops, something I very rarely have time to do. He came back with an eye-achingly pink outfit for Iona Flora, and I bought a wildly expensive Swedish log saw for Patrick.

In truth, I would have been quite happy to return to the car park now and go home, but nevertheless we sat ourselves down in a corner of the public bar of the Blue Boar and sipped our orange juice. I had offered to treat James to his favourite tipple to celebrate as I was driving but he declined, saying he regarded himself as being on duty. Not to mention still having to take pills.

DI Hough had told us that we could not miss 'Jacko' as he was a tall man with short grey hair and a thin moustache. He usually sat on a settle near the fire in the winter and at a small table in the opposite corner at other times, both of which the regulars avoided when he was due to arrive around an hour after opening time. He usually stayed for a couple of hours, yarning, but did not drink heavily.

Someone who was unmistakably Jacko duly arrived, on time, and seated himself, not in his summer position but on the settle near the fireplace as someone else, a visitor perhaps, had got to the other seat first. He did not seem to mind. The picture I had built up in my mind of some kind of saturnine and intimidating man of the criminal night was utterly wrong. This man looked like a retired bank manager.

'I have seen this man, or a photograph of him, somewhere before,' Carrick murmured and got to his feet. I remained where I was and watched as they exchanged a few words and then James went to the bar and bought him a tot of whisky. He then beckoned me across and I went, taking our drinks. We sat down.

'This is Jack Masters, one-time Chief Constable of Surrey Police,' James informed me in little more than a whisper.

SEVENTEEN

'Hough rang to tell me you'd brow-beaten him into saying where I could be found,' said Masters with a smile. 'And congratulations. I understand you got your man.'

'What's left of him,' Carrick replied and then went on to give him a few more details, as he seemed interested.

'Although it's a while since I retired I still keep my ear to the ground,' Masters continued in jovial fashion. 'People, those on the job, that is, tell me I ought to forget it and retire completely. But it keeps me out of mischief.'

He was indeed older than first impressions had suggested. And recently bereaved? There was a sadness about him.

I said, 'There's a titled one-time senior army officer who used to be closely involved with MI5 who ostensibly retired to his castle in Sussex to grow roses. He was brought in as an adviser when SOCA was first set up and now not only has his hands firmly on the reins but is regarded by those in the know as being the tender of all grapevines. I have an idea you're like that, only more modestly.'

'That would be Richard Daws,' was the immediate response.

'Touché,' I said.

He held up his glass in silent acknowledgement. 'I started in the Met and during a long career built up quite a network of people, mostly on the wrong side of the law. It seemed a pity to chuck it all away when I could carry on being useful.'

Carrick would probably not have had the nerve to ask my next question but curiosity has always been a weakness of mine. 'So what do they get out of it?'

'The same. Information. I trade in it.'

'Couldn't that be construed as giving assistance to criminals?'

He did not become angry with me. 'Oh, I'm careful what I pass on. Sometimes people get a warning that some rival mobster or other's going to move in on them or their family. Things like that. And everything I get to hear is sent to various investigating officers first.' A big smile. 'I'm a radar set, really.'

'Hamsworth's on your screen?' Carrick said.

'I gave Hough the only details I know about him. He said you knew that already.'

'Only recently. Someone's been asking around,' I said.

'That someone being one of your operatives.'

'That's right.' I didn't want to go into any more details, not altogether sure I trusted him. 'Does Hamsworth live at the club in Woodford?'

'It's likely, but I can't deny or confirm it,' Masters answered. 'And I have to tell you that he cultivates an atmosphere of fear around himself. People are terrified of crossing him or breathing a word about his movements. As it is, the man goes everywhere in cars with tinted windows so it's impossible to spot him in the ordinary way of things. He also employs ex-army personnel as bodyguards and hit men, a few of whom are always with him.'

'We've both had experience, directly and indirectly, of that,' Carrick put in.

'Well then, folk won't talk because the risks are too great. Your man needs to exercise great care. Has he come face-to-face with him in the past?'

'Yes,' I said. 'But he's working undercover this time.'

'I think you should pull him out. That criminal knows things he shouldn't know and hears things he shouldn't hear. But the Met'll arrest him eventually when he gets too clever and makes a mistake. They always do in the end, you know.'

'I've no authority to give orders,' I told him. 'But when he makes contact I'll pass on your concerns.'

What use were concerns? Patrick was fully aware of the dangers. I was thinking that we would end up having to change tactics and arrange that all vehicles leaving the club with tinted windows were tailed. I was also made even more aware of our failure in not arresting Hamsworth in Bath. My greatest fear now was that, in desperation, Patrick would do something completely crazy. He had said himself that in order to get results he would have to forget that he was a policeman.

'Well, thank you for your advice, sir,' Carrick was saying.

'Your loyalty to the Met is natural and highly commendable,' I said to Masters. 'But I don't entirely believe you.'

Did I imagine James drawing in his breath through his teeth in horror? Possibly not.

I continued, 'SOCA, as you must know, is shortly to be absorbed into the new National Crime Agency. We now deal with serious crime of this kind. Commander Greenway is already liaising closely with the Met over this and there's *no* competition, no prizes, no round of drinks to those who arrest Hamsworth first. If you have any information that might lead to this man that so far you've only given to some crony who might not even be in one of the Met teams investigating what I'll call associated crimes then it's your duty to share it with us as well. Time moves on!'

'You don't mince your words, do you?' was Masters' only reaction for a few moments. Then he said, 'There's one small detail but it's useless by now as it's already been investigated and nothing was found. It's rumoured that Hamsworth trains his people and takes them to an old warehouse he may or may not own somewhere in Thameside, east London. Word has it that he actually rehearses crimes like bank robberies and occasionally they seem to have what I'll call exercises using live ammunition. You must understand that this might be hearsay – all kinds of crackpot stories swill around the criminal underworld and most of them are just that – stories.'

'But surely people living nearby would report the sound of gunfire,' Carrick said.

'This isn't a built-up area,' Masters replied. 'It was once, now everything's mostly demolished prior to redevelopment – in a word, dereliction. People don't go there as there's no reason to.'

And to me, 'I suppose you could always take a look at the place. But for God's sake, don't go there alone.'

'Where is it?' I asked.

'All I know is that it's supposed to be near a rubbish incinerator. But don't be surprised if you can't find it as the rumour's not a new one and the building's probably been flattened by now. Personally, I think it's an alcohol-fuelled myth.'

We chatted for a little longer, Carrick bought him another drink and then we left. I thanked him sincerely as I was feeling a little guilty about the way I had spoken to him in one of my occasional bloody-minded stand-by-your-man moments. Once in the car I sent Patrick a text, outwardly vague, but using code words that would tell him I had something to say that might be important. Then I had second thoughts and sent him another, giving him the information I had just received.

I drove us back to London – the quickest route for James to get home by train – and then booked into the usual hotel. He had been reluctant to leave me on my own, worried that I might be tempted to head off looking for Patrick, but as I made clear to him, there was little point in my seeking out Salvation Army hostels, defunct canals or disappearing warehouses. Not only that, if I did, we, Patrick and I, would both be hazarding ourselves, breaking our working rule that, once we got split up, one of us should always stay in a reasonably safe place for the children's sake.

It had been a long day.

At eight-thirty the following morning Commander Greenway rang me. 'I contacted James Carrick to see how things fared with him and was delighted to hear that he's definitely off the hook as you found the murder suspect. Congratulations. Where are you now?'

I told him.

'Oh, come in to the office. I have some news that'll interest you.'

The grey clouds and rain had been blown away and the sun shone brightly, the pavements steaming in the warmth. I decided to walk to HQ as it would only take around fifteen minutes. There was a spring in my step and the journey seemed to take no time at all. First James, now good news of Patrick?

Greenway was in buoyant mood as well, this explained when he presented me with coffee and a piece of iced fruit cake, saying it was his birthday and he and Erin were going out that night to celebrate. I wondered if things had been patched up between them and that was the real reason for his obvious happiness.

'The good news is that we've struck lucky with Jonno Smithson,' Greenway began.

When I'm writing I avoid the expression 'my heart sank' as it's very hackneyed but the sensation is nevertheless real and horrible.

'He's been interviewed and admitted, when told about the discovery of his mobile phone, that he had done a couple of jobs for a man called Nick who liked to be called Raptor. Initially, he denied that it was anything to do with his father but, under questioning, admitted that he had been put under great pressure to give details of DS Paul Smithson's movements, the registration number of his car and his address as he and his wife had separated. Jonno was quite well paid for even the smallest amount of information, apparently – money that he hid in his bedroom where we knew his mother found it. Don't worry, nobody said that she'd come across it. The ten-pound note she gave Patrick did have traces of an illegal substance on it, by the way, but the email I received didn't say exactly what.'

'Jonno was very nervous,' I recalled. 'Was he made to listen to the recorded messages?'

'He was, and had obviously forgotten about the one that actually referred to "your old man". First of all, apparently, he shouted and raved that the police were framing him and that the message was a fake. Then he burst into tears and said he'd been told that his mother would have acid thrown over her if he didn't do exactly as he was told. At that point the man became beside himself, incoherent, and they had to stop the interview, but it would appear that his father was rendered unconscious and they – we don't know exactly who "they" were yet – somehow forced whisky and sleeping pills down his throat using a funnel.'

We both fell silent for a few moments at these ghastly revelations.

'The man was cremated so there's no chance of a second PM to try to spot any damage to the throat that was missed at the first,' Greenway went on. 'God, I can hardly bear to think about this. But I have to. When Patrick surfaces, with or without the location of that mobster, he can question him.'

'You want him to question Kev, the doorman at the Bath night club as well if there's no real progress with the case,' I reminded him.

'Yes, you're right.'

I took a deep breath. 'I really wish you'd pull Patrick out of this job. I have a very bad feeling about what he's doing.' I then went on to tell him of our conversation with Jack Masters, including the rumours about Hamsworth's occasional use of a warehouse as a training ground.

My 'feelings', or 'cat's whiskers' as my father used to call them, have earned a certain amount of respect since I began working for SOCA.

'I *have* learned to leave him alone and trust his judgement,' Greenway responded.

A gentle reproof from the boss, perhaps?

'I think the ball's definitely in his court, don't you?' Greenway continued.

'Well, as usual then, I'd better sod off,' I said with a big bright smile.

'Ingrid . . .' he began.

I went, or rather stormed out, while he was sitting there failing to think of something useful to say.

I found myself unable to bear going home. It seemed pathetic – a betrayal even though that was what Patrick had asked me to do. There was little point in looking for the warehouse as the chances of anyone being there were as good as zero and, for another, I had an idea that Masters, one of the old school, had encouraged me, with all due cautions, in that direction as he thought I ought to be got out of the way of 'the professionals' working in other directions on the case, or even, may his dentures turn green, that I shouldn't worry my pretty little head about it.

'Bugger everything,' I said as I got back in the car.

I returned to the hotel, deferring any decision, every part of me desperate to stay in London, to be near Patrick. Once there, I rang Elspeth, who informed me that everything was well and that the children had had no further traumas.

Restless, I went out again and strolled aimlessly until I came across a small park and sat in the sun for a while. This pleasant open space was busy with young mothers pushing prams and buggies – some perhaps nannies and au pairs – the toddlers doing the usual things: playing with balls and chasing pigeons. One, just like Justin at that age, was having a tantrum.

'You ought to be doing that,' I muttered to myself. 'Taking Mark out for a little walk with Vicky. Being normal, not some misfit who can't write books all of a sudden either. What was a good idea while you were young is not now you aren't. And it's no use moaning to Greenway when Patrick's given a desk job and then panic when he's assigned to something more potentially dangerous.'

I would go home.

And be a fantastic mother who writes, nay, dashes off, bestsellers.

Bugger everything.

I struck away a tear from my cheek and got to my feet. As I did so my phone rang.

'Just making contact,' said Patrick.

To my utter shame I burst into tears of relief, sobbing helplessly.

'Greenway's told me to come off the job,' said his voice quietly in my ear. 'I got the impression he took some serious reservations of yours to heart.'

'Have I messed up anything?' I gulped, my first reaction.

'No, and I'm not going to.'

'Oh.'

'I need to know where you are.'

'In a little square not far from HQ.'

'Go back to the hotel. Please. I really don't want you wandering around like this. Please, Ingrid!'

I did not argue and, heavy-hearted, set off. Once there and aware that someone would probably be cleaning my room now, I sat in a coffee bar in the cavernous marble-floored reception area bar, consuming an Americano and a muffin I did not really want.

An hour went by and staying in a public place seemed to be a good idea.

Finally, after another thirty minutes had leadenly ticked by and I had actually risen to my feet with a view to going to my room, I glanced in that direction just as a man, one of a steady stream of people coming and going, pushed through the revolving doors. Three other people were immediately on his heels but they went their different ways. After looking around and about to move off, his gaze came to rest on me. He came over and my first thought was relief that I was in an exceedingly public place. This time the Smith and Wesson was in my pocket, not my handbag. My right hand curled around it snugly.

'Miss Langley?' said the man.

'Who wants her?' I asked.

This threw him a bit as he'd obviously been expecting a straight 'yes' or 'no' answer. Then, despite being well over six feet in height, probably in his late forties and looking as tough as slowly roasted leather, he stammered, 'I was – er – told to say that it's a message from your – er – ever-loving Patrick. Patrick Gillard.'

'Yes, that's me,' I said. 'How did you know what I look like?'

'He said you were dark-haired, slim and glamorous. So perhaps I've struck lucky and don't have to ask someone to phone your room to see if you're there.'

Still being very, very cautious, no code or pass words given, I said, 'What is this message?'

'He wants you to come with me to a safe place.'

'I feel perfectly safe here, thank you.'

My reply created no hint of aggression, just, eyes heavenwards for a moment, a rather fetching impression of tried patience. Then he said, 'If you didn't believe me he said to say that Graham said it's OK.'

'It's OK, then,' I responded, the mention of my father's name no kind of password either but nevertheless telling. Perhaps I would have to trust this man.

My cat's whiskers were frantically indicating otherwise. Patrick wouldn't use my father's name in such cavalier fashion. I said, 'Did he speak to you personally or phone you with his request?'

'He spoke to me personally.'

'When?'

'About half an hour ago. I got a taxi.'

'And who are you, exactly?'

'An old chum.'

'Name?'

The butter-wouldn't-melt-in-his-mouth demeanour vanished. 'Just do as he asks, all right?'

No, sunshine, it wasn't all right. I took a firmer hold of the handgun.

One of the other people who had arrived through the revolving doors at the same time, on whom I only now focussed my attention, had been standing by a display case containing leaflets advertising London attractions directly ahead of me across the foyer.

I eyed my visitor and said quite loudly, 'No, sorry, I'm not going with you.'

The other man turned and then strolled over.

'No luck then?' he said when still several yards away.

'Who the hell are you?' asked the first man.

'He knew you'd screw it up. So he sent me. And it's Paddy.'

'I haven't screwed anything up!'

'Screwed,' whispered Paddy right in the other's face, Irish to the core by the sound of him. 'I heard what she said. She's not fallen for it and going with you, is she? Not today, tomorrow or even bloody next year!'

'I've never seen you before in my life!'

'Keep your voice down. No, you won't have done. You don't know even a fraction of our friend Raptor's empire. I'm one of those who stays in the background, part of what some not at all late-lamented Bath newspaper hack referred to recently as his private army. And *he* finished up in a skip with his throat cut.'

'I heard about that,' the man said a little hoarsely.

Paddy turned his gaze, sub-zero, state-of-the-art pitiless, to me. 'There's two of us now.' Then, to the man, 'Your name?'

'Lane.'

Paddy, stubbly beard, the rest fairly presentable, returned his attention to me. 'And, after last time, Raptor doesn't care too much if you arrive alive or a little, shall we say, damaged. You won't get away this time. Shall we go?'

'I shall just have to start screaming,' I said through my teeth.

The knife must have been in his hand all the time and now was right in front of my face, the blade springing with that ghastly slicing click. No one else saw, no one noticed, no one came to my rescue. Good old London.

'Take care,' Lane muttered, only to be completely ignored.

'Or I could just leave you dead right here,' Paddy said to me with a big smile that told Lane of his personal preference to do just that as it was an awful lot less bother.

He never knew how much self-control it took not to rat everything up by giving him a big kiss. Instead, despondently, I said, 'Then I have no choice.'

The knife disappeared and Lane was asked, 'Do my orders countermand yours? Do we take her to the club in South Woodford?'

'That's what I was told.'

'Good.' And, on an apparent afterthought, 'Is he there?'

'Yes. Surely you must know that if he gave you your orders.'

'He rang me. No other details. You know what he's like.'

'So where were you if you're supposed to be one of his private team?'

'At the warehouse overseeing preparations for the next exercise. You ask too many questions. We'll take a taxi and she' – he jerked a grubby finger in my direction – 'can pay.'

With Paddy's arm around my shoulders in proprietorial fashion, we left the hotel.

I recollected that he did not know exactly where the club was situated, hence the need to stick with Lane. Lane, his attention on looking for a taxi, did not see the smile I gave Patrick and the way his right hand squeezed my shoulder. All we had to do then, I reasoned, was get to this place and, somehow, phone in with its whereabouts. Something told me that it wasn't going to be anywhere near as easy as that and I could not imagine for one moment a situation where Patrick would be content merely to be the messenger boy and stand back while the Met raided the premises. He is not a standing on the sidelines sort of person.

A taxi was waved down and we got in. Patrick had already intimated to Lane that he should do the talking, saying it would leave him free to keep an eye on me in case I made a bid for freedom. This low-key and smooth way of giving orders so that people hardly realize they are being told what to do has always impressed me and I suppose stems from his army days. I did not hear the address Lane gave the driver but it hardly mattered now.

It was quite a long journey, right across a suitably grey and drizzly London, with several hold-ups due to heavy traffic. Both men stared stonily out of their respective windows for the entire journey with me sandwiched in the middle. The one on my left I knew was working on strategy, sifting through his choice of tactics in response to any given situation; in other words, flying by the seat of his pants.

EIGHTEEN

'This'll do,' Patrick said to the taxi driver as we turned into the entrance to a long, curving drive. One corner of the house was just visible in what must be at least an acre of grounds, the road strictly residential and leafy with high hedges.

'It's a fair walk,' Lane protested.

'Security reasons,' he was told, with a meaningful jerk of his head in the direction of the driver. 'Everything's far too lax.'

I paid the fare with my debit card, for some reason stupidly wondering if I could claim it on expenses. One might not live to do so, might one?

'Go on, go with him,' Patrick chivvied as I paused when he did. 'I'm bursting for a pee.' And with that he hurried into the shrubbery.

'Security reasons – crap,' Lane sneered as we set off again. 'Too big for his boots, if you ask me.' After a few yards he rounded on me. 'Can't you walk any faster than that?'

'My ankle hurts,' I snivelled. 'I twisted it yesterday.'

He took a handgun from his packet. 'Does this make it feel any better?'

'No,' I wailed. 'Why have you horrible men brought me here?'

'So we can have bargaining power with that husband of yours, that's why. To get him here as Raptor's got a score to settle. And don't play the innocent – I happen to know that you work for the law as well.'

The irony of the remark was quite lost on him.

Determined to prolong this soundtrack from a gangster B-movie for as long as possible and praying that no one in the house would hear, I shrieked, 'But he won't come here! He's going to divorce me soon anyway and go off with some trollop he met in Italy!'

'Then we'll just have to kill you anyway, won't we?'

'Please, please let me go,' I begged. 'He won't come, I tell you.'

I fashioned a good storm of tears and, faced with the choice of having to shoot me dead there and then, thereby suffering the consequences from the boss or merely shove me in front of him down the drive, Lane thankfully chose the latter. I limped along.

Patrick did come, as I had hoped, my sound effects covering his footfalls as he arrived at speed, struck Lane down from the rear and dragged him to one side.

'You don't happen to have any of those handy cable ties with you, do you?' he asked.

They make very good replacement handcuffs and he put a couple, linked together, around the man's ankles as well. Lane was then consigned into a group of very prickly bushes. *Berberis buxifolia*, I noticed in a detached kind of way.

'You phoned?' I said as we stood out of sight of the house.

'Yes, but I only had to give a code word and the address.'

'How did you know someone was going to trick me into coming here?'

'I didn't. How could I? But I thought there was every chance that someone was following you – they seem to have been keeping an eye on HQ – and that's why I was worried. The fact that I arrived at the same time as he did was a lucky and complete coincidence. Look, the Met'll be here in no time at all. I'll escort you back to the road and get you a taxi. Please go back.'

'You want to be in at the kill.'

Patrick bared his teeth in a humourless smile. 'Yes. I'll settle for arresting him, though.'

'Me, too,' I said stubbornly.

From down by the house came the sound of cars being started up and we just had time to conceal ourselves behind some evergreens before vehicles came racing down the drive. Peering through the foliage I saw that the first was a stretched limo, the other two conventional saloon cars. All were black, with dark windows.

Patrick swore and then walked away for a short distance, swearing a lot more.

'Perhaps they've gone to the warehouse,' I suggested.

'They may well have done.'

'There's no guarantee that he was with them.'

'No, it could have been any number of resident hookers going off to the local tanning parlour,' was the response I got for that before he called HQ back. Then he made a further call. My mutiny appeared to have been put on hold.

It was dangerous to make a move towards the house as we had no idea who was there and we definitely needed initial reinforcements. As Patrick put it, looking at his watch for the third time in so many minutes, he had no wish to be shot on sight. As it happened, there was little time to wait and very shortly afterwards the Met arrived, *fortissimo*. We gave it around thirty seconds while there was a lot of shouting in the distance and then everything went quiet. Circumstances now being different, I went with Patrick as he headed for the house.

The proceeds of serious crime had bought an extremely desirable property that must have cost in the region of one and a half million pounds. On two floors and possibly dating from the thirties, it was built of red brick and had a more recent L-shaped extension on the ground floor. This consisted of several garages, the doors painted bright red, as was the front door of the house, a row of large plastic butterflies on a wall and some tubs, also plastic, planted with red geraniums. I have never known a crook who had good taste.

'Flown,' an individual wearing the obligatory designer mack said disgustedly when he saw us. 'Just a few staff. But we've arrested them anyway as there's obviously some kind of unlicenced use of this place going on.'

'No, we aren't part of this criminal set-up,' Patrick told him, always annoyed, yes, with lax security, when not asked for some kind of ID. 'Although for obvious reasons I'm not carrying my warrant card. My wife is, though.'

'Relax,' said the man. 'I was told to keep my eyes open for a scruffy-looking tall bloke possibly accompanied by a good-looking lady as they were SOCA.' He grinned. 'And you didn't make a run for it, did you?'

Someone really clever wouldn't necessarily have done so under the circumstances, was the thought that immediately crossed my mind.

'I was warned on the way here that a number of vehicles had

left this property,' the man went on. 'Any idea where they might have gone?'

'No,' Patrick answered. 'And we're in a hurry. May we have a look at those you've arrested? We're familiar with these people and may be able to put a name to some of them.'

'Help yourself, mate.' He wandered off, lighting a cigarette.

'I thought cops like that were only on the telly,' Patrick muttered as we wended our way between a number of vehicles.

The suspects were in a large entrance hall, red carpet, black walls, and just about to be led out, five men and two women. The latter looked like Philippinos and were wearing blue overalls, almost certainly domestic staff. They were extremely upset, crying. One of the men, who had a strong Scottish accent, was protesting that he was only the gardener.

I showed my ID to a woman who appeared to be in charge of this part of the operation and went up to him. 'Remember me?'

'No,' he replied, blank-faced.

'I think you're Dave MacTavish. You were at Jingles on the night my colleague was seriously beaten up. You were one of those who were going to rape me and before that had given your skene dhu to Paul Mallory, which he then used to cut Benny Cooper's throat. Yes?'

He said nothing.

I moved on to the next one, a vision of bloodshot eyes and bad teeth. 'Ned Freeman?'

'No, I ain't.'

'Yes, you damned-well are!' roared the man to his right. 'I'm buggered if I'm goin' down without you after all the things wot you've done!'

'It's good to have chums, isn't it?' Patrick said to me out of the corner of his mouth.

'You're Squinty Baker,' I said to the man who had shouted.

He opened his mouth to speak, looked at Patrick, who I did not glance at but had an idea was emanating extreme malice aforethought, and shut it again.

'Where have they gone?' Patrick demanded to know.

'Dunno,' said Squinty, looking nervous.

'To commit another bank robbery perhaps, or a jewellery raid? Come on, man! Speak!'

'No, nuffin like that.'

'A training session, then. All your jobs have been very well organized. A couple of witnesses said they were carried out with almost military precision.'

'I don't know nuffin abaht it and wasn't there.'

'It has to be somewhere where you're not required, no doubt on account of your all being as thick as a brick shithouse!' Patrick yelled in his face.

Squinty took a step backwards. 'It's nuffin to do wiv being thick. Just . . . well . . . er . . . we . . . don't do guns, that's all.' He looked around wildly at the others. 'Do we, lads? So don't try and stick that on us!'

'By that do you mean they've gone off to use weapons? I seem to remember you carrying them in the club that night. Tell the truth!'

'Er . . .'

'I'll ask you again. Have they gone to some kind of training session?'

'They . . . er . . . might have done. But I don't know where so I can't tell you,' Squinty finished by saying triumphantly.

The arresting officers were writing busily against a background noise of regulation shoes tramping all over the house.

'So you lot are just the beat-em-up mob,' Patrick said cheerfully.

'Yus.'

'You stupid cross-eyed arsehole!' bawled Dave, throwing a punch at Squinty before anyone could stop him, which resulted in a fight starting between the two of them. We stood demurely out of range while the officers of the law sorted it out.

'No further questions,' Patrick said.

The remaining two men did not say anything, just glowered at us, which suggested that they were unlikely to be innocent bystanders. I did not recognize them and neither did Patrick.

'Right,' he said, turning to leave. 'There's nothing else for us here.'

I was wondering why he had not been truthful to the man in overall charge and stood aside when he went up to him on the gravelled drive.

'Any chance of SOCA borrowing a vehicle for a while?' he enquired. 'We arrived by taxi and I don't want to have to hang around waiting for someone from our department to pick us up.'

'I do need you both to make a report as to the circumstances of your being here.'

'Will it be OK if I email you a copy of what I write for Commander Greenway plus adding in all the background info of the case? Only we work directly for him, you see.' This was followed by a smile that would have had Sauron making daisy chains.

'That would be very useful to me . . . so perhaps I can accommodate you on that,' the man said slowly and hesitantly. 'But—'

'I'll make sure it's returned,' Patrick wheedled.

Amazingly, we were presented with a Land Rover Discovery, perfect for me as I once drove one around half of Wales, mountainous bits and all. Patrick had to have our automatic Range Rover specially adapted with a hand throttle and only drives other cars for short distances if he has to.

Someone's satnav was in the vehicle, just poked into a shelf on the dash. I waved it under Patrick's nose. 'Do we know where we're going?'

He emerged from strategy wrangling. 'Oh, sorry, yes. Thameside.'

I had already known that, of course.

'Ingrid, for the second time in this case we've been incredibly lucky.'

Hadn't I always wanted to drive a police car with sirens wailing and blue lights flashing? Unlike some partners, Patrick made no comment about this. Partly, I think, because I could detect that he now had a sense of real urgency and also the fact that we have both completed several advanced driving courses. However, as we approached Thameside, a large, one-time industrial area by the river that I knew was undergoing complete regeneration, I did not have to be told to slow down and proceed as unobtrusively as it is possible for a police car to be.

'Thameside East,' Patrick said suddenly, indicating a road sign. 'The old warehouse is between, but not that close to, a sewage works and the rubbish incinerator you mentioned when you texted me.' He added, 'I tracked it down yesterday.'

'There was a notice on it then?' I said. 'Raptor's training shed?'

'Bullet holes in the doors.'

'Oh.'

The housing estates, mostly consisting of high-rise blocks of concrete flats resembling long-departed Clydeside factories, petered out and the traffic thinned. We entered a typical estuary area that at one time must have been a haven for water birds, a place of willows and silence and reed beds. Now, notwithstanding the new roads that appeared to lead nowhere and hopeful and colourful notices proclaiming future plans, it was just a wilderness of demolished buildings and piles of stone and bricks. A few new buildings had been erected and a large area near the river, according to the sign once an old canal basin, had been excavated to make a wild fowl lake and visitor centre, the latter already under construction.

After a mile or so we came to the rubbish incinerator, a massive and hideous building, its chimney belching smoke, admittedly clean-looking. Dustcarts – we had passed several – were constantly going in and out.

'Drive in,' Patrick said. 'We can leave the car in that area by the offices reserved for visitors and walk the rest of the way.'

I parked next to a coach that appeared to have brought children on a school trip, then turned to him and said, 'We seem to be a raiding party of two.'

Patrick shook his head. 'No.'

I let that go but it still felt all wrong. 'Your oracle can only utter the usual tedious reservations.'

He leaned over and kissed me. 'For which I offer grateful thanks plus the promise of a lavish dinner out followed by a night of unremitting passion. Coming?'

A trifle mulishly, I climbed out of the Discovery. I was then required to go into the office, show my warrant card and ask to borrow a couple of hi-viz jackets and hard hats. These were forthcoming after someone went away to raid a cupboard and we put them on. I had already discovered a bar of chocolate that had been with the satnav which we ate there and then. I immediately felt a lot more positive.

Although it had turned into a fine summer's day, the easterly breeze had the chill of the North Sea and brought with it a salty, mudflats smell with a hint of drains, no doubt something to do with the sewage works, which I guessed was the other large building in the distance.

I felt the situation to be utterly surreal, no one's idea of a police operation, nothing of the all-bells-and-whistles-tyres-squealing swoop about it, just a man and a woman walking along a practically deserted road. Patrick had said that in order to deal with this mobster he would have to forget he was a cop. So was it to be him, us, against a warehouse full of armed criminals? I began to feel nervous and for the first time, ever, questioned his judgement.

Our destination was the only standing structure set among several massive heaps of rubble and wood, the result of the demolition of some kind of factory complex. A large rusting water tower lay on its side, the bent and twisted supporting girders of the structure piled on top of it together with other metal components and iron roof beams and pillars. Flocks of pigeons and crows pecked among the wood piles, no doubt finding wood-worm and death watch beetle larvae. On seeing us, they flew off.

A short distance away, at the head of the road that led to it, was yet another noticeboard trumpeting the regeneration scheme. Also today there was a suspect Ministry of Defence sign, or one stolen from somewhere, which indicated in large red letters that access was strictly forbidden to the public on account of a military exercise taking place within. The three black vehicles that we had seen were parked close to the warehouse, together with a couple of other cars I did not recognize.

'The building's windows are blocked up on this side,' Patrick said. 'But keep your head down and try to walk like a rough sort of bloke in case someone's on watch. We're bods from the demolition company come to eye up the last part of the job, but our truck has broken down along the road.' He chuckled. 'Demolition. That's the word.'

'You still taking those antibiotics?' I wondered aloud.

'When I remember to.'

Perhaps that explained it. But here he was, the boy I had fallen in love with at school and married, for better or for worse, for richer or for poorer, for the opportunity to take part in a firefight in a derelict warehouse or stay at home and do the ironing. Perhaps I was raving mad.

As we got closer we could hear voices within and what sounded like heavy pieces of furniture or wood being moved around, dragged for short distances and then dropped. There was then a much louder crash followed by angry shouts and an even louder voice telling everyone to shut up. The shifting of wood noises resumed.

Here, the front of the building had several windows high up and, as Patrick had said, they were also boarded up. Below them were two wide arch-shaped entrances with massive wooden double doors, one of which, the farthest from us, had a steel bar across it with industrial standard padlocks at each end. The other, from which we were now about twenty yards, had the remains of the fixings but the bar and padlocks had gone. Both entrances had a single smaller door set into the one on the right-hand side, which now, I thought, surely would be locked from the inside.

Patrick jerked his thumb to the right and, moving as quietly as possible, we made our way around the corner of the warehouse and walked towards the rear. There was not a lot to see when we arrived, more piles of bricks and stone, two of baulks of timber and more birds hunting for food, ripping out pieces of rotten woods. They also flew off. An old van was parked across a rear door, just the one here but identical to those at the front.

'Please stay here,' Patrick whispered and walked away for a short distance, looking upwards, at the windows, I assumed. For some reason he pointed at three of them and then glanced behind him as though working out distances. A small chunk of wood at the top of one of the heaps slid for a short distance and then rolled down to the bottom, which he noted and then ignored. Just the birds, then.

'Right,' he murmured, coming back. 'I don't *think* anyone's seen us.'

'Just go in?' I questioned, feeling as though I was now having some kind of weird dream. Yes, I must have gone to my room at the hotel, put my feet up on the bed and fallen asleep.

'Yes, let's finish this.'

Back at the front double doors, the one that looked as though it had been forced open, Patrick positioned me well to one side, picked up one of the stray pieces of brick and beat on the small inner door with it. He then drew his Glock, moved quickly aside and shouted, 'Police! This building is surrounded and you're all under arrest! Come out one at a time with your hands up!'

Predictably, a hail of lead smashed into the doors, some of which penetrated in a cloud of splinters. Much less predictably, seconds later, the big doors burst open and several men dashed out. From the comparative safety of my new position, half behind the left-hand door, I registered that they were carrying handguns the moment they began firing them wildly. In the next couple of moments a couple dropped where they stood, the sound of these shots coming from Patrick's position. One man spun around to point his weapon in his direction and I took a shot at him, this taking him, amazingly, in his gun hand. He sank to his knees and then keeled over, perhaps having fainted. The rest of those left standing bolted back into the warehouse.

There was then a distinct chattering sound and an authoritative voice inside yelled, 'Drop 'em or die!'

A sub-automatic machine gun fired another short burst and then there was silence for a full twenty seconds. I know, because I counted.

Then, at speed, Patrick momentarily appeared around the edge of my door and, palm facing me, gave me an unmistakable order to stay exactly where I was, before entering the building. After a few minutes he reappeared and gave me a thumbs up.

The thickness of the doors had prevented any hint of what had taken place within to reach our ears. I went in and was completely unprepared for what was before me. Four soldiers in camouflaged battle dress carrying what I was sure were Heckler and Koch sub-machine guns were standing over the prone figures of around eight other men, the latter's weapons – handguns – remained where they had been dropped or thrown down. Ropes hung down the walls from three of the windows.

'One ran off and is hiding somewhere over there, sir,' one of them said. 'And you previously ordered us not to kill anyone so we didn't open fire.'

'Thank you, Sergeant Meyers,' Patrick replied. 'Does he still have a weapon?'

'A pistol, sir. Unless there are others concealed there.'

'Over there' referred to a large and untidy collection of various lengths of wood, sheets of plywood and corrugated iron, tarpaulins, rope and boxes of various sizes that they had obviously collected and used as 'props'. The way it had all been stored in the corner had created a kind of labyrinth with narrow 'corridors' in between used for access.

Those on the floor were unceremoniously booted over on to their backs for identification purposes and Patrick walked down the row, gazing into their faces. They had obviously taken one look at who they were up against and surrendered.

'It's Hamsworth,' he reported, coming over to me. 'Just like in corny old operas, the baddie runs off and the hero then has a sword fight with him on a staircase, which results in him getting a small flesh wound in a shoulder before he spits his man right in the guts.'

The last few words had been uttered with sufficient venom to poison a small town. After then speaking very quietly to two of the soldiers he waved them into position, one on each side of the collection of what was, in effect, demolition debris, and then, while I retreated a little behind the comforting presence of a massive iron pillar, positioned himself in between the men to one side of the widest 'tunnel'.

'There are three of us right here,' Patrick said briskly, addressing the hidden Hamsworth. 'Should you wish to blow your brains out then please feel free to do so as it will save everyone a lot of paperwork. If, on the other hand you prefer to re-enact the Alamo then that will be a bit more paperwork but rest assured you'll still get a bullet, if not several. That's the choice.'

'Choice!' Hamsworth shouted from somewhere inside. 'That's no choice!'

'That's it. Choose. Quickly.'

'You said we were all under arrest.'

'You are. But you decided that was not for you.'

'OK, I've changed my mind.'

'Then throw out the gun and come out with your hands in the air.'

'I can't throw it from where I am.'

'Then move until you're somewhere you can. Slowly. I warn you, I'm a bloody good shot.'

Nothing happened for a few seconds and then there were sounds of movement and a handgun came flying out through the gap to thump on the dusty floor.

'Now you,' Patrick called.

'Not very good at your job, are you?' Hamsworth jeered. 'You should pick it up to stop me from grabbing and firing it.'

'So I should.'

He stayed right where he was.

It happened so quickly that if anyone had blinked they would have failed to see the end of it. Or died in the hail of bullets. Those who were not lying prone already threw themselves down as the man emerged at a run, rounds smashing into everything from the rapid-firing weapon in his hands as he swung it around. I fired and so did Patrick – we both hit our target, the man pitching on to his face and falling on the weapon, which fired a few more rounds into the floor and then became silent.

Patrick checked that the man was dead and then walked away, leaving the weapons where they were.

NINETEEN

Miraculously, no one else had been hurt but for a few scratches and minor cuts from flying splinters, as in his haste, or panic, Hamsworth had fired slightly high. I was not feeling guilty at having been partly responsible for his death – my shot had taken him in the chest – because, as far as I was concerned at the time, in the next second or so he would have re-adjusted his aim. The instantly fatal shot had been Patrick's, to the head.

The four soldiers, all from Patrick's old regiment, The Devon and Dorsets, now subsumed into The Rifles, had been 'borrowed'. He still has good contacts. They had not fired a shot but for the short warning bursts into the air by Sergeant Meyers, the situation exactly as intended, or rather ordered.

This much I learned before Commander Greenway arrived in the wake of the Metropolitan Police and several ambulances. Patrick, apologetically, had also told me that he had only arranged assistance, provisionally, the previous afternoon after I had given him the information about the warehouse and he had gone in search of it. There had been no indication when, or even if, anything would come of it or even if it would succeed. Better to err on the safe side.

The remainder of the cache of weapons, from which Hamsworth had snatched one, had been immediately found hidden under a pile of old plastic bags at the back of the conglomeration of debris. The commander duly inspected this before coming over to where we were engaged in a somewhat edgy conversation with the woman in charge, Inspector Jinny Taylor.

'They're with me,' Greenway told her, having introduced himself. 'It'll save time if they report to me and I forward everything to you.'

'How do I explain *this* though, sir?' she asked, greatly bothered and gesturing towards the military quartet, who were preparing to depart.

'You have it on good authority – mine – and you can write it down, that I understand they're part of a unit training with the Met in order to assist during any terrorist activity in London. But don't spread it around – it's not for general consumption. It seemed a good opportunity for an exercise due to the expectation that these mobsters were armed with semi-automatic weapons, which has been proved to be quite correct. The Heckler and Koch belong to you, the Met – the Ministry of Defence can't be expected to provide firearms as well – and will be immediately returned.'

She looked relieved and went away to carry on supervising her team.

'I think that's as you gave it to me,' Greenway said to Patrick. 'Did I get it right?'

'Word perfect,' was the reply.

'How did they get here?'

'In the old van out the back.' Faced with slight bafflement, Patrick added, 'No, not in an armed personnel carrier.'

He then went over to thank them.

Able to examine my surroundings properly for the first time I looked around and then, needing a few quiet moments, strolled away from everyone. A forensic team was over by Hamsworth's body, the usual photographs being taken. There would be an inquiry into events by the Independent Police Complaints Commission and it occurred to me that I might end up losing the Smith and Wesson, which I do not carry with any kind of official blessing.

A start had obviously been made into building some kind of 'set' which was thrown up over by one wall, I supposed to practise for the next raid, robbery, or whatever had been planned. Part of it appeared to have collapsed – the crash we had heard.

The warehouse was a typical Victorian building with the same massive iron roof beams and pillars as were piled outside. Soon, the last of the group would succumb to the wrecking ball. Although passionately keen on Britain's past being conserved, I would shed no tears for this one.

A couple of days later, the Ring o' Bells seemed the most suitable place to have a non-official debriefing, the official ones having all taken place. Unfortunately Commander Greenway could only be represented by an email he had sent Patrick that morning, which he read out, the six of us – we had been joined by Carrick, Joanna, David Campbell and Lynn Outhwaite – sitting in a quiet corner of the lounge bar.

'"Congratulations on a case well conducted and brought to a satisfactory conclusion. I thought you would be pleased to know that, following a search of the premises at South Woodford, during which more weapons, drugs and counterfeit money were found, a safe was opened that contained, among items already mentioned, a list of names, including photographs, of police officers who were to be targeted, for intimidation purposes or physical attack. My name was in the second category. I especially want to thank you for your warnings and personal endeavour in this matter and, in case anyone else feels like having a go at me, will take your advice with regard to my own safety when Erin and I return from a last-minute planned holiday to Italy. Good shooting!"'

'You must have saved lives by killing him,' Campbell observed. 'Hamsworth could have created a bloodbath with that weapon.'

Manifestly, having been through his ordeal by fire, he had been reluctant to join us but Lynn had told him, point blank, that he ought to, this detail whispered in my ear by her when we had first met this evening. As Patrick and James had hoped, the man soon relaxed when a glass of his native brew was in his hand and I was aware that he had already profusely apologized to Carrick for what had occurred.

I am still not sure why it had.

Later, at home, I said, 'Greenway guessed, didn't he?'

'I reckon so,' Patrick answered.

'What'll happen about Nathan Forrester?'

'I discussed it with Carrick and we're going to drop the charges. He'll be given an official caution.'

I smiled to myself, both at this news and remembering, before we had come out, the expression on Jonno's face when Patrick had given him back his ten-pound note.

Lightning Source UK Ltd.
Milton Keynes UK
UKOW01f0220170218
318028UK00002B/29/P